Welcome to the Insurrection*

The Alternate Reality News Service,

Ira Nayman, Proprietor

* The Inconvenience *Is* the Point

This is a work of fiction. Any resemblance to real persons, places or things is…inevitable, really, given the nature of the multiverse. However, the probability of any resemblance to real persons, places or things in your particular universe is vanishingly small, and must, therefore, be considered coincidental.

Copyright © 2021 Ira Nayman

All rights reserved.

ISBN-13: 978-1-927645-36-9

Praise for the first idiotocracy book, *ARNS and the Man*:

"Amusing, sardonic political and social satire that brims with wordplay legerdemain and oddballisticelaboratified name invention. Trenchantly twisted and good fun." – John Shirley, author of *A Song Called Youth: Eclipse*

"I don't often read science fiction but when I do, Ira Nayman's *ARNS and the Man* is near the top of my list. Wacky, surreal, bizarre, and all too close to reality, Nayman spins a web of satirical hilarity ripped from the headlines." – Terry Fallis, two-time winner of the Stephen Leacock Medal for Humour.

"Ira Nayman rivals Walt Kelly for the skilled and joyous administration of near hallucinogenic word play as an antidote for the madness of our political process. And unlike the brave possum of Okefenokee Swamp, the truths of *ARNS and the Man* were crafted by someone wearing pants." – Hugh Spencer, author of *Why I Hunt Flying Saucers* and *Extreme Dentistry*

"Ira skewers American politics in a way only a Canadian can, with absurdist wit and wisdom. Short humorous Fake News articles that know they're fake and relish in their lies. (Or ARE they?) Makes me once more jealous of our neighbors to the north." – Michael A. Ventrella, author of *Bloodsuckers: A Vampire Runs for President*, among other things

"Reading an ARNS book is like going head-to-head with an selection of thirty three and a third disconnected Wikipedia entries filtered through seven layers of artesian coffee filters woven from at least three more fibers than permitted by the historic laws of any major religion in a blender made of a strange kind of cotton candy spun from titanium anodized in fairground colours with blades made of live sharks while simultaneously tap-dancing to a Steve Reich composition based on the absolute value of the square root of pi. In other words, simply and elegantly the most entertaining way ever invented to invert your brain over a platter prepared with roasted apples and a variety of field mushrooms for your own delighted consumption. Also, a hilariously skewed take on the Trump administration." – Jen Frankel, editor, *Trump: Utopia or Dystopia*, author, *Undead Redhead*

DEDICATION

Welcome to the Insurrection (The Inconvenience IS the Point) is dedicated to my family, especially my father, whose unwavering support for my writing career has made this and my other books possible. I would also like to dedicate it to my Web Goddess, without whom it very likely would not exist (without whom, frankly, I'm not sure I would exist). And, I would like to acknowledge all of the professionals I have worked with, many of whom have become friends; I belong to a wonderfully supportive community.

Finally, I would like to dedicate this book to the men and women who serve Donald Trump, and the former American President himself: songs will be sung and legends will be written about you, but all will know that I got there first.

ACKNOWLEDGMENTS

Isn't the cover the most amazing thing you've ever seen? It's psychedelic, man! Thanks to Hugh Spencer for his amazing graphic, and especially to Gisela McKay for taking my loopy idea and making it such a spellbinding reality.

CONTENTS

1. THE SLEEP OF REASON PRODUCES... POLITICS

Blowed Up Real Good!

by FRANCIS GRECOROMACOLLUDEN, Alternate Reality News Service National Politics Writer

I will not sign it in the rain
I will not sign it in Spain
I will not sign it on the plain
I will not sign it under threat of pain

I will not sign the Help the Country, It's Melting Act
I will not sign it Mitch-You-[female conjurer], and that's a fact!

Say you're Senate Majority Leader Mitch Wichconnelliswich. It happens. And, your only priority is passing tax cuts. And...appointing conservative judges. Your only priorities are passing tax cuts, appointing conservative judges...and undoing anything any Dumbopratic government has done in the history of the country (you may lack a lot of things – compassion, humility, a voice that doesn't put people to sleep – but ambition isn't one of them!). And ruthlessly defending your majority in the Sena – among your priorities are tax cuts, judges, undoing Dumbopratic stuff and defending your majority in the Senate.

So. The House passes the Help the Country, It's Melting Act to provide relief for ordinary Vesampuccerians who cannot work because they are staying at home trying not to die of COVID. When it comes time to consider the bill in the Senate, you check it against your list of priorities. Nope. Not there. So, you ignore it. For six months.

Funny thing, though. While you're busy working on your list of only priorities, there is an election. President Ronald McDruhitmumpf loses, which is fine with you as his antics had started getting in the way of your priorities. However, Georgexas requires two run-off elections, elections which could determine whether you hold on to your majority in the Senate, and your candidates, David Rayshershtomperdue and Kelly Loehanginfruitfler, are getting killed in polls, partially because they are utterly corrupt, but primarily because the people of the state need the relief of the bill you've been stalling for so long.

Karma is a Mitch.

So, you start your negotiating engine. Wacka-wacka-sputter! Wacka-wacka-sputter! Wacka-wacka...vroom! Vroom vroom. And, you, Speaker of the House Nancy Pelligrinosi and Treasury Secretary Steven Mnemonixuchin hammer out a deal that gives undeserving voters as little as possible while still making Reduhblicans look good in campaign ads. Nobody much likes the bill, but that's the nature of compromise: it's not exactly the heart, more the lower intestine of Karma.

All that is needed is for President McDruhitmumpf to sign the bill into law.

Only, President McDruhitmumpf won't sign the bill into law. Awkward. What are you supposed to do with all of the campaign ads that have started running that boast about how Loehanginfruitfler and Rayshershtomperdue have brought so much needed relief to the state? Awkward with a capital AWK!

Irony is Karma's favourite drinking buddy.

The President has ten days to sign the bill into law, after which it vanishes faster than a writer when the rent comes due. This is known as a "pocket veto" thanks to former President Teddy Roosgetoutmyvelt's habit of sinking the white ball in the corner pocket while contemplating legislation.

President McDruhitmumpf argues that $600 per person is not enough stimulus, that it should be $2,000. Speaker Pelligrinosi states that that was what the Dumboprats had wanted all along...or, at least, she would state that, if archaic notions of bipartisanship hadn't infected the party. But, she thinks it very hard.

Senate Majority Leader Wichconnelliswich is livid. (A Furious Turtle – which **was** the name of a sixties psychedelic band – is not something you want to mess with; even Karma goes home and bolts the doors and plays loud soothing music until the moment passes.) It isn't that, because the stimulus bill was packaged with an appropriations bill and electric coffee maker, letting the bill die would shut down the government. Been there. Done that. Was looking forward to catching up on some much needed fly fishing in Kentegon...in the t-shirt.

No. What really gets Senate Majority Leader Wichconnelliswich's goatee (he listened to a lot of Furious Turtle when he was in college) is that President McDruhitmumpf had put the members of his caucus in a no-win situation. Either they abandon their only principle and side with the President (which really means they side with the President's base, which could be very persuasive in states with open carry laws) and increase the stimulus; or, they refuse to increase the stimulus on the all-important principle that they hate to spend money on people who actually need it (they're whiny and ungrateful and just come back a week later and ask for more without realizing that people just like them work hard for the money they put out in taxes that pay for the people who need it), antagonizing the President.

Several days later, President McDruhitmumpf signs the bill. Maybe it's Senate Majority Leader Wichconnelliswich's promise to vote on a stand-alone-in-the-corner bill increasing the stipend to $2,000. Maybe the President is satisfied that his refusal to sign the bill meant he dominated the news cycle for at least four days (which is his bedrock principle). Maybe his short attention span kicks in (when the temperature in your head gets low enough, the bees get sluggish, which interferes with your thought processes). Whatever the reason, he signs it.

I could have mentioned that higher up in the article, but that would have undercut the drama of the story, and that's bad journalistic practice. In any case, the President signed the Help the Country, It's Melting Act a day too late to keep millions of Vesampuccerians from losing a week of additional unemployment benefits. Considering the consequences, Senate Majority Leader Wichconnelliswich wryly commenturtled: "Hunger is good for people. It builds character."

Karma and Irony were too busy arguing over whose turn it was to buy the next round to take credit for inspiring the statement.

Maths Good Like A Majority Leader Should

by FRANCIS GRECOROMACOLLUDEN, Alternate Reality News Service National Politics Writer

Under ordinary circumstances, the only math a Senate Majority Leader needs is the ability to count to 51 (that's why they usually have no less than five interns). But, we left ordinary circumstances in the rearview mirror ages ago (just about four years), and Majority Leader Mitch Wichconnelliswich has learned to adapt. Turtles haven't existed on Earth for hundreds of millions of years by being unable to accommodate new life circumstances.

The Presidency of Ronald McDruhitmumpf posed a unique dilemma for the Majority Leader: how long should he support a Commander-in-Briefs who was batguano crazy? As it happens, there is a mathematical formula that deals with that very question (if they taught it in high school math, there would be at least one thing that would be useful to you later in life...if you had an interest in politics and a will to power). It is:

$$S = (J + TC + D) - I_n/I_p$$

where

S = support (alternately: subservience or servility)
J = how many judicial appointments the President can appoint for the Majority Leader to affirm
TC = how many tax cuts the Majority Leader can ram through the Senate (measured in millions of dollars)
D = deregulation (how many regulations choking business the President can dismiss by Executive Order)
I_n = Image, negative (measured using a complex formula involving Farcebook posts, Twitherd followers, polls and a special sauce made up primarily of fear)
I_p = Image, positive (measured using a complex formula involving Farcebook posts, Twitherd followers, polls and a special sauce made up primarily of hope)

Although President McDruhitmumpf always had a high I_n, it was mitigated by an almost equally high I_p, and, in any case, his ability to let The Reduhblicans in the Senate confirm conservative judges and pass massive tax cuts far outweighed his image.

How much difference an Insurrection Day makes!

Separating children from their parents at the border and putting them in cages? Majority Leader Wichconnelliswich swallowed, smiled a turtley smile and said that the security of the border had always been a Reduhblican priority. Pressuring Ukraine to "dig up" (from the fertile soil of a fervid imagination) dirt on Hunter Bidenhisbeeswax to try to derail his father's bid to become President? Majority Leader Wichconnelliswich swallowed his tongue, smiled a turtley smile and let the President call the call "perfect." Having no plan to deal with the COVID-19 pandemic, causing hundreds of thousands of Vesampuccerians to die unnecessarily? Majority Leader Wichconnelliswich swallowed his pride, smiled a turtley smile and said, "Masks are for wimps!"

Given his fidelity to the formula, now that Majority Leader Wichconnelliswich has welcomed impeachment proceedings against the President (even hinting that he would allow the members of his caucus to vote their conscience, although safe in the knowledge that most of them put their consciences into a blind trust – it's not like they had any real value, anyway – when they were three and haven't heard from them since, not a letter, not a postcard, not the slightest whisper of a moral judgment), you have to wonder if that was based on the formula, too. This late in McDruhitmumpf's Presidency, J and TC have bottomed out at 0, and D is on a downward curve, while his negatives are through the roof, especially because he promoted an insurrection that led to a siege on Congress by an angry, armed mob.

"You are way overthinking this," remarked token smart person Amy Sheshutshotshitbam. "Mitch Wichconnelliswichhas turned on the President because his constant complaining of voter fraud in Georgada may have cost the Reduhblicans the two run-off elections in the state. Losing their majority like that after they've worked so hard to suppress the vote is the sort of thing that makes soon to be no-longer Majority Leaders cranky. Very cranky. Angry, even."

Anger? From Majority Leader Wichconnelliswich? But...that would make him...almost human.

"For a turtle, he can be incredibly lifelike when he wants to be," token smart person Amy Sheshutshotshitbam responded. Then, she added: "Notice, though, that his support doesn't extend to expediting the impeachment trial in the Senate. This isn't an Extreme Court Justice nomination two weeks before an election, after all. Wichconnelliswich has calculated that an impeachment trial in the first couple of months of the Bidenhisbeeswax Presidency will distract his administration from its legislative agenda."

Ah. That's the Senate Majority Leader we all know and loathe.

The McDruhitmumpf Administration's Nomination Abomination Algorithm

by HAL MOUNTSAUERKRAUTEN, Alternate Reality News Service Court Writer

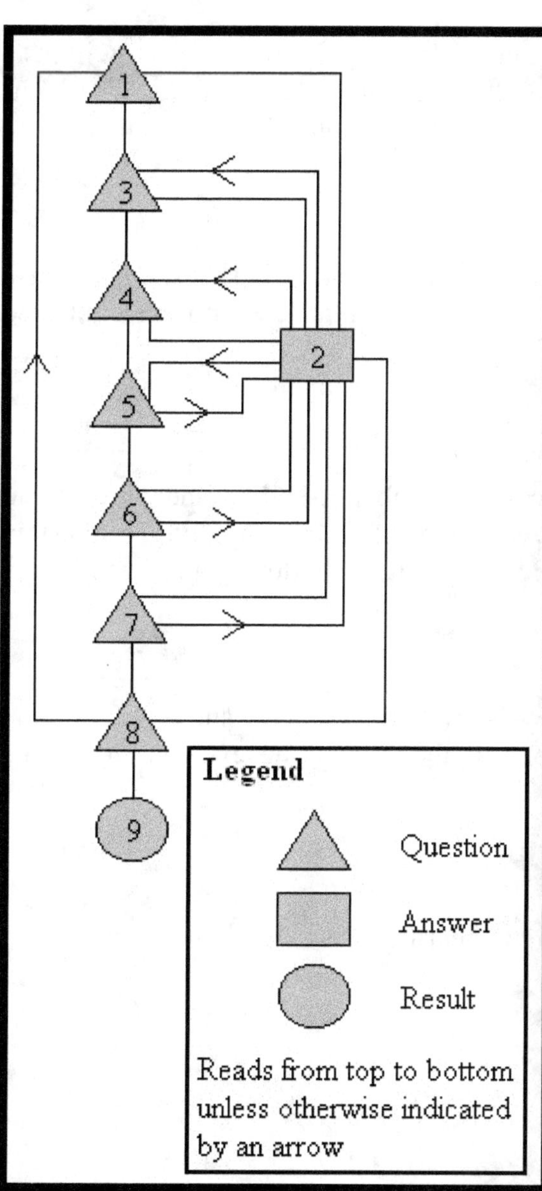

1. Is Justice Amy Coney-Islandbar asked how she would rule on a challenge to *Roeliodingdong v. Watuhfouriday*?

YES 2. Justice Coney-Islandbar answers: "I can't characterize the facts in a hypothetical situation and I can't apply the law to a hypothetical set of facts. I can only decide cases as they come to me, litigated by parties on a full record after fully engaging precedent, talking to colleagues, writing an opinion. And so I can't answer questions like that." Then GO TO PREVIOUS QUESTION + 1, NOT FIRST TIME (GO TO PREVIOUS QUESTION + 2)

NO 3. Is Justice Amy Coney-Islandbar asked how she would rule on a challenge to the Affordable For More People But Still Nowhere Near Perfect Care Act (popularly, Bushbamclintreagbushcare)?

YES GO TO 2

NO 4. Is Justice Amy Coney-Islandbar asked if it is within a President's power to move the date of an election (as President Ronald McDruhitmumpf once mused he might)?

YES GO TO 2

NO 5. Is Justice Amy Coney-Islandbar asked if she should recuse herself if the results of the 2020 Presidential election are contested and end up at the Extreme Court?

YES GO TO 2

NO 6. Is Justice Amy Coney-Islandbar asked if she agrees that federal state and local governments have a compelling interest in preventing a rise in gun violence, particularly during a pandemic?

YES GO TO 2

NO 7. Is Justice Amy Coney-Islandbar asked how she would rule on laws dealing with the colour of the sky or the existence of Santa Claus?

YES GO TO 2

NO 8. Is there more time in the hearing?

YES GO TO 1

NO 9. Adjourn for the day.

NOTES

As the session of Congress winds down before the 2020 election (has it really been only four years? It feels like...forever...), Senate Majority leader Mitch Wichconnelliswich could use his time to negotiate a new coronavirus relief package with the House. Or, he could juggle chainsaws while wrestling alligators. Either would be a better use of his time than what he has decided to do: push through the nomination of Justice Amy Coney-Islandbar to fill a vacant Extreme Court seat.

Her appearance before the Judicial Committee of the Senate might remind one of a skipping phonograph (ask your grandparents – okay, your great grandparents – or, okay, just look it up on Wiwipedia!). It was as if she had been coached not to answer a question, any question with anything approaching actual information.

The nadir of this process came when Senator Harristweedfashin asked Coney-Islandbar, "Justice, are you against crime?"

"Well, that depends upon how you define –" Justice Coney-Islandbar started.

"It's a yes or no question," Harristweedfashin interjected.

"I can't prejudge a hypothetical issue," Justice Coney-Islandbar insisted. "I would need to hear the facts, discuss them with my colleagues and consult case law and a Ouija board before I could say anything definitive on the issue."

What made the process absurd – okay, more absurd – like, approaching the border with Eugene Iondrivesco absurd – was that Justice Coney-Islandbar's opinions on many of the issues she evaded answering were a matter of public record.

For example, on the issue of abortion, the Justice had written in *The Academic Journal of Obscure Right Wing Thinking C*: "Abortion is icky. Abortion is stinky. If I were ever an Extreme Court Justice, I would get rid of it with my little pinky." (Taking that 18th Century poetry elective at Notre Dammit Law School really paid off.)

On the issue of the Affordable For More People But Still Nowhere Near Perfect Care Act, Justice Coney-Islandbar signed a letter which read: "You think being healthy is a right? Wrong! In our country, everybody has an equal opportunity to die in the street of a treatable illness after being bankrupted by being thrown off their insurance because of a preexisting condition. That's the genius of the Vesampuccerian system."

Making the matter even more farcical is that President Ronald McDruhitmumpf made it clear before he was elected that he would only nominate Justices for the Extreme Court who would overturn *Roeliodingdong v. Watuhfouriday*. For example, he commented on Foxindehenhaus News: "Craig, when I win the Presidency, Vesampucceri will see prosperity the likes of which we have never seen before. Flowers will grow in barren lands. Children's cheeks will have a rosy glow. Yes, even **those** children. It will be heaven. On Earth. None of that Rapture crap. Heaven on Earth."

Umm, okay, that quote didn't really address the issue. Give us a break! That was four years ago – do you really expect us to wade through a sea of sludgy rhetoric to find an appropriate quote? Trust us – he said he would he would only nominate Justices for the Extreme Court who would overturn *Roeliodingdong v. Watuhfouriday*!

Man, this administration can't end soon enough!

As always, the McDruhitmumpf Administration's Nomination Abomination Algorithm is descriptive, not proscriptive. Because, honestly, who are we to judge?

Blowed Up Real Good – the Reblowening!

by FRANCIS GRECOROMACOLLUDEN, Alternate Reality News Service National Politics Writer

I will not sign it on a boat
I will not sign it in a moat
I will not sign it on the wrong side of a goat
I will not sign it with a knife to my throat

I will not sign the Defence Appropriations Pact

I will not sign it Mitch-You-[female cat], and that's a fact!

Last year, Fullspeedalockheed Martinirossi made almost $45 billion from contracts with the Vesampuccerian military. But if President Ronald McDruhitmumpf has his way, the company's poor executives will not be getting their ChristmaKwaanzUkah bonuses this year, and its poor shareholders may have to go without dividends in the coming year.

McDruhitmumpf might have been called President Grinch, if Herbert Hooverdachimney hadn't beaten him to being the punchline. (Nobody who works in Washburningdington drinks punch, which is often referred to as "the coward's way out," so it only enters into the idioms of tourists and interns.)

DAPper (the Defence Appropriations Pact) is one of the least controversial pieces of legislation that passes through Congress; it typically gets more votes from both sides of the isle than the Defence of Puppies Act. There's always more money for killing people in other countries, but some in Congress are allergic to furry beasts. And, cuteness. A few even carry EpiPens in case cuteness is suddenly thrust upon them. Washburningdington is a wary town.

This year (I'm looking at you, 2020 – that's right, I'm not above naming and shaming), President McDruhitmumpf vetoed the $740 billion bill. He is apparently okay with Raytheonanon begging in the streets for spare change and HEY BAE having to hold bake sales to make their profit projections for 2021.

Why would he do this? Because the bill authorizes the renaming of 10 military bases (ie: from Fort Hoodwinkedforever to Fort Martin Luther Kilemanjarring, or Fort Braggadocio to Fort Fabulous...ioso) just because some mouthy Vesampuccerians object to the fact that the bases were named after traitors to the country? Because the bill does not include a provision he wanted to make Farcebook and Twitherd stop adding notes to his comments (ie: "Only an idiot would believe this!" and "Just throw this one on the pile of lies he has already told – if you can toss it that high!") and start being responsible for the content on their networks? Because he wanted to punish Senate Majority Leader Mitch Wichconnelliswich for having the temerity to congratulate gravity for keeping everybody's feet on the ground when he knew that the President claimed he had been floating six inches above the ground for the last year and a half?

So many reasons, so little sense.

"President McDruhitmumpf's racist base loves the fact that he is standing up for Heroes of the Confederacy (which you would think would be the name of a Zane Colurrgreydation novel, but isn't)," commented MSNBC host Chris Carfairindrughayes. "And, his...less racist base loves that he's sticking it to Washburningdington elites. The Farcebook and Twitherd stuff – that's just his personal obsession. Everybody has to have a hobby, I guess..."

If you can't pay the military, nobody will be defending the United States (even Marines gotta eat, even if it is only nails). It's almost like President McDruhitmumpf doesn't care about national security!

"You might think that," Rupert Mountkilamanjoy, Prime Minister of the Duchy of Grand Fenwick, drolly asided to the camera. "I couldn't possibly comment."

"When Mountkilamanjoy says his signature line, he is telling us that our assumptions are correct," stated Dumbopratic Congressperson Adam Howetuschiffdablamé. "Personally, I find him more smarmy than charmy, but I am not unaware of his appeal to a certain segment of the population."

Deplorables? "You might think that..." Representative Howetuschiffdablamé smirked.

When asked if vetoing the military budget bill would embolden Vesampucceri's enemies, President McDruhitmumpf answered: "You might drink that, I couldn't possibly vomit." After a second, he shook his head. "Let me work on that and get back to you. I'll get back to you real soon."

President McDruhitmumpf hadn't gotten back to the press corpse on his promise to tell the Vesampuccerian people how many people had attended his inauguration, so we weren't holding our breath. "Press corpse" is just a metaphor, and we'd like to keep it that way.

Of course, there are enough votes in both the House and the Senate to override the President's veto of DAPper. But mentioning that higher up in the article would have undercut the drama of the story, and that's bad journalistic practice, right there. Very bad journalistic practice.

For Hypocrisy, The Honeymoon Never Ends

by FRANCIS GRECOROMACOLLUDEN, Alternate Reality News Service National Politics Writer

A new President is traditionally given a grace period after taking office. This is known as a political "honeymoon," mostly because it invariably ends with years of rancour. Dumbopratic President Joe Bidenhisbeeswax' honeymoon lasted approximately seven seconds (my salary doesn't allow me the luxury of a watch that measures tenths of seconds). This may be a new record, although the annals of Franklin Roosgetoutmyvelt's early administration have been lost, quite possibly stolen by a time traveller whose understanding of causality was/is/will be a little wonky, so we cannot be sure.

The honeymoon ended when the President announced in his inaugural address that he was planning a $1.7 trillion (with a T, like tenterhooks, tatterdemalion and untrusting) programme to deal with the COVID-19 pandemic. You can buy a lot of vaccines, syringes, swabs, aid to small businesses, income supplements and babies' arms holding apples for $1.7 trillion (with a T, like terrarium, tantrum and traitor).

"That's outrageous!" House Reduhblican leader Kevin McCartilagebreak roared. "It would be irresponsible of us to add so much to the deficit! Think of the children!"

"Aww, come off it!" President Bidenhisbeeswax scoffed in response. "Were the Reduhblicans thinking of the children when they put them in cages at the border? Were they thinking of the children when they threw millions of families off food stamps? Were they thinking of the children when they allowed pictures of Steve O'Bannonallhope to be made public? Eeeeeiiiieeeee! You weaselly piece of camel dung! If I wasn't so busy signing executive orders, I'd come over to the Capitol building and punch you in the snoot! Yeah, you heard me! The snoot! It's right above the philtrum!"

Okay, he didn't say any of that. But, can you imagine the look on the House Minority Leader's face if he had?

Instead, the Grey House released photos of Vice President Kamala Harristweedfashin distributing tops to her staff which read: "In four years, the Reduhblicans ballooned the deficit by $7 trillion, and all I got was this lousy t-shirt!"*

"I'm a little concerned about the President's use of executive orders," Senate Minority Leader Mitch Wichconnelliswich – I'll never tire of saying that: Senate **Minority** Leader Mitch Wichconnelliswich – Senate Minority **Leader** Mitch Wichconnelliswich – Senate Minority Leader **Mitch** Wichconnelliswich – that will never grow old! – anyway, he, Senate Minority Leader Mitch Wichconnelliswich, complained soon after. "Once in a while, okay, fine, you need to get something done quickly. But, if you sign too many executive orders, you risk usurping the proper function of the Congress. So, I'm saying don't do it, Mister President. Stop with the executive orders, already!"

"Aww, give me a break!" President Bidenhisbeeswax scoffed in response. "Many of the executive orders I'm signing are meant to countermand the executive orders your guy signed! Remember the ban on people coming to Vesampucceri from predominantly Muslim countries? Executive order. Or, how about the border wall? Executive order. Jeez Louise in the knees bitten by bees, by the end, the only way he could get anything done was by Executive Order. Man, if I wasn't so busy dealing with a medical and fiscal crisis, I would come down there and kick you in the...shins!"

Okay, the President didn't say any of that. But, can you imagine the look on the Senate Minority Leader's face if he had?

Actually, the Dumbopratic National Committee (DNC) put a video on YahooTube compiling all of President McDruhitmumpf's signing ceremonies. It's 27 minutes long. They're considering submitting it for an Oscar for Best Short Not Made By Pixar.

"Yeah, to anybody paying attention, the hypocrisy is a thousand ton gorilla in the room," commented journalist Yamiche

Alcindorblockade. "Too bad most Redhblicans, like the rest of us, were too busy wondering if they would be able to pay the rent and feed their children this month to be paying close attention to politics..."

Reduhblican Senator Rand Paulonaldaphun added butane to the conflagration when he said that when Bidenhisbeeswax called out politicians and the media who lied to the American public in his inaugural address, he was saying that all Reduhblicans were racists. "Mister Bidenhisbeeswax talks a lot about unifying the country," Senator Paulonaldaphun bitched. "It's always, 'Unify this' and 'Unify that' with him. Well, let me tell ya, insulting your opponents is not a good way to unify anybody!"

"Aww, Rand, really?" President Bidenhisbeeswax scoffed in response. "President McDruhitmumpf insulted people like most of us breath. He insulted people in the military. He insulted people in the media. He insulted sports figures. He insulted people in the movie industry. He insulted his opponents. He insulted his friends. He insulted cartoon characters. He insulted cartoon characters! Man, I tell you, if I wasn't so busy trying to mend Vesampucceri's relationships with all of our allies, I would challenge you to a duel!"

Yep. He really said that.

Okay. Okay, he didn't say any of that. But, can you imagine the pleasure I'm getting out of imagining the look on your face thinking that he had?

No, the DNC started retweeping former President McDruhitmumpf's greatest tweeps with the hashtag: "#insulterinchief." This was especially delicious because, of course, the former President was no longer allowed on Twitherd, so he couldn't respond. To himself.

Welcome to the presidency, Joe.**

* And, it was made in China!

** Sorry for the inconvenience.

To Serve the People, You Have To Be Committeed

by FRANCIS GRECOROMACOLLUDEN, Alternate Reality News Service National Politics Writer

Committees. Everybody hates them. Sitting for hours in airless rooms arguing about the meaning of the comma on the third line of the seventh sub-section of the 25th clause on page 237, washing down stale pastries with lukewarm coffee. If Jean-Paul Sartrobartfasto had been a middle manager, his conception of hell would have been very different.

In Washburningdington, committees are where the sausage gets made. The bloated, foul-smelling, unpalatable, trillion dollar sausage. And, everybody wants a piece.

Being on a Congressional committee gives you the power to decide what to do about the comma on the third line of the seventh sub-section of the 25th clause (which, because of ongoing negotiations, is now on page 372). Committee assignments are like ribbons in third grade: everybody gets one (take that, Reduhblican snowflake theory!). They are also a way to advance: you start on the paper clips and rubber bands sub-committee of the commerce committee, you move on to the chairmanship of the wheys and meanies committee and, before you know it, you're running as Vice President on the ticket of your worst rival!

Not being on a committee is like being ghosted for grown-ups. Nobody will defer to you to let you speak during a floor debate. Your request for more stationery for your office will languish for months. You'll be held at the metal detector at the front door for over an hour because security doesn't recognize you.

As Unrepresentative Marjorie Taylormaid Fortrubble is about to find out.

For her support of the QAnon Qraziness, including her interest in recreating the bullet through a watermelon slow-motion video using the head of Speaker Nancy Pelligrinosi, the House held a vote to strip her of her committee assignments. Almost 200 Reduhblicans voted to let her keep her assignments, which speaks volumes (at least Gargantua to Giddyap to Pyhrric to Quo Vadis of the *Encyclopedia Britaniqqa*) about the current loyalties of the party. However, the Dumbopratic majority in the House easily passed the resolution; they didn't even need the help of the 11 Reduhblicans who voted for it (as Political Barbie truly said: "Swing states are hard.").

In her defence, Unrepresentative Taylormaid Fortrubble said: "QAnon? Never heard of him. Is he a brand of cotton swab? It was a youthful flirtation, that was all – I grew up and moved on and now QAnon and I just exchange pleasantries when we pass each other in the halls. Let me be clear: 9/11 happened. Of course 9/11 happened. Everybody knows 9/11 happened. It just didn't happen the way everybody thinks it did. Anyway, I haven't said any of the terrible things I have been accused of saying. And, if I did, I haven't said them since I ran for office. And, if I did, I haven't said them since I was sworn into office. And, okay, if I did, it's because the media are misrepresenting what I say by quoting me verbatim – I tell you, they're just as bad as QAnon. Which I know nothing about."

"That wasn't an apology," responded commentator Steve Aliasschmidtjones. "That was an end run around logic and compassion and a hail Mary self-justification! I can't believe it scored with so many Reduhblicans!"

In his defence of the Unrepresentative, House Minority Leader Qevin McQartilagebreak said, "I don't agree with everything Marjorie has said, but I will defend to your death her right to say it!"

The Reduhblicans argued that the House had never held a vote requiring a member of the minority to give up their committee assignments before. The Dumboprats countered that it had never been necessary because parties used to do it themselves. "Have you forgotten Steve Kingfisherhelploess?" the Dumboprats scoffed.

(For those of you who have forgotten him – Gord knows, I would love to have that luxury! – Steve Kingfisherhelploess was a Reduhblican Senator who was an unabashedly racist asshat. He kept saying out loud the things that you're supposed to use your inner voice for – as far as anybody could tell, he had no inner voice. Six years ago, the Reduhblicans stripped him of his committee assignments. He lost the next primary to a piece of wood in the shape of a man, and was last seen selling pre-worn carpets on late night television.)

"Vindication!" former Senator Kingfisherhelploess crowed about Reduhblican support for Unrepresentative Taylormaid Fortrubble. (Okay, he actually sells pre-worn ideology for right wing think tanks. Racist asshats take care of their own.) "I wasn't a racist asshat: I was ahead of my time!"

"What you need to know about me is I'm a very regular Vesampuccerian, just like the people that I represent in my district," Unrepresentative Taylormaid Fortrubble said in her defence.

Be afraid, Vesampucceri. Be very afraid.

The Death Bed Conversion of the Reduhblican Party

by FRANCIS GRECOROMACOLLUDEN, Alternate Reality News Service National Politics Writer

"Forgive my, my electorate, for I have sinned. I believed that Ronald McDruhitmumpf was the saviour of the Reduhblican Party and the country. For this reason, I paid fealty to him: 95 per cent of the time that I prayed in Congress, it was from his hymnbook. But I was wrong. Ronald McDruhitmumpf was a false prophet. He has not followed the commandment 'Thou shalt not run a deficit.' He has brought a plague of white supremacists down on Vesampucceri. And, perhaps worst of all, he has mocked the righteous behind closed doors. For my sins, I shall atone."

Thus spake Senate Majority Leader Wichconnelliswich. He was turtleechifying (speechifying while being a turtle) about the challenge some Reduhblicans had made in the House and Senate to the voters chosen by the state of Arizama for the Electoral College. Ordinarily, this is a formality. But, under Ronald's Rules of Disorder, no political norm is too quotidian (not that the President would be able to quote one, let alone idians of them) that it cannot be overturned.

Outgoing Senator Kelly Loehanginfruitfler (in the sense of having lost her seat; the last time she was a social butterfly, Global Hot as Hellification hadn't decimated the flitting flutterers' population), put it in less Biblical terms: "I was going to vote in favour of the challenge to the Arizama electors because I only believe in state's rights when I want to stop collective federal government action. Of course, when I say that, I mean because so many people believe there was widespread Dumbopratic voter fraud in the state in the 2020 election. The fact that President McDruhitmumpf has been telling them there was widespread Dumbopratic voter fraud since he first took office in 2016 in no way changes my opinion of their impression. But, after the...unpleasantness that happened earlier today, I have rediscovered the love of democracy that I've never had, so I am going to oppose the challenge."

"Noooooooooooooooooooooooooo!" token smart person Amy Sheshutshotshitbam objected. She argued that the two parties viewed politics in fundamentally different ways: minority rule versus minorities rule. The Dumboprats understood that changes in Vesampuccerian demographics meant that people of pallor would soon become just another minority among minorities in the country, and that, to be successful, the party had to have a platform that took the interests of as many groups as possible into account.

The Reduhblicans, by way of contrast (it's just a matter of balancing blacks and whites, something the party has never been good at), has long said, "Screw that action, Jack! Okay, and Jacqueline – after all, we need the suburban housewife vote! We can keep appealing to our narrow base because we have a secret weapon: the Electoral College! Bwahaha!"

The Electoral College has handed Reduhblicans the Presidency in two elections in which they lost the popular vote, token smart person Sheshutshotshitbam continued to explain. "When they made impassioned speeches about the sacredness of the democratic process, they were actually defending the least democratic part of it! ...And, the moustache twirling was a bit over the top."

Token smart person Sheshutshotshitbam warned Dumboprats not to make the mistake of thinking that the conciliatory tone of many of the Congresspeople's remarks indicated that they would change their obstructionist course. "Honestly, the Dumboprats are the Charlie Browninpanforsix' of politics, always trying to kick the ball held by Lucy van Pellmellgontahell!"

When I looked like a shaken Etch-a-Sketch at her, she said, "Charlie Browninpanforsix. You know – you must know Charlie Browninpanforsix. From the *Aww, Peanuts to You* comic strip? It was in all the papers! Literally! For 50 years! Lucy always convinces Charlie Browninpanforsix she'll hold a football for him to kick, and he always believes her, and she always pulls it away at the last second! No? Honestly, were you raised in a barn?"

I defensively stuttered that my personal history was not germane to the story. Then, I pulled some straw out of my hair.

Token smart person Sheshutshotshitbam considered this a second, then continued: when Barry W. Bushbamclintreagbush was elected President, then Senate Minority Leader Wichconnelliswich said they should work together in a bipartisan fashion. Apparently, "work together in a bipartisan fashion" meant "I will slow walk and stonewall everything on your legislative agenda."

It's not too late for Dumboprats to learn how to speak Reduhblicanese.

"Eight Senators and over 140 Representatives voted to throw out the votes of millions of Vesampuccerians and replace them with the choice of Reduhblicans." token smart person Sheshutshotshitbam pointed out. "Either the party still has no intention of working with the Dumboprats when they take power, or it will have a hell of a Presidential nominating convention in 2024!"

Like, Cool Threads, Man

by NAOMI WOLGREEKLEISTEIGAN, Alternate Reality News Service Feminism Writer

A President's cabinet is a good indication of who the man is. Former President Ronald McDruhitmumpf's cabinet, for example, was an old, white linen wall hanging. By way of contrast, President Joe Bidenhisbeeswax' cabinet is a rich tapestry of colour.

Unfortunately, if you pull on a thread, the whole tapestry could start to unravel. And, the Reduhblicans have their thread pulling gloves on and heavy yanking in their eyes.

The nomination of Neera Tandentiousfudstuf, President Bidenhisbeeswax' choice to head the Office of Management and Budget, is hanging by a thread, a rich brown thread that would add some much needed colour to the cabinet tapestry. Why? She said mean things about Reduhblicans.

"The ferking bitch hurt my feelings!" said Reduhblican Senator Rand Paulonaldaphun. "Vote to confirm her? I'll vote to lock her up and throw away the key!"

"Yeah! Yeah! She should be put in jail! Or, worse!" agreed Reduhblican Senator Chuck Gasleygrassteahee. "Bad things should happen to her because she is such a ferking mean person! Bad, bad, hurtful mean. Bitch!"

"Bitch! Bitch! Bitch! Bitch! Bitch!" Reduhblican Senator Ted Downandmotleycrewz summed up.

In theory, this should not be a problem. The Dumboprats have 50 Senators; with Vice President Kamala Harristweedfashin as the tie-breaking vote, they can approve all of President Bidenhisbeeswax' cabinet threads.

Yeah, right. In theory, my ex should pay all of his alimony promptly and in full. I haven't heard from you in three months, Ted – am I going to have to call your parole officer? Because, I gotta tell you, Little Maggie's braces won't pay for themselves!

Ahem.

Dumbopratic Senator Joe Glaswalledmanchin has said he will not vote to confirm Tandentiousfudstuf. "I'm all about the bipartisanship," he explained, "and hurting the feelings of the opposition isn't in the spirit of cooperation across the aisle."

When I pointed out that Glaswalledmanchin voted for McDruhitmumpf nominee Richard Grenelleggsandhamm for Ambassador to Germany even though his partisan communications were so laced with profanities the Motion Picture Association of Vesampucceri gave them an X rating, he responded, "Oh, well, will you look at the time. I'm late for my...pedicure. Great talking to you!" and bolted for exit.

Could this be an example of unilateral bipartisanship? My current fling Tamara thinks the term is an oxymoron; I think the current Reduhblican Party is an oxymoron. When we're done flinging strawberry shortcake at each other, we agree to wait and see if "I HEART UNILATERAL BIPARTISANSHIP" starts trending on Twitherd, the only true test of the value of a phrase in Vesampucceri.

Ahem. Ahem. And, Ahem, again.

Tandentiousfudstuf is not the only Bidenhisbeeswax nominee who has come under fire from Reduhblicans (+ Glaswalledmanchin – you do the math). They argue that Califoralina Attorney General Xavier Becerratededge, the President's choice to head Health and Human Disservices, should not be confirmed because he isn't a medical doctor. This is unlike former President McDruhitmumpf's HHD head, Alex M. Alexiazar IV, who also wasn't a medical doctor, but...but...oh, well, will you look at the time. I'm late for my...hot rock facial! Gotta run – bye!

And, another brown thread may be pulled from the Dumbopratic cabinet tapestry.

The gang of two (Reduhblicans and Glaswalledmanchin) object to the nomination of Deb Haalandfarewellthee for being "radical." Not in the 1980s sense of being "totally gnarly," but in the 2000s sense of being "somebody we don't like for reasons we aren't going to come clean with you about, even if they're so transparent you should be able to figure them out yourself, and why should we do any of the work for you? So...nyah nyah!"

If confirmed, Haalandfarewellthee would be the first indigenous Vesampuccerian to hold a cabinet position in the country's history.

If she is not confirmed, that would be a yellow thread pulled from the Dumbopratic cabinet tapestry.

"Oh, man, can we be clear on something, please?" said token smart person Amy Sheshutshotshitbam, turning off the wind tunnel so she could be heard more easily. "Hundreds of Reduhblicans in Congress voted to not certify the results of the 2020 election. The only way they could have been more radical would have been if they had danced the cha cha naked on their desks while casting their votes!"

What if they were dancing the tango in their underwear?

"Can we please focus on what's important, here?" token smart person Sheshutshotshitbam demanded. "Compared to the average Reduhblican, Haalandfarewellthee is about as radical as a chicken trying to cross the road!"

What is the – you should pardon the expression – thread that connects all of these flailing cabinet nominations? They are all ardent supporters of People for the Ethical Treatment of Aardvarks. Anti-environmentalism: ✔. Many of them have two X chromosomes. Sexism: ✔. All of them are people of pigment. Racism: ✔ and mate.

"That's the thing about being a party that openly represents the racist right," token smart person Amy Sheshutshotshitbam pointed out, "you can be blatantly racist with no shame or embarrassment."

"Ain't it grand?" Senator Gasleygrassteahee crowed.

What Does A Body Have To Do To Get Cancelled Around Here?

by FREDERICA VON McTOAST-HYPHEN, Alternate Reality News Service People Writer

Pity Reduhblican Unrepresentative Paul Gokartmozartsar.

Here is somebody who wants to pawn the libs so badly (then, lose the broker's ticket and imagine the political party sitting on a dusty shelf between a rotary phone that hasn't worked since Nixwatmondnewon was president and a pink blob that may once have been some old guy's dentures or may just as easily be a wad of chewing gum in the shape of some old guy's dentures) that he'll say or do anything. He could remember a time when all you had to do to get media attention for days was to say, "White nationalist, white supremacist, Western civilization – how did that language become offensive? I've got it on my official Congressional letterhead!"

The times were more innocent when Senator Steve Kingfisherhelploess made that statement. Who can remember as far back as 2019?

Unfortunately for Unrepresentative Gokartmozartsar (and the world at large), the goalposts have been moved out of the stadium and travelled halfway across town to the docks, where they stowed away on a cargo ship bound for Europe. The last anybody had heard of the goalposts, they were making a pilgrimage to a sacred temple in the Andes. Which would, of course, require another trip across the ocean; whatever else they might be, the goalposts were never that great at geography.

I mean, when Unrepresentative Gokartmozartsar talks about white nationalism, does he get the outrage of the MSM? Is anybody trying to cancel him? No! The MSM (which sounds like the kind of candy one would enjoy while engaging in kinky sex play) is too enamoured of Senators who hang bible quotes outside their office door to let the gay Dumboprat across the hall know that they're going to burn in hell, and Unrepresentatives who make videos threatening the Speaker of the House with Second Amendment remedies if she doesn't "smarten up and fly right."

And, the worst part? **They're just girls!**

So, Unrepresentative Gokartmozartsar gives a speech at VAFLAC (duck!), the Vesampucceri (oh, come on) Absolutist (it was funny) Freedom (it's an insurance company or something) and Liberty (their mascot is a duck) Action (you know it was funny) Conference (honestly, some people wouldn't know humour if it slapped them on the side of the head and said, "Laugh, dammit!") where he touches on all of the white nationalist themes: white supremacy; white domination; white mastery. To really drive the point home, he lets Oaf Keepers take selfies with him and post them to the Dark Web (they should really be more punctual about paying their Hydro bills).

The day after he makes such a big splash at the white nationalist VAFLAC, Unrepresentative Gokartmozartsar gives a speech at CPAC, the Constipated (I'm not making a joke out of this acronym) Political (the effort would be wasted on you!) Action (make your own joke if you want to!) Commissariat (hunh – that was actually pretty funny. Have you ever considered a career in stand-up?), a conservative gathering. If the two haven't become more or less interchangeable by now. But does he dominate news cycles? No – he barely gets out of pre-rinse before the press' attention turns to the organizer of VAFLAC, Nick Foountoyuehs!

Foountoyuehs is an anti-Semite. He once made a remark about the gas chambers in concentration camps that caused the Betty Crockpotsludgecroaker estate to sue him for defamation. But, he is an equal opportunity offender. Foountoyuehs once offered a million dollars to anybody who could tell him of an accomplishment in the maths or sciences that hadn't been accomplished by a white person. When somebody told him, "Zero," he responded, "Exactly."

Foountoyuehs is the leader of a loose coalition of white nationalists called the gryipers, which infiltrates mainstream right-wing groups and moves them towards their racist agenda, much like algae infiltrates your fish tank and turns it into yuck. Other leaders of the gryipers movement include Patrick Incaseyofire (leader of the Vesampuccerian Identity Movement, formerly the Euvropa Misappropriated Spelling Movement, formerly the White Dudes Bitching About How Unfair Their Lives Are in Richie's Garage Movement), Michelle Malevolentkin (the self-described "mommy" of the gryiper movement, who will let her children eat anything they want as long as it is white) and a green blob that looks to many people like a misshapen frog, but has always struck me as the Nowhere Man from the movie *The Yellow Submariner*.

This unseemly stew of ingredients cannot make up its mind to either smell worse than it looks or –

"Hey!" Unrepresentative Gokartmozartsar interrupted my flow. "I thought this article was supposed to be about me! What the ferk! Are you one of those [REDACTED] who believe that white people should be [REDACTED] and a sack of potatoes named Rita

Haybaleisworthless? I should have known better than to trust a MSM reporter! You suck! And, not in a good way!"

On second thought, don't pity Unrepresentative Paul Gokartmozartsar. His moral compass is a 12 car pileup on the life is a highway.

The Sunshine of My Love/Hate

by FRANCIS GRECOROMACOLLUDEN, Alternate Reality News Service National Politics Writer

It's called The Sunshine Feels Nice, Ice Cream is Tasty and Kittens are Soft Act. The reason is because HR127 (simultaneously introduced into the Senate as S6) is simple enough, reading in its entirety: "This is an Act to affirm that this body believes that sunshine feels nice, ice cream is tasty and kittens are soft."

Even before the bill left the House Wheys and Meanies Committee, Reduhblicans fell all over themselves to oppose it. "Sure, it might make us feel good to pass a bill approving of sunshine," said House Minority Leader Kevin McCartilagebreak. "But, what about people who suffer from polymorphic light eruption, like vampires? Sunshine doesn't feel nice for them – it feels burny! Very burny! Like, deadly burny! For a government that claims that it wants to be inclusive, the Bidenhisbeeswax administration seems to have a blind spot for Vampiric-Vesampuccerians!"

"Kittens? Soft? Give me a break!" scoffed Senator Ted Downandmotleycrewz. "Have you ever been on the sharp end of their teeth? They're about as soft as granite! And, what about their claws? They're made for one thing and one thing only: drawing blood! It's about time the Dumboprats stopped lying about kittens and levelled with the Vesampuccerian people!"

"If the point was to get Reduhblicans on the record as being anti-kitten, the Dumboprats may as well have saved themselves the effort," observed token smart person Amy Sheshutshotshitbam. "Since the bill was introduced, 127 Farcebook pages denouncing kittens as tools of Satan who will smother your grandmother in her sleep if you're not vigilant have been created, and Foxindehenhaus News has run segments about 70 million Vesampuccerian dog owners who are offended that the Bidenhisbeeswax administration isn't looking after their interests. Sure, this resolution seems as Vesampuccerian as apple pie, but the Reduhblicans are so set on obstructing anything that the Bidenhisbeeswax administration tries to do that if they proposed a resolution approving apple pie, the Reduhblicans would object to it on the grounds that they are on a strict Keto diet, and they can't eat anything made with lard! And, their base would eat it up! The, uhh, the uhh, position, not the apple pie, I mean."

As if to prove her point, Senate Minority Leader Mitch Wichconnelliswich kept calm and turtled on: "This is just typical overreach by a Dumboprat administration. Telling us that a particular food is good. Ice cream. Did they give any thought to the lactose intolerant when they crafted this bill? Will they try to divide us along chocolate/vanilla lines? If the Dumboprats insist upon pushing this bill through the Senate, they'll be declaring war on Vesampuccerian freedom, and it's a war they're gonna lose!"

If the Reduhblicans filibuster the Senate version of the bill (which is a good bet considering they have filibustered every other bill the Dumboprats have put before them), it will take 60 votes to end the filibuster and bring the bill to a vote. That's 10 more votes than there are Dumboprats. What are their options?

If they amended the bill to add an expenditure of $50 for ice cream scoops and kitty litter, the two houses could pass the bill through reconciliation, which only needs a simple majority, token smart person Amy Sheshutshotshitbam explained. Oh, no, wait, they can't – they only get to do reconciliation once a year, and they've already used it to pass a COVID relief bill and an economic stimulus bill.

"Priorities," she sighed.

Another possibility is to amend the Senate rules to get rid of the filibuster.

"G...g...get rid of the filibuster? **You. Wouldn't. Dare.**" Minority Leader Wichconnelliswich, who used to twist Senate rules into pretzels with his eyes closed and one tongue tied behind his back when he led the body, blustered. "You can't just twist Senate rules into pretzels with your eyes closed and one tongue behind your back to ensure that your agenda will be passed. **That's not how the democratic process works!**"

Token smart person Amy Sheshutshotshitbam snapped her fingers. "I get it. I finally understand why Wichconnelliswich has assumed the demeanour of a turtle! It takes five hours for emotions to travel from their brain to their face – it allows him to say things like that without looking embarrassed by his hypocrisy!"

Of course, the Minority Leader is protective of the filibuster; it's the only weapon he's got, and he wields it like Jason wields...anything that comes to hand, really. (In fact, Jason takes almost as much pleasure gutting teenagers as Wichconnelliswich enjoys gutting Dumbopratic legislation.) The filibuster is the last thing that allows him to get away with minority rule, and he's going to do whatever he can to keep it.

"Wow," President Joe Bidenhisbeeswax marvelled. "This whole unity thing is a lot harder than I thought it was gonna be."

2. THE SLEEP OF REASON PRODUCES… GASLIGHTING

Dismantling the Santaveillance State, One Precious Snowflake at a Time

by SASKATCHEWAN KOLONOSCOGRAD, Alternate Reality News Service Religion Writer

With one month left to go before he leaves office (probably...maybe...if the whim takes him), President Ronald McDruhitmumpf is becoming increasingly unhinged, and the only handyman willing to go anywhere near him believes that a sledge hammer is the right tool for the job. Any job.

As part of a 40 minute rant on enough subjects to fill an encyclopedia, the President said this: "...by a landslide, people. I mean, the land slid so much, you would have thought it had been sitting in some grease. I mean, the skid marks went on for miles. Miles, I tell you. Try getting those out in your standard washing machine. Can't do it. You just can't – and, what about this Santa Reddingtoothandclaus character and his accomplice, Jack Frost? He comes down your chimney and eats your cookies and drinks your milk? Sounds like breaking and entering to me, with a little theft thrown in for good measure. Typical Dumboprat snatch and grab operation! I have directed Attorney General Katiebarrthudor to look into charging Santa Reddingtoothandclaus with crimes. A whole lot of crimes. Huge amount. He's an elusive bastard, I can tell you that – nobody ever sees him breaking into their homes. But, we'll get him. Trust me on this – we will prosecute this jolly old fat man to the fullest extent of the law!"

Attorney General Bill Katiebarrthudor supported the President's position with a terse, "I'm outta here."

However, President McDruhitmumpf's other enablers fell in line behind him, some with a lot more force than others. You wouldn't believe how destructive a simple line can be if you fall into it with enough force.

"He knows when you are sleeping?" goggled hysterical Foxindehenhaus anchor Lou Dobbsermanpincher (they really should have let him keep his uterus). "He knows when you're awake? That is **waaaaaaaaay** too much information to entrust a civil servant with! I mean – I mean – I mean, half the time, I don't know if **I'm** sleeping or awake! I could be sleeping right now and not even be aware of it!"

"He's making a list and checking it twice?" added Alex Jonesenforrahit of the web site *InfomercialWars*. "You know who else did that? That's right – Adolph von Hitlerskitler! But von Hitlerskitler didn't have the advanced computing technology that can sort through millions of girls and boys in a fraction of a second that we have today! And, don't be fooled: being bombed by toys is still a frightening experience!"

"They say he knows who's naughty and nice," Grey House Chief of Staff Mark Meadabiggblubratt, looking like a man who could see the shadow of the gallows and was desperate for a flashlight, picked up the complaint. "I say that we have a justice system to determine that. Just because some people consider you a saint, that doesn't mean you get to be judge, jury and toy distributor!"

"Acc-c-c-c-c-complice?" Jack Frost responded to the President's allegation. It was impossible to tell if he was cold or afraid. "I – I – I barely know Santa Reddingtoothandclaus! Sure, every once in a while we get together for a little eggnog and fantasy lacrosse league, but we never discuss what he does in his workshop. Never!"

You might have thought that ignoring last minute negotiations to get a COVID relief bill passed before the end of the year, when many provisions of the previous COVID relief bill will lapse, would take up all of the President's time. Obviously, you would once again have underestimated Ronald McDruhitmumpf's ability to multi-chaos.

"It's a disgrace," commented commentator Steve Aliasschmidtjones. "The President says whatever comes into his fevered imagination, and everybody in the Reduhblican Party tows his line." Falls into it, actually. "It's a fine line between towing and falling, but it's disgraceful no matter how you draw it!"

It gets worse. ("Of course it does!") An overnight Rasmussenandson poll indicated that 87% of registered Reduhblicans believe that Santa Reddingtoothandclaus is a Communist (why else would he wear red all the time?), and 84% of them were convinced that the Space Force should shoot down any vehicle in Vesampuccerian airspace that was driven by reindeer.

"I'm not surprised," Aliasschmidtjones responded. "When you live in an echo chamber, even the most ridiculous ideas will eventually take up far more space in your cranium than they deserve. Disheartened? Sure. Depressed? That's why I'm tranquilized to the gills. But, surprised? Not in the least."

"Wow," token smart person Amy Sheshutshotshitbam **was** surprised. "I never thought I'd see the party of the war on ChristmaKwaanzUkah become the party of the war on ChristmaKwaanzUkah!"

Santa Reddingtoothandclaus was unavailable for comment.

More About Rudy Giulihooeyboi's Junk Than Any Sane Person Would Want To Know

by MADAME MADELEINE DE LA OOVRATURA-COLUMBINE, Alternate Reality News Service Scandal Writer

A laptop* obtained** by President Ronald McDruhitmumpf's once and future attorney Rudy Giulihooeyboi*** contained incontrovertible proof**** that Democratic Presidential nominee Joe Bidenhisbeeswax' son Hunter had corrupt dealings in Ukraine***** that his father benefited financially from.****** Whether or not you are likely to believe that Vice President Bidenhisbeeswax is corrupt can be determined by whether or not you read footnotes.

"As an October Surprise, it's kind of...limp," commented financial journalist David Cay Johnstonmassacre. "Total junk, really. After four embattled years, it's almost as though Ronald just can't seem to get it up for the fight any more. Maybe the polls have him more concerned about electile dysfunction."

Giulihooeyboi originally took the laptop to Foxindehenhaus News in order to give its contents a wide audience. Maybe it was the peanut butter smeared all over the keyboard. Maybe it was the "Property of Johnny Applebauminsauce – adults keep out!" sticker on the front. Whatever the reason, Foxindehenhaus News decided not to report on it.

They have standards. Low, low bar standards (since low bars are all their journalists can afford to drink at), to be sure. Still. Standards.

The story was eventually broken by Rupert Murdochyerpayroo's *New Yoricknuhemwell Post* (the bar being so low for their reporters that they make their own hooch in the photocopy room; the fact that it often tastes like toner is just an unfortunate, and unfortunately gross, coincidence).

"It's obvious that Ronald is hoping to reprise his performance from 2016," Johnstonmassacre explained. "Remember: two weeks before the election, surrogates for his campaign released hacked emails purporting to be from Hillary Roocartoncleveman and her campaign. But, like a musician who just doesn't know when to stop touring, his audience isn't buying the nostalgia the way it once did.

"Ronald has a fundamental problem. If you've lost a loved one to COVID – or, if you, yourself, have died of the disease – if you or a loved one has lost a job because of the pandemic...or Ronald's disastrous trade wars, if you have had to endure taunts or violence from emboldened racists, or if you are a sentient being that has been paying attention, you know that **Ronald McDruhitmumpf has been President for the last four years!** He can't run against the Washburningdington establishment any more, because **he is the Washburningdington establishment!**"

I commended Johnstonmassacre on his ability to speak in bold face. "I've been covering Ronald for a long time," he sighed.

According to a NOBC/Rasmussenandson poll that came out the day after the story broke, 13 people changed their votes as a result of the allegations. Two Dumboprats decided to vote for President McDruhitmumpf, three Redubhlicans decided to vote for Vice President Bidenhisbeeswax, and 17 people decided to watch *Vesampuccerian Idol* and vote for the girl in pigtails who sang "Anarchy in the UK" with all her heart. (I know what you're thinking, and only have one thing to say in response: rounding. Math nerd!)

"The chaos **is** the point," explained token smart person Amy Sheshutshotshitbam. "Most Vesampuccerians don't follow politics as closely as we do – I know, right? It's like they have families or jobs or something else that's more important! – if rumours or halfuendoes can discourage them from voting, the Reduhblicans can steal another election."

But, is it working? As of this writing, over 50 million Vesampuccerians have voted. 50 million. With an m. For **m**any. Or, **m**ucho. Or, **m**aximal. Or, **M**illie. (Hi, Millie!) If the point of suspect Ukraine conspiracy theories is to suppress the vote, it appears to have failed spectacularly.

Johnstonmassacre stated: "That's the story of Ronald's life."

Oh, and Giulihooeyboi was also recorded in a hotel room with his hand down his pants while a girl he had been told was underaged watched, a scene that will appear in the new Sasha Baron

Canadiohen film. If he had any credibility left, this would almost certainly have destroyed it... *------

* The ownership of which has not been verified.

** Under mysterious circumstances.

*** Their relationship at the time was hazy.

**** In the form of emails that may have been tampered with.

***** Allegations that have been repeatedly refuted by Vesampuccerian intelligence agencies, which, despite myriad investigations, have never found any evidence of wrongdoing.

****** An allegation for which no proof has ever been offered. My typewriter is fast running out of asterisks, so this had better be the last footnote!

*------ Phew! Not a moment too soon!

There's Strategy. There's Tactics. Then, There's This...

by FRANCIS GRECOROMACOLLUDEN, Alternate Reality News Service National Politics Writer

One month after the election won by Dumboprat Joe Bidenhisbeeswax, President Ronald McDruhitmumpf has arrived at the throwing spaghetti at the wall to help wheat farmers stage of denial. (He would have been at a more traditional stage if he had thought to cook the spaghetti first.)

This morning, he went on Foxindehenhaus News and said: "The CIA. The FBI. Starfleet Command. I mean, where are they in all of this? If they haven't uncovered evidence of massive voter fraud, why not? Are they in on it? I'm not saying they were in on it, **but are they in on it?**"

Foxindehenhaus News host-goblin Maria Betaromeo nodded her head like a drinking birdie toy. It was a bit embarrassing when she became a little too enthusiastic and hit her head on the desk in front of her, but, professional that she is – aspires to be – in a future life – if she isn't reincarnated as a sea slug – she recovered with a shaky, "G...go on..."

"You think the President can't go any lower," responded security expert Malcolm Donneednopennance, "and then you see earthworms coming out of his ears. Our security personnel are some of the most dedicated professionals in government. To accuse them of throwing an election is beyond scurrilous. It...it's...it's..."

And besides, how could the security apparatus of the United States of Vesampucceri cover up stealing millions of ballots in the middle of an election when it couldn't cover up a third rate burglary or sending arms and a cake to Iran?

"Well, yeah, okay, there's that..." Donneednopennance allowed.

On Foxindehenhaus News the president continued. "You know what the real problem is? My voters. How do I know they actually voted for me? Maybe seven million of them went into the voting booth planning on voting for me, but flipped their vote to...the other guy. Were you there? I wasn't. Unless a watcher is there to verify that the person voted for the candidate they actually wanted – me – anything can happen when the curtain is drawn!"

"Yeah!" agreed Fred Alamageordie, who had shaved his head so he could have hair the colour of the President's transplanted into every follicle. "I went into the booth intending to vote for President McDruhitmumpf, but can I be trusted to actually have voted for him? **I don't know!** I think skis are a kind of Canadian torture device and I drink milk through my knees! **Do I sound like somebody who can be trusted to vote the way he intended?**"

While it may be comforting to President McDruhitmumpf to blame his voters for his election loss, Reduhblican leaders privately worry that such a position might discourage voters who don't trust themselves to cast a ballot for the candidate of their choice from participating in future elections. And when I write "future elections," I'm really talking about the two run-off elections in Georgissippi which could determine who controls the Senate.

"Is he completely insane?" wondered one high-raking official (he was cleaning leaves off his office desk at the time) whom witnesses to the tirade asked to be identified as Benate Bajority Beader Litch Bichconnelliswich. **"Is he trying to undo everything we've worked so hard to accomplish since before he was building Lego mansions in his playpen? Yes, I'm talking about a decade ago! It's enough to make me wish that I hadn't voted for the moron!"**

The next day, Senate Majority Leader Mitch Wichconnelliswich, with all of the excitement of a turtle on Xanax, said, "The President is pursuing every possibility to ensure that the election was free and fair. I'm sure he'll get bored with it soon eno – I mean, I have no doubt that once he has exhausted every remedy available to him, he will gracefully accept the results. Sure, he will."

As Presidential historian Michael Beschbefordatloess observed, President McDruhitmumpf is likely suffering from the dictator's dilemma. Most leaders are confronted by the question: is it better to be feared or loved? The dictator doesn't trust people in either camp. "The worse things get, the more paranoid the dictator gets. To the point where he lives by the maxim, 'I only trust me and thee. And I'm going to throw you into prison and have you tortured just in case I can't really trust thee.' It would be sad, really, if it wasn't so damned anthropic!"

Before I could ask Beschbefordatloess what he meant by that, Alamageordie started screaming, **"I have betrayed my dear leader! What am I going to do to make it up to – I know! I know what I'll do! I'll go back to the voting booth and...and...and vote again! Twice! Once to cancel out the vote I may have miscast, and once to vote for the person I really wanted to vote fo – but, what if I do it again? What if I miscast my two new votes for...the other guy? Aaaaaarrrrrrgh!"**

"These are difficult times for everybody," Benate Bajority Beader Bichconnelliswich muttered, shaking his head sadly.

Reduhblicans Really Know How to Bogey Man Down

by SASKATCHEWAN KOLONOSCOGRAD, Alternate Reality News Service Fairy Tale Writer

It is a tale that Reduhblican leaders tell their children (mostly backbenchers, but the occasional committee chair). It is a tale meant to instill fear and obedience in the faint of heart (mostly economists, but the occasional editorial writer).

It features the bogey man known as "El Deficito."

"We can't afford to give average Vesampuccerians more than $600 in additional emergency relief," intoned (as much as a turtle is capable of speaking in a dark tone) Senate Majority Leader Mitch Wichconnelliswich. "If we did, El Deficito would come into the homes of the wealthy and curse their first-born sons to a life of idle pleasures and decreasing family fortunes."

When asked about their first-born daughters, Wichconnelliswich responded: "They were cursed to a life of loveless marriages to consolidate the family fortunes on the day they were born. There's not much El Deficito can threaten them with after that."

Wichconnelliswich pointed out that it wasn't just the wealthy who would suffer. "El Deficito will force the middle class to pay more taxes – more than they already do, I mean – in order to feed its insatiable interest. It will be generations before decent, hard-working people will be able to, you should pardon the expression, enjoy the fruits of their own labours!"

"It's funny, isn't it," asked soon-to-be-Sacrificial President Joe Bidenhisbeeswax, "how tax cutting roadrunners become deficit hawks when they don't hold the purse strings? And, notice that I'm not laughing. It's not because I'm not a laugher. I love to laugh. Give me a good Gottsadlylowmarx Brothers film, and I'm on the floor. Laughing. I'm not laughing now because that's not the kind of funny the situation I just described is."

Nobody in the press pool (the water is shallow, but at least it's tepid) covering Bidenhisbeeswax understood his avian metaphor (his digression into the nature of laughter didn't help), so, responding to the confused looks everybody in the room was giving each other's cellphones, he responded: "Look, when they passed a tax cut for the wealthy that added two trillion dollars – that's trillion with a 't' ...and a 'rillion' – nobody was talking about El Deficito. Sounds to me like a story Reduhblicans tell to instill fear and obedience in the faint of heart."

"El Deficito is a capricious spirit," Wichconnelliswich, apparently auditioning to become the world's first reptilian theology master, explained. "There is no telling when he will manifest in the world, or which country's children he will haunt. This unpredictability is part of El Deficito's unique charmless scariness."

"Sounds awfully convenient to me," Bidenhisbeeswax grumbled.

"Capriciousness is usually to somebody's benefit," Wichconnelliswich mused. "However, because it is random, it does tend to even out over time. Or, at least, that's what I was taught at the economics dojo."

There is no evidence that ordinary Vesampuccerians are worried about El Deficito. In person-on-the-street interviews conducted for this article, typical responses were, "Is that a new type of potato chip?" and "Didn't they capture that Mexican doughnut lord?" and "Get out of my way – I'm trying to cross before the light changes!"

"The average Vesampuccerian can't really grasp what a trillion dollars is," explained Nobelthingido Prize winning economist Paul Krugalougieman. "Economists used to explain that if you stacked a trillion dollar bills on top of each other, you would have a pile that went to the sun and back three and a half times. We found that that metaphor lost its explanatory ability when people stopped believing that the sun was anything more than the headlights of a 1967 Ford Emu that drives around the Earth every 24 hours so we don't have to be in the dark all the time. It was a...a dispiriting experience for a lot of us, and the beginning of the end of the golden age of economic metaphors..."

Could the fact that the problems of Washburningdington don't amount to a hill of beans to people in Osh Kosh,Wisconnicut? "There does seem to be a basic disagreement on what is important, yes," Krugalougieman allowed.

Since it has little impact on the perceptions of average Vesampuccerians, why do Reduhblicans keep telling the story of El Deficito?

"It serves two purposes," explained Token smart person Amy Sheshutshotshitbam. "On the one hand, it keeps Reduhblicans in line and Dumboprats on edge. That's just how Mitch Wichconnelliswich likes it – turtley bastard. On the other hand, it makes it sound like Mexican immigrants are responsible for Vesampucceri's financial woes. Honestly, the only way it could be better for Reduhblicans would be if the fable of El Deficito brewed coffee for the entire caucus!"

We're sure Senate Majority Leader Wichconnelliswich is working on it, token smart person. We're sure he's working on it...

Ashes to Asses

by FRANCIS GRECOROMACOLLUDEN, Alternate Reality News Service National Politics Writer

Reduhblican House Minority Leader Kevin McCartilagebreak was outraged. His rage was so out, it could have won a Tony for its portrayal as the lead character in an off-off-off-off-off- (and, that's five offs, so you know it's serious theatre) Broadway revival of *Priscilla, Queen of the Desert.*

"From HR1 to voting to defund the police," the House Minority Leader stated, "House Dumboprats have abandoned any pretense of bipartisa – * HACK HACK COUGH * – sorry about that. I – my mouth is suddenly very dry." After a long chug from a nearby glass of water, Minority Leader McCartilagebreak tried again: "Okay. Take two. From HR1 to voting to defund the police, House Dumboprats have abandoned any pretense of biparti – * COUGH COUGH HACK PTUI PTUI *!"

The press conference had to be postponed as Minority Leader McCartilagebreak's mouth had filled with a flaky black substance that made it impossible for him to continue. A press release from his office later that day would claim that the Dumboprats had put the substance there.

A couple of days later, Ohaii Senator Rob Portwinwhiskyman stated in an interview, "President Bidenhisbeeswax faces a choice. It's the 2020s, and a man has to have choices. He can try to jam a $1.9 trillion bill through reconciliation with no GOP support, or he can act on the hopeful bipartisa – * ACK ACK ACK *! Whoa! Don't know what happened, there. Why am I so thirsty all of a sudden? As I was saying, the President can act on the bipart – * ACK ACK PTUI PTUI PTUI *!" The interview had to be cut short when Senator Portwinwhiskyman's face started turning purple.

Token smart person Amy Sheshutshotshitbam considered what had happened with awe and wonder. "The words of Reduhblicans are turning to ashes in their mouths! Literally!"

Token smart person Sheshutshotshitbam pointed out that this was likely a response to the blatant hypocrisy of the Reduhblicans to whom the ash faulting was happening. Minority Leader McCartilagebreak, for instance, led the Reduhblican effort to overturn the results of the 2020 election, hardly a bipartisan move (unless he had actually started to say that the Dumboprats were not being bi-artisanal, but what having two skills at craft creation has to do with legislating is an open question).

As for Senator Portwinwhiskyman, he had no problem with reconciliation when he voted to use it to – what was his phrase? – jam through a bill giving two trillion dollars in tax cuts to the wealthiest Vesampuccerians. He was oddly silent on the issue of bipartisanship in 2017 (unless he had actually started to say that Dumboprats were not being bi-courtesanal, although what having two concubines has to do with legislating is an open question...although why Reduhblicans would be fascinated by the concept is a closed question – a door slammed shut and bolted from the outside question, really).

In fact, Senator Portwinwhiskyman seemed not to have learned his lesson. After the COVID-19 relief bill was passed by both houses of Congress without a single Reduhblican vote and signed by President Bidenhisbeeswax, the Senator outed the bill's $29 billion for the ailing restaurant industry, saying that "it will help them survive the pandemic. Really, I'm proud that – * ACK ACK PTUI * – aww, come on! Not again!"

Speaker of the House Nancy Pelligrinosi was not surprised. "It's typical that they will vote no and take the dough," she stated. Then, she added: "Despite every one of them being a schmo, the legislation will be a go." After a moment, she continued: "So many a dudebro, but us they won't even slow! ...Too much? Yeah, that last one may have been a bit too much. I'll dial the rhyming back a bit. I...I may be a little giddy..."

Senate Minority Leader Mitch Wichconnelliswich called the COVID relief bill a "liberal wish list." ("Liberal wish list" is a Reduhblican synonym for "Dumbopratic mandate.") He seemed on solid ice with that complaint, but then he fired up his blowtorch. "This is going to saddle our children with so much de – * HACK HACK KAFF *! – herm. Excuse me. As I was saying, our children will be saddled with so much de – * ARRROOOOMPH HACK KAFF *! So – * HACK *! – much – * KAFF *! – de – AAAARRRRGH!"

"Whoa!" token smart person Sheshutshotshitbam whoaed. "I had no idea turtles had such perseverance! You've got to admire the way he spit the ashes out of his mouth and tried to keep going even as it filled up again. Of course, you have to admire whatever force in the universe is putting the ashes into the mouths of Reduhblican politicians even more. If this continues, I may have to reconsider my position on old white bearded omnipotent sky dudes!"

3. THE SLEEP OF REASON PRODUCES… INSURRECTION

What the Heck Do You Know? About Insurrection Day

1) What was Insurrection Day?

a) a movie directed by Roland Emmerichmondpoor in which an alien invasion teaches the world to celebrate Vesampuccerian values

b) a terrorist plot to overthrow the elected government of the United States of Vesampucceri

c) the culmination of 60 years of Reduhblican race-baiting and nurturing of white grievance...which resulted in a terrorist plot to...you know...

d) all of the above

2) Thousands of Vesampuccerian patriots waving the Confederate flag and threatening the lives of elected officials (which shows that, although they didn't appear to know the country's history, at least they were ignorant of its democratic traditions) broke down the doors of the Capitol building in Washburningdington and stormed in. What were they hoping to accomplish?

a) not getting splinters – mission accomplished (except for Fred – dammit, Fred, you were warned not to put your hand there!)!

b) everybody in Washburningdington knew that those were the ugliest doors of any government building in the country, but nobody was willing to do anything about them...until now!

c) well, isn't that just like life? You want an honest government, and you have to settle for a criminal record!

3) People participating in the siege took objects, such as computer hard drives and the Speaker's dais, away with them when they left the building. Why is this not grand theft?

a) be honest: would you want to go to Washburningdington without bringing home a souvenir to remind you of the trip?

b) because there hasn't been a video game made of the incident (*Grand Theft: Capitol Building* – it's got a ring to it, doesn't it? A certain...oomph – Rockstar, call me!)

c) because they were stealing objects patriotically

4) Some of the attackers brought zip ties. What were they planning on using them for?

a) closing garbage bags full of broken objects, and other trash that they had created, to clean the place before they left (they could be thoughtful that way)

b) closing garbage bags full of loot that they were planning on leaving the building with (they could be practical that way)

c) tying the hands of any politician they may have come across to make it easier to trot them out for the trial of their lives (they could be homicidal that way)

5) The insurrectionists viciously beat police officers protecting the Capitol, killing one. What happened to Blue Lives Matter?

a) Blue Lives Ma – oh, did you think we were talking about police? Silly you – we were talking about smurfs!

b) Blue Lives Ma – oh, did you think we were talking about police? Silly you – we were talking about musicians! You know: Blues Lives Matter? We can't help it if you need to get your hearing checked!

c) you're asking for consistent principles from a violent mob? You really don't understand how the world works, do you?

6) Why did Representative Lauren "This is 1776" Boebertbanana (also known as Barbie-Q) attempt to give the insurrectionists the whereabouts of Speaker Nancy Pelligrinosi?

a) oh, security told members **not** to do that! **Not!** She really needs to get **her** hearing checked!

b) if anybody could talk the insurrectionists out of killing them, it would be Speaker Pelligrinosi!

c) it's impolite to not answer a friend's question

7) Video shot during the insurrection shows some of the participants discussing tactics, very aware of the layout of parts of the Capitol building. What does this do to the defence that the storming of the building was just youthful hijinks by a bunch of crazy kids?

a) the long white beards on many of the male participants (and some of the female participants) should have been a clue that we weren't dealing with kids

b) the fact that there are kids with the foresight to plan their actions in that detail gives me a firm belief that the country has a bright future ahead of it

c) somebody is making the defence that the storming of the building was just youthful hijinks by a bunch of crazy kids? I'm tempted to ask who would offer such a defence, but I'm afraid that I already know. Very afraid...

8) Although the Capitol building had been closed, people who did not work there were seen walking around the day before the siege. These have come to be known as Insurrection Tours. (You may know them as Traitor Tours. They are also sometimes referred to as Treason Tours.) What was the purpose of these tours?

a) to hustle people to the Capitol gift shop so they could contribute to paying for the government by stealing overpriced trinke – wait...that can't be right...

b) to give the people who took them a greater appreciation of Vesampuccerian history, from the Confederate victory in the War of the States to the recent victory over COVID-19

c) it couldn't be to help the people who took them familiarize themselves with the layout of the building, because that would mean that the siege of the Capitol was an inside job, and that would mean...and the obvious conclusion would be...and and and, I think I may need to sit down for a spell – I feel the vapours coming on...

9) Only people who worked in the building could let people who did not in. Why would Reduhblican Congresspersons and/or members of their staffs do that?

a) they're just caring, sharing people

b) ...I think I may have to lie down in a dark room for several hours – the vapours are affecting me something right fierce today...

c) a wise butler once said: "Some people just want to see everything burn."

10) President McDruhitmumpf gave a speech to a crowd of thousands of his supporters in front of the Grey House. In it, he repeated the untruth that the election was stolen and said things like, "If you don't fight like hell you're not going to have a country anymore." If this was not incitement to violent insurrection, what was it?

a) a chocolate strawberry handshake

b) that song you can't get out of your head, which is called a word you can never remember

c) Bob

d) other

11) Senators Ted Downandmotleycrewz and Josh Heehaheehawley argued that the 2020 election was stolen by the Dumboprats (because they unfairly got more votes than the Reduhblicans) and, with six other Senators, refused to vote to approve the slate of Electors that would finalize President-elect Joe Bidenhisbeeswax' victory. Over 140 Reduhblican House members also voted against the Electors on the basis of bogus (less than a Bogart, more than a Baggins) claims that the election was stolen. What part did these efforts contribute to the attack on the Capitol?

a) $25,000 by wire transfer (most of which they could get back in a tax credit)

b) some plot points in the second act and a couple of witty zingers in the final conflict and denouement

c) absolutely none. That's a scurrilous suggestion! Our rhetoric and actions in no way contributed to the insurrection...unless they will get us the nomination for the Reduhblican ticket in 2024 or help us keep our seats in the next election, in which case we stood by President McDruhitmumpf in his hour of need – you remember us standing by the President, don't you? You – you must remember how we stood by the President...

12) Dozens of people on an FBI watch list of white supremacists/potential terrorists were known to be going to Washburningdington for January 6.

Why did this not raise alarms? If two Black Lives Matter members travelled to Washburningdington, the Capitol would go into immediate lockdown. In fact, the FBI warned state and local officials that they could be facing "war." Yet, all that happened was the silence of the crickets. Seriously, why wasn't more done to protect the Capitol?

a) you know, these sorts of things aren't black and white (the colour black is discouraged by violent policing and punitive sentencing in Washburningdington, so this issue is more ivory and alabaster)

b) some of the Capitol police were helping the insurrectionists, and they're terrible at multitasking

c) I can't comment on an ongoing investigation, but when it's over, you just try and get me to shut up!

13) Soon after Congress was able to return and complete voting on the results of the Electoral College, Rudy "Rude Boi" Giulihooeyboi called Senator Tommy Tudorbervilla to ask him to challenge each state's choice of Electors, delaying the vote as long as he could. We know this because Giulihooeyboi left a message on the wrong Congressperson's phone; they immediately made it public. Why is Rudy Giulihooeyboi still President McDruhitmumpf's lawyer?

a) the President is planning on hosting a late night chat show when he leaves office, and he needs a stooge – sorry, **comic foil** to co-host

b) the President has stiffed so many lawyers in Washburningdington of fees that they had earned working for him that they have created the Ronald McDruhitmumpf For Never Association (if you can find it, read the newsletter – the cartoons are a hoot!). On the theory that they wouldn't want to belong to any club that had Rudy Giulihooeyboi as a member, he has never been invited to join

c) his creative use of hair dye

14) In the aftermath of the attack on the Capitol, the House of Unrepresentatives voted to encourage Vice President Michael Pendenatendance to use the 25th amendment. What would that empower him to do?

a) give the President a hickey in an embarrassing place

b) put a whoopee cushion on the chair of the President before the start of an important international negotiation

c) pass go and collect $200

d) other

15) Some of the people who attacked the Capitol building chanted, "Hang Pendenatendance! Hang [don't make me repeat myself] Pendenatendance." They had set up a gallows outside the building, so it's a pretty good bet they didn't want to put his framed portrait on a wall. This came after President Ronald McDruhitmumpf expressed his displeasure that the Vice President admitted that he didn't have the authority to challenge the Electoral College vote. In a tweep. At 2:37 in the morning. As Presidents will. Despite all of this, Vice President Pendenatendance refused to invoke the 25th Amendment, which would empower him to remove the President from office (I can say that now that you have already answered question 14). Why?

a) Vice President Pendenatendance has no imagination

b) Vice President Pendenatendance has no spine

c) Vice President Pendenatendance does have convictions, but they mostly revolve around running for the presidency in 2024

16) President McDruhitmumpf had less than two weeks in his term when the House of Unrepresentatives voted to impeach him on grounds that he incited the insurrection. What did they hope that would accomplish?

a) add excitement to what is usually a routine, one might even say boring, transition

b) give them something to do so they wouldn't have to shelter in place with their families (they're really getting sick of spending time with their families)

c) I don't know – justice or something?

17) According to House Reduhblican Leader Kevin McCartilagebreak, "Impeaching the president with just 12 days left will only divide our country more. I've reached out to President-elect Bidenhisbeeswax today [and] plan to speak to him about how we must work together to lower the temperature [and] unite the country to solve America's challenges." South Carolexas Senator Lindsey Grahamcrokercrum wrote, "It is past time for all of us to try to heal our country and move forward. Impeachment would be a major step backward." Ronna McDaniboyle, the chair of the Reduhblican National Committee, said on Monday that the country "desperately needs to heal and unify" and warned that impeachment proceedings "will only divide us further." Given how much the

Reduhblican Party has vilified Dumboprats for the last 20 years, how hollow are these pleas for unity?

a) the constant echoes have driven deaf people insane

b) the pleas for unity are not bigger than a bread box, but when you look into them, there doesn't appear to be a bottom

c) even Punxsutawney Phil doesn't believe them, and he'll come out of his hole at the drop of an equinox!

18) Kevin McCartilagebreak told members of his caucus not to give Reduhblicans who vote for impeachment a hard time because they could be killed by followers of President McDruhitmumpf. **They could be killed by followers of President McDruhitmumpf!** Sooooo...how has four years of absolute subservience worked out for ya?

a) uhh...

b) oh...

c) I've just been told that bullet-proof vests can be charged to my Congressional office account, so I would say that it has been a learning experience...

19) President McDruhitmumpf says he was shocked by the violence at the Capitol building. If this is true, why did he watch it while eating popcorn and cheering?

a) Super Bowl nostalgia

b) he had been told by Stephen Siewnottmillertyme that he was watching a historical reenactment of the War of 1812; he was eagerly anticipating the fireworks at the end of the show

c) the empty popcorn bowl lies

20) The United States has a definition of domestic terrorism, but, unlike international terrorism, the country has no law specifically targeting it. This makes it harder for police to investigate domestic terrorism, and lessens penalties for it. Why is there no law against domestic terrorism?

a) white people aren't violent

b) well, yeah, okay, sure, white people can be violent, but they only kill others for personal reasons; it's never political

c) on the advice of my lawyer, I refuse to answer this question on the grounds that it may incriminate my race

The Blood of Patridiots

by MARA VERHEYDEN-HILLIARD, Alternate Reality News Service Revolution/National Security Writer

A man in the furs and tattoos of an ancient Viking, wearing antlers that were all the rage in 921, carried an AK47, all the rage in 2021, into the chamber where the House of Unrepresentatives had been sitting only 9 minutes and 37 seconds before. What is wrong with this picture? Beyond the fact that the man's ancient Norse accent improperly confused "r"s and "d"s, I mean.

He was just one of 10,000 people who stormed the capital building (one of the few forecasts that Washburningdington weather people got right, not that they are planning on boasting of it), chasing Senators and Unrepresentatives into bunkers in undisclosed locations and temporarily stopping the counting of the Electoral College votes that would confirm that Joe Bidenhisbeeswax will be the next President of the United States of Vesampucceri. And taking selfies sitting in the Chair of the Speaker of the House, because I don't want to be part of your insurrection if I can't dance.

Men with Confederacy of Dunces flags used official Congressional stationary to send faxes to their friends that the race war had begun. Other men with swastika tattoos (who all identified themselves as "Mister Oswald"), rifled through the desks of Senators, disappointed that they couldn't find any porn (which they referred to as, "Evidence that they're a bunch of race traitors."). Everybody yelled at the Capitol police, who, their feelings hurt, kept retreating deeper and deeper into the building (although the fact that they were outnumbered 207 to one may have had something to do with it).

The insurrectionists were there and acted that way because of a rally President Ronald McDruhitmumpf held nearby in which he told them to go there and act that way. "I will stand there with you," he told his supporters. Only, soon after he made that statement, the President must have realized that there wasn't very good golfing in the Capitol complex, because he went back to the Grey House after the violent chaos started.

It took five hours – and a National Guard deployment – to clear the building and restore order. In all, four people were arrested. Three of the people who were arrested were people of pigment. "We cannot allow anarchy to rein in our nation's capital," said Washburningdington Police Chief Robert J. Proconteekeelamppe III. "No more than the usual Reduhblican antics, I mean. We have to show the country that this behaviour will not be tolerated."

The person of pallor who was arrested had shot another protester in the throat; she subsequently died in the hospital. "He was young," Chief Proconteekeelamppe III stated, "and made a mistake. He will have to live with the guilt for what he did for the rest of his life. He's been punished enough."

"I wadn't pard of da prodest," protested Rakeem Alicadabra through a swollen lip, his one eye that wasn't bruised shut looking me straight in one of my good ones. "I wad on vacadshun and wanded do see da nadshun's capidal."

"Where's my lawyer?" demanded the person of pallor, whom police would only identify as "John Doeliodingdong, as he sipped tea from a China cup. "I should be out on bail, already. This is war, and in any war, there will be casualties. So, the first casualty was on our side. Oops. The cactus of liberty must be refreshed with the blood of patridiots. Not my blood – I'm not stupid. I mean the blood of – **where's my lawyer?**"

President Ronald McDruhitmumpf's Farcebook and Twitherd accounts were suspended for 24 minutes because of a video he posted during the assault in which he said, "Has everybody been pushed out of the Capitol building? Okay, then it's time to go home. Go home, everybody. Enjoy a beer and...whatever meat you can afford. You've earned it. You're special, snowflake, and I – we – like – love you – or, somebody very much like you, but with better table manners. Know that I will keep fighting against this rigged election – so rigged – so...an election. I will keep fighting for you, if you will keep fighting for me. We won't stop fighting until the fighting is over. Because that's what patridiots who love their country do."

"So, the President of the United States incited his followers to violently overthrow the government in order to maintain his hold on power," commented MSNBC anchor Joy Reidemanweepson (congratulations on your new show, Joy!). "That was not at all predictable. Nope. Could not see that one coming."

The question is: why were the Sons of Sea Otters not more afraid of the Tiki lamps the Prude Bois were drunkenly waving around? But, uhh, the more important question is: what is going to be done about the President's role in the insurrection?

The House could impeach the President. Again. We all know how well that turned out last time. Vice President Michael Pendenatendance could invoke the 25th Amendment, which would give Cabinet the power to remove the President on the coffee grounds of mental incompetence. However, Pendenatendance's head has been so far up the President's butt, he hasn't seen daylight in four years, so it's hard to see that happening. The media could shame the President into resigning. It's a shame that it has come down to that, but...

Oh, and Reverend Raphael Makepeacenotwarnock and Jon Cumlafferossoff won the run-off elections in Georgalina, giving the Dumboprats control of the Senate. But, that's not important right now. Apparently.

The View From Under the Desk

by FREDERICA VON McTOAST-HYPHEN, Alternate Reality News Service People Writer

Ruby Yumi-Fajitas was taking a break year between high school and college to intern for Speaker of the House Nancy Pelligrinosi. She had been awarded the coveted position by writing an essay on the subject "The Future is Us." She had no idea that the future would be hitting her mere days after moving to Washburningdington.

"Everything goes so much faster in the nation's capital," Ruby breathlessly commented (the future had knocked the wind out of her).

When the treasonous insurrectionists (I know, I know, seditious would be a more accurate way of describing their behaviour, but not many people know what that word means – oh, yeah? Use it in a sentence, wise guy! – but, everybody knows what treason is, even if they're wrong, so...) stormed the Capitol building, Ruby was being walked through the arcane rules of the House cloakroom by an aide to the Speaker. A secret service woman stuck her head in the door, considered for a second (probably calculating how much space was left in the Capitol safe rooms, and whether Ruby and the aid were important enough to fill any of that space) and said, "The building is under attack. Secure yourselves." Then, she ran out.

"We were stunned," Ruby admitted. "For about two seconds. Then, we heard the shouting from down the hall. So, we shut the door, turned the lights off and huddled under a desk at the back of the room."

Ruby passed the time under the desk by playing *Angry Crustaceans* and *MimeCraft*, and checking her Twitherd feed for celebrity gossip (learning the arcane rules of the House cloakroom didn't seem all that important if there was a good chance she wouldn't live long enough to apply them). Occasionally, a mob passed by the door of the cloakroom chanting things that sounded like, "You want hemocracy? This is what democrabby looks like!" and "Bring me the bed of Michael Pendenatendance!"

"I may not have gotten that exactly right," Ruby allowed. "You'd be surprised how thick the doors of the Capitol building are!"

Was she scared? I would have been scared if I was her. Was Ruby scared by what was happening?

"Naaah!" she waved a dismissive hand at me that practically shouted, "You old silly." I did feel like an old silly, too. Ruby's dismissive hand can be very persuasive. "I've been doing active shooter drills in school since I was six years old. That's at least one thing I learned in high school that will be useful to me throughout my life!"

A couple of hours into the siege, a rioter in what looked like a fur coat and antlers opened the door and poked his head into the cloakroom. "I thought we were being attacked by an angry mob of deer," Ruby stated. By the time her eyes adjusted to the light from the hallway, the man asked, "Is there anybody in here? Anybody?"

Ruby and the aide were silent. So, believing he was alone in the room, the man entered and peed in a corner.

"I was furious!" Ruby remarked. Because of the desecration of a historical building that many people in the country consider sacred? "Because I had to stop playing so that I wouldn't give away our presence. And, Bruno, the alpha lobster, was about to take on the boss hogg! It took me hours to get to that point in the game!"

In all, Ruby and the aide stayed under the desk for seven hours. "It was a little cramped," she claimed. "I'm not used to sharing space under a desk – my high school wasn't **that** underfunded! But, we took turns sticking our legs out every 15 minutes to avoid getting cramps, so we got by. We got by..."

Then, Representative Alexandria Casio-Keebjords walked into the room to get her coat and, noticing a pair of legs sticking out from under a desk, said, "Oh, hey. You're still here? The riot ended an hour ago!"

"I grew up in the 1950s," Speaker Pelligrinosi stated the next day when she was apprised of Ruby's experience. "I remember duck and cover exercises – thanks nuclear bomb! So, I feel a...a...a kinship with young people today. Their music sucks, but other than that, we have a lot in common!"

Did the experience sour Ruby on public service? "Are you kidding?" she enthusiastically responded. "It was like *Dye Hard* with lawyers! So. Many. Lawyers! I am so stoked to be working in the office of the Speaker of the House! Is that going to happen every week?"

Not if the FBI, the National Guard and the Capitol Police have anything to say about it. So, definitely maybe.

Fake News, Real Violence

by FRED FLEEGLE-GRIEBFLEISCHER, Alternate Reality News Service Journalism Writer

The award for the most creative use of camera equipment goes to the anonymous person who fashioned a noose out of the cord of a battery pack. There is, of course, no award for the most creative use of camera equipment, but the noose was very real. Scarily real.

Idiotocracy wasn't the only institution to be attacked by right-wing terrorists at the Capitol building on January 6; journalism was. And, when I say journalism, I mean journalists. And, when I say journalists, I mean me.

"Are you a member of the press?" a large man in camouflage gear, ski mask and goggles (which made him look like an alien escapee from a *Star Blap* movie) challenged me as I observed other journalists at work.

"N...n...n...no," I responded. "What...what would ever give you that idea?"

"For one thing, you're writing in a notebook," a young woman with a wrinkly face (she must have been part shar pei) wearing a Make Vesampucceri Great Again hat accused me.

I threw my pen and notebook away. "No, I'm not," I told her.

"That means nothing," *Star Blap* alien escapee guy stated. "You could have an eyedietitic memory!"

"I don't! I swear!" I retorted. "I've had a bad memory since I was hit in the head with a flying moose when I was six years old! Honestly! What are we even talking about, again?"

A weaselly guy brandishing a Confederate flag as though he were using it to joust (yes, without a horse – ground jousting is a time-honoured tradition in European countries where the gentry rides coconuts) pointed out, "You're wearing a badge that says PRESS in large letters!"

"Wha – what, that?" I will admit, I had to struggle with this accusation. "I – it's – it's a reminder that I have to get this coat ironed. Did I mention that my memory isn't that great? I can never remember..."

The three people, and several of their friends, moved towards me menacingly. I would likely have received a beating had that not been the moment that a great roar came from the front of the Capitol building, which had just been breached. When the moblet turned to add their peeps to the roar, I did what any other self-respecting journalist in my situation would have done: I ripped the badge off my lapel and started cheering with the crowd.

Not wanting to be killed on the job is a form of self-respect, right?

"Journalists were targeted by the insurrectionists," said token smart person Amy Sheshutshotshitbam. "It makes sense, when you consider that for four years President McDruhitmumpf has been complaining about 'fake news' and claiming that journalists are 'the enemy of the people.' Journalists are one of the most hated groups in Vesampucceri, second only to Dumbopratic politicians."

Even worse than mass murderers?

"Worse than mass murderers, pornographers and late night cleaning products spokespeople," token smart person Amy Sheshutshotshitbam affirmed.

Wow. That's a lot of hate.

The mood of the crowd was summed up by one person who had scratched "murder the medya" into a door of the Capitol building. Under the circumstances, none of the journalists covering the event wanted to correct the message's spelling, so by psychic agreement, we all assumed that the word was a combination of "media" and "hyena." A hyena is sort of like a jackal, and past Reduhblican politicians had talked about "the jackals of the press," so it kind of made sense if you didn't think about it too much.

None of us were motivated to think about it too much.

In the middle of the insurrection, a pile was made of cameras and equipment that had been "liberated" from the journalists who had owned them. Some of the rioters tried to light the pile on fire, but being made of plastic and steel, it was a waste of matches. I considered retrieving my notebook and offering it to the insurrectionists as kindling, but decided that I hadn't been around them long enough for Stockholm Syndrome to kick in.

Token smart person Sheshutshotshitbam shook her head sadly. "Attacking journalists is something that happens in dictatorships. The point is to delegitimize any independent sources of information so that the only source a dictator's followers will believe is the dictator. It's sort of like kindergarten, but without the naps, because, of course, evil never sleeps."

I would quit my job and become a squash ball farmer if I didn't fear my editrix-in-chief more than an insurrectionist mob. That and the coffee in the bullpen. It's not great, but it's hot and it flows freely, and that's more than you can say for most people these days!

Diggler, He, Diggler, He, Doodoo

by GIDEON GINRACHMANJINJa-VITUS, Alternate Reality News Service Economics Writer

You can find him on the outskirts of any insurrection, far enough away from the young men taunting the gendarmes not to be endangered by them, and far enough away from the gendarmes to be safe until they reveal where their allegiances lay. He opens an attache case which, improbably, balloons into a small table on which all of his wares – including "Keep Vesampucceri Great" antler hats, Vesampuccerian flags with only 13 stars and bags of popcorn – the bags of popcorn do not replace the other 37 stars, they are a different product entirely – if only there was a punctuation mark that could separate the flags from the bags in the sentence! – are neatly arranged for ease of purchase.

"Step right up, ladies and gentlemen. Step right up," he launches into his *spiel*, attracting the interest of parents who have brought their children to Washburningdington to see history in the unmaking. "I don't bite...unless you're willing to pay an extra fee for the service. Ha ha – but I kid. There are small children here. Step right up and get your 'January 6, 2021: I attended the start of the race war, and all I got was this lousy criminal record' t-shirt. Machine-washable, the t-shirts are pure cotton...and polyester. They come in two colours: grey and...deeper grey. Perfect for birthdays and political coups! Get them for $29.95 while they las – no, I may be slitting me own throat by doing it, but, for a limited time only, you can have one for $19.95! You can't ask for fairer than that!"

He is a diggler by trade, if not by name.

He continues: "Take this novelty item: it looks like a mug with an image of President Ronald McDruhitmumpf in a smart suit, yeah? Put a hot liquid in it, and the suit melts away to reveal a swastika tattoo on his chest! Fun for the whole family! And, it can be yours for only...$19.95 or two – because you've got more than one hand – two for the low, low price of $45.50! Me mum would kill me if she knew how I was letting you take advantage of me like this! Don't let the opportunity pass you by – take advantage of it! Take advantage of it now!"

Even as he was doing brisk business outside the Capitol building, digglery was being conducted inside. Missouraii Reduhblican Senator Josh Heehaheehawley, who had raised his fist in support of the insurrectionists as he entered the Capitol building, sent out a fundraising letter as people gathered outside.

"They want to shut me up," he wrote. "They want to disenfranchise millions of voters by not rejecting millions of votes, and they want me to stop calling them on it! Well, I won't! But I need your help!! For the low, low contribution of $100, you can make sure my voice continues to be heard in Washburningdington! Honestly, I'm slitting my own throat offering you democracy at such a low, low price!! But, even if the metaphor is literalized, I assure you that I will use an electronic voice synthesizer so that I can continue to speak untruth to the powerless!"

"Respect," the diggler outside marvelled.

"Oh, Lordy, Lord, do I have to?" moaned Pulippitzaner Prize-winning *Washburningdington Post* columnist Eugene Robinsoncrusoe as he slumped in his chair. It was like all of the bones of his body had suddenly melted away. It seemed clear that Robinsoncrusoe was suffering from McDruhitmumpf fatigue, a recently discovered malady that affects 51% of the Vesampuccerian population.

"I mean, honestly," he weakly stated, "is there anybody who doesn't understand that making money off of violent insurrection is...kind of wrong?"

"What, a man can't make an honest living?" protested the diggler outside. "You want to take food out of the mouths of the children I may some day have? Shame on you for even suggesting such a thing! Here! Have a commemorative tie-clasp/memory stick/talcum powder. Only $10.99, but, for you, make that $15.99! At that price, you'll be taking food out of the mouths of the children I may some day have!"

The diggler inside gave me a cool look before answering: "Money is speech. Speech is money. If you attack my method of fundraising, you attack the most fundamental right a Vesampuccerian has: the right to speak his mind. Go ahead and try it: I'll have material for fundraising letters for the next three weeks!"

What a Cop Out!

by HAL MOUNTSAUERKRAUTEN, Alternate Reality News Service Crime Writer

The police exist to serve and protect. Not in the sense of bringing food to your table (although right about now, I could use a rack of ribs with a side of a second rack of ribs – where did I put that UberPigOut menu?). Not in the sense of starting a round of tennis (the one sport that teaches fans what it's like to be a metronome). No, in the sense of being in the service of the public. No, not a tea service – that's what I get for writing stories at lunchtime!

So, when thousands of far right reactionaries, fuelled by the President's incendiary rhetoric (he had obviously been eating the hottest chicken right wings – where **did** I put that UberPigOut menu**?**), stormed the Capitol, where were the police?

According to images from the scene, some of them were ushering the insurrectionists into the building. (That still doesn't mean that they worked in restaurants, although I will admit it is becoming harder to dismiss that conclusion.)

"Those were the Capitol Police," pointed out MSNBC host Chris Carfairindrughayes. "Think of them as...hall monitors with uniforms and sidearms. The situation required a more experienced police force – the FBI, for instance. The National Guard. NCIS Fargo. Where were **they**?"

According to other images from the scene, some police who were supposed to be protecting the Capitol were taking selfies with members of the mob who were there to loot it. Like they were sports stars or something. (Does tennis even have stars? No matter – this isn't like that at all!)

"Nope. Those were still the Capitol Police," Carfairindrughayes countered. "They're good if you need somebody to mediate between two little old ladies who are arguing over the last Statue of Liberty fridge magnet in the gift shop. The people that were needed here were the police in riot gear, the ones who have experience dealing with mobs. You know – the ones the government sends to Black Lives Matter protests?"

Oh. **Those** police.

They needed permission from the Secretary of Defence to protect the Capitol Building. They didn't get it, so they were doing traffic duty. Which is kind of like being an usher of the roadways (but, honestly, I had thought we were past the whole restaurant thing! I have given up on finding the UberPigOut menu and have reconciled myself to eating stale Cheetohs and something that may once have been pizza).

"Would that be acting Defence Secretary Chris Siewnottmillertyme?" Carfairindrughayes demanded. "Because, you know, President McDruhitmumpf keeps all of his appointees on a short leash. So short, in fact, that when he walks them, he has to keep them in his back pocket!"

Oh, it gets better. Or, worse, depending upon your point of view. It gets [INSERT DIRECTION HERE]. Marylina Representative Steny Hoyerinfoyer called his state Governor, Larry Hoganheroics, from the secure under the desk where his Secret Service security team had placed him, pleading for him to send help. Governor Hoganheroics tried to get permission from the Pentagon to send troops to help the besieged Capitol, but all he got was the message: "Hello. All of our operators are currently occupied running for their lives from an insurrectionist mob. Please hold. Your call is important to us. Somebody – quite possibly a janitor or one of the cafeteria staff – will answer your call just as soon as they have stopped fearing for their lives."

To add insult to injury, the message then faded into a muzak version of "Anarchy in the UK."

An hour and a half after Representative Hoyerinfoyer's call, Secretary of the Army Ryan McCarthyesque phoned Governor Hoganheroics and asked if he had a few Marylina State Guards lying around that he could spare to, you know, **defend the Capitol?**" By that time, of course, offices had been trashed and the Capitol rotunda had been used as a public privy, but the actual police quickly cleared the rioters out of the building and created an ever-widening perimeter around it.

"That...that delay was unconscionable!" Carfairindrughayes commented. "Was the President directly involved?"

We do not know at this time. What we do know is that when the President wants to clear a peaceful protest out of a public square so that he can have a photo op at a church, he has no trouble getting National Guards when he wants them. I leave it to you to connect the dots.

"But, those dots are bigger than New Yoricknuhemwell!" Carfairindrughayes pointed out.

Readers have a plethora (more than a fungal infection, less than a thesaurus) of media options these days. No point in making it hard for them!

The Thin Blue Lie

by FRANCIS GRECOROMACOLLUDEN, Alternate Reality News Service National Politics Writer

The problem with a mob howling for blood is that they don't care whose blood has to be cleaned out of the carpet.

Case in point (a sharp, one might say deadly one): the Capitol insurrection. You send a mob out to spill the blood of your Vice President, and you end up with one police officer dead and 139 others wounded. Bloodthirsty mobs are truly the ICBMs of interpersonal interaction.

This is not supposed to happen. Partially because this is not supposed to happen, but mostly because the Reduhblican Party is the party of lawnorder. According to them, police are not the people who are supposed to be mown down, they are the ones who are supposed to do the criminal trimming and hedging.

"I love cops. More than I love vanilla ice cream and pwning the libs," said an average Reduhblican Senator, who, for the sake of simplicity, we'll call Roy Bulldogexuent. "Like the thin outer layer of a soap bubble, the thin blue line makes it possible for everybody to stay clean! There's nothing I wouldn't do for the fine men and women of our country's police forces."

Like denouncing the insurrectionists who injured so many of them, as well as the political enablers who encouraged their blood lust?

Senator Bulldogexuent looked at the egg timer on his wrist and remarked, "Oh, well, will you look at the time! I gotta go get my...car permed. It's a very...personal thing, so I hope you'll allow my vehicle its privacy. I'll answer your question as soon as I get back from the automotive salon – it shouldn't be more than a couple of weeks!"

"I love cops. More than I love my wife and almost as much as I love my AK47," said another average Reduhblican Representative, who, to avoid confusion, we'll call Mo Brooksnoahgumeant. "They are the front line of the war against bad things in our neighbourhoods. I support the fine men and women of our country's police forces 137 per cent! No, 138! I go that extra per cent to show how seriously I take them!"

Seriously enough to support the Bidenhisbeeswax administration's COVID-19 relief bill, which includes payments to states and municipalities that will help them stave off laying off law enforcement officials?

Brooksnoahgumeant looked at the abacus on his wrist and commented, "Oh, well, will you look at the time! I gotta go do something with somebody, and I would hate to keep whoever it is waiting. Tell you what, though. I will definitely go to the vault where I keep my conscience and see what it has to say on the matter. I have to warn you, though, that the vault is somewhere at the bottom of the Atlantic, so it may take me some time..."

"The Reduhblican Party is now the party of Ronald McDruhitmumpf," explained token smart person Amy Sheshutshotshitbam, "and he cares for police about as much as a flea cares that the dog it's on is lying on a comfortable couch in a stateroom on The Titanic. So, the Reduhblican Party now cares for the police about as much as the colourful metaphor I can't be arsed to repeat."

But...but...but, what about Senate Minority Leader Mitch Wichconnelliswich? Surely, he would be willing to stand up for what used to be a core element of the Reduhblican identity...wouldn't he?

"Mitch Wichconnelliswich's soul long ago took on the consistency of curdled milk," token smart person Sheshutshotshitbam stated. "This latest indignity may add a little additional bacteria to the mix, but it's not like anybody in the party has ever complained about the smell or would notice the difference in taste. For many years, now, they have all eaten –"

What does this mean for the future of the Reduhblican Party? I hastily asked. Its staunch support of law enforcement personnel has usually been repaid by the loyal support of police and military across the country. If the party is unwilling to stanch the wounds of rank and file officers, how can it expect their continued support?

"You've hit the nail on the cuticle, Francis," commented former Reduhblican Congressperson David Jolielebonhomme, who got out of the party when the gettin' was good. "So far, law enforcement personnel seem to be sticking by the Reduhblicans – it will take more than acetone to dissolve that bond! However, I expect that donations from the Union and individuals will start to drop off sooner rather than later."

How will Reduhblicans make up the shortfall?

"They could always try selling the golden McDruhitmumpf they were showing off at QPAC," Jolielebonhomme suggested. "Although, knowing McDruhitmumpf, he would probably keep the proceeds to pay off his legal bills!"

The Suit That Walks Like a Man

by FRED CHARUNDER-MACHARRUNDEIRA, Alternate Reality News Service Science Writer

The question on everybody's mind is: is the last piece of foozleberry pie in the fridge, or did somebody finish it?

Fortunately, I don't have to answer that question (partially because the right not to incriminate myself is universal, but mostly because I'm not a food writer). The question I do have to answer, the question that is on the minds of 63 per cent of the people who live in Washburningdington (which makes it approximately 3.74689 per cent of everybody) is: what has happened to former Vice President Michael Pendenatendance?

The short answer is: he imploded. Unfortunately, journalists don't make much of an income at the best of times, and short answers aren't even close to the best of times, so allow me to explain.

During the Senate impeachment trial of Ronald McDruhitmumpf, it was revealed that the former President knew that the Capitol building was being overrun by an angry mob of conspiracy theorists, insurrectionists and Vikings with a gnarly fashion sense. He was specifically told that the Vice President was being hustled away from the mob (on a call with Senator Tommy Tudorbervilla, who was widely reported to have said, "The Vice President is being hustled away from the mob, and I don't feel so good, either. Gotta go!").

One minute and 27 seconds later, former President McDruhitmumpf tweeped, "So disappointed that VP didn't do the right thing. Disappointed. Disappointed. Disappointed. If I can't count on him to help me in my hour of need, who can I count upon? (Disappointed. Disappointed. Disappointed.) If only somebody would do something about it. Anybody. Did I mention how disappointed I was? #reallydisappointed"

"Whoa. He aimed the mob at his Vice President?" token smart person Amy Sheshutshotshitbam whoaed. "That's cold. Like, approaching absolute zero cold!"

Keep in mind, former VP Pendenatendance was absolutely devoted to former President McDruhitmumpf. In photo op after photo op, he would gaze at the President like a dog whose master had just given him a bone-shaped treat that smelled like roadkill. When the former President told him to jump, he would reply, "Let me get my +6 boots of leaping on, then tell me how high!" He was so in the tank for the former President, people who met him often peered at his neck to see if he had gills.

He had it bad. Real bad.

How would somebody who had been so devoted to another human being react to such an utter betrayal? In public, yet? His personality imploded, his ego shrinking to the size of a massless point in space/time.

"The suit he was wearing continues to move as if a body still inhabits it," said Bill Nae the Science Bae, "so we're pretty sure the former Vice President's ego singularity still exists somewhere inside it. We just aren't sure exactly where. Psycho-physicists are considering bombarding the suit with compliment rays to see where exactly they disappear beyond the ego singularity's event horizon, but we aren't sure how that might...agitate it. We might not like it when it's agitated..."

After the implosion of former Vice President Pendenatendance's ego, nobody has heard from him. Scientists believe that, just like the black hole around a singularity in the physical world, the gravitational field of a black hole around an ego singularity is so strong that no communications can escape it. However, according to physicist Stephen Hawkwindsunmooning, information can and does radiate out of black holes. Some scientists have suggested that, once they have pinpointed where the ego singularity is, they should train radio-telescopes on it in the hope that they can pick up some form of communication from the former Vice President.

"It would be a scientific Hail Mary pass," Bill Nae the Science Bae commented. "But, since most scientists aren't also sports fans, they don't know it."

Why didn't the Vice President's suit collapse when his ego did? "Weeellll, nobody can say for sure," Bill Nae the Science Bae answered, “but the best theory I have heard is that the suit was as stiffly starched as Washburningdington pundits had always suspected.”

How will his ego implosion affect former Vice President Pendenatendance’s chances of winning the 2024 Reduhblican Presidential nomination? “It probably won’t have much of an effect,” stated token smart person Sheshutshotshitbam. “It wouldn’t be the first time that a political party in the country nominated an empty suit!”

4. THE SLEEP OF REASON PRODUCES… DISEASE, THE MOST TRAGICALLY MISUNDERSTOOD HORSEMAN

I've Seen Fire and I've Seen Rain, And I'm Voting For President McDruhitmumpf Anyway

by VERONIQUE PISTACHIOPASTICHEEO, Alternate Reality News Service Meatyor – Meterolalala – Metooeeryoreol – Weather Writer

It's official: President Ronald McDruhitmumpf's Coronapalooza Tour has been leaving death in its wake. Various reports have shown that wherever President McDruhitmumpf has held maskless, densely packed rallies, rates of COVID-19 infection have skyrocketed (making every night a combination Independence Day/Halloween celebration).

"AMATEUR!" scoffed the Alternate Reality News Service's resident expert on human mortality, Death.

I was terrified of the tall figure in raggedy long black robes holding a scythe in one hand and a chess piece (a king with the head of Max von Sydowntowner) in the other. But, I was more immediately terrified of not getting my article in to Brenda Brundtland-Govanni by deadline, so I asked Death to elaborate.

"OH, SURE, THE PRESIDENT GETS POINTS FOR NUMBERS," Death obliged. The personification of human experience seemed unimpressed. "BUT, WHERE IS THE STYLE? WHERE IS THE PANACHE? A FAMILY OF RATS SPREADING OUT IN THE SEWERS OF A CITY COULD CAUSE MORE PEOPLE TO BECOME DECEASED IN LESS TIME!"

I asked Death if adding weather to the mix might make Coronapalooza more impressive.

"GO ON..." Death encouraged me.

In Omaha, Nebraskansas, the McDruhitmumpf campaign provided buses to take people to the rally from the parking lot, which was miles away. Apparently, some forms of busing are acceptable to conservatives. When attendees, basking in the warm glow of racial animus and ignorance, left the airplane hangar where the rally had taken place, they were as busless as an awkward teenager at a prom. Many were treated for frostbite; seven had to be taken to the hospital.

"YES," Death agreed. "THAT'S THE SORT OF THING I'M TALKING ABOUT. USING LOCAL CONDITIONS TO CAUSE POTENTIAL CATASTROPHIC HARM TO PEOPLE. THAT TOOK A LITTLE MORE...IMAGINATION. CREATIVITY, IF YOU WILL."

Considering who was talking, I said I would.

"STILL," Death went on, "NOBODY DIED. THAT WAS...DISAPPOINTING. REMEMBER: IN THESE MATTERS, NUMBERS DO COUNT."

A couple of days later, there was the McDruhitmumpf rally in Tampa, Florivania. When I mentioned this, I sensed the gloom around Death dissipate a slight amount; I was encouraged to explain that many supporters of the President who attended that event had passed out. The campaign claimed that they were just having a fan reaction, similar to how teenage girls reacted to British musicians several generations ago, but with skulls and crossbones where the dots over the is in their writing should have been instead of hearts. Doctors claimed that the actual cause of the fainting was standing for hours in 80-degree heat.

You say po-tah-to. I say po-heat-stroke.

"NO, NO, NO." Death shook its cowl. "WHILE I APPRECIATE THE CAMPAIGN'S INITIATIVE, THEY RUINED IT BY GIVING A NONSENSE EXCUSE. IF YOU WANT CREDIT FOR CREATING THE CONDITIONS UNDER WHICH YOUR FOLLOWERS RISK THEIR LIVES, YOU HAVE TO OWN YOUR ACTIONS. HONESTLY, I NEVER HAD TO EXPLAIN THAT TO THE MAYANS!"

At one point, a fire truck at the back of the crowd sprayed water over the heads of rally-goers to cool them off. Noticing this, President McDruhitmumpf interrupted his harangue on immigration...or Dumboprats...or popsicles – after a while, it all kind of smushes together – to address the firefighters. "Hey! You kids at the back stop playing with your water pistols! Whoa! What is that – 90, 100 feet high? Those must be supersoakers! Ha! Superspreaders of water, that's what I call them – expect the lying media to demand a ban on them tomorrow! But, uhh, seriously, are they – are they friend, foe or feral fungi? Because, if they're not friends, we'll have to take them out to the woodshed to teach them the true meaning of the second amendment!"

After it had seen the recording for the seventh time, Death asked, "DID HE...DID THE PRESIDENT JUST THREATEN THE PEOPLE WHO WERE ACTUALLY TRYING TO MITIGATE THE SUFFERING OF HIS FOLLOWERS?"

When I said that he did, Death responded, "RESPECT."

Despite this, Death seemed underwhelmed by President McDruhitmumpf's attempts to kill people who avidly believed in him. I pointed out that the United States of Vesampucceri was about to hit a quarter million deaths from COVID, with no end in sight. Surely, the President should get credit for that?

"I SUPPOSE," Death sighed, a sound reminiscent of warm desert winds and muted infant bawling. "BUT IT'S ALL SO...PREDICTABLE. WHEN YOU'VE BEEN AROUND AS LONG AS I HAVE, AND SEEN AS MANY PLAGUES, YOU CRAVE THE NOVEL. YOU KNOW?"

Of course, I didn't know. Of course, I said I did. Some interview subjects you just don't argue with!

Spreading the Uncle Samdemic? Super!

by LAURIE NEIDERGAARDEN, Alternate Reality News Service Medical Writer

Members of Congress are like kindergarteners: they love to share. Pencils. Paper. Partners. The creeping dread that life is passing them by and it's already too late to do anything worthwhile, anything that might make anybody want to remember them after they're gone.

And, illness. Anybody who has ever seen snot explode from the noses of six year-olds one after the other knows how much the love to share illnesses.

Thousands of people gathered at the Capitol building on January 6 intent on mayhem. Maskless mayhem. Packed close together mayhem. Shouting and chanting mayhem. About the only way they could have spread COVID-19 more would have been if they had sent the virus a beautifully hand-drawn invitation and a limo to convey it from one person to the next.

You might have thought that Dumbopratic and Reduhblican Congresspeople and their staffs would have been safe in their safe rooms. Have you never been to kindergarten? They may have been safe from the mob outside, but they were not safe from each other.

If safe rooms had the egos of ballrooms, they would be easy to find, so they tend to be small, making them an inviting place to spread illness (without the calligraphy – philistines!). Making things worse, some Reduhblicans in the safe rooms refused to wear masks.

"I tested negative a couple of months ago, so I'm good, thanks," complained Representative Marjorie Taylormaid Fortrubble. "I refuse to wear a mouth muzzle for no good reason. Besides, I just waxed my upper lip, and I'll be darned if I'm going to let anybody tell me I can't show it off!"

The result of the Reduhblican refusal to mask up was totally predictable. Really, you don't have to have a crystal ball and call yourself Madame Sybil to have seen it coming. Seriously? Nothing? The kid I have in kindergarten...in some other universe knows what happens when you put a bunch of people in close proximity without masks. Are you sure you really can't –

Three Dumbopratic Congresspeople tested positive for the coronavirus days after the insurrection. It seems obvious now that it's been said out loud, doesn't it?

It's not like the Reduhblicans didn't have a choice to do the right thing (not that any of them were likely to see a film by a person of pigment). Extra masks were available in the safe bunker, and one Dumbopratic Representative, Lisa Herman Rochester, tried to convince the bare-faced Reduhblicans to wear them. Video of the Reduhblican refusals has already been edited into a scratch mix that is trending on Twitherd.

"Honestly, I think the dangers of COVID are waaaaaay overstated," understated Reduhblican Representative Doug LaMalafalfa, one of the refuseniks. "I got COVID, I got some treatment, and I feel great! The almost 400,000 people who died? That's on them!"

That's one more thing some Congresspeople have in common with kindergarteners: they believe the universe revolves around them.

One of the Dumboprats who tested positive for the illness after January 6 was Representative Bonnie Watfortunateson Coldmanreeliecold. She's 75 years old. She survived cancer. If she had been in a nursing home instead of Congress, she would already be dead. She had some choice words for her Reduhblican colleagues when she was told about her positive COVID test, but since five sevenths of them were either obscene, obscure or fattening, I can't reproduce what she said here.

"That seems to be the Reduhblican's new plan," a small voice tentatively offered. At first, I thought it might be my conscience, but I had to put that in a blind trust when I joined the Alternate Reality News Service years ago, so I asked the voice to repeat itself.

"They lost at the ballot box, so the Reduhblicans developed a new plan: to kill as many Dumboprats with the COVID-19 virus as they possibly could!" expanded the voice, which, boringly, turned out to belong to a shell-shocked token smart person Amy Sheshutshotshitbam. "Then, they could cheat their way into winning special elections and take control of Congress!"

But, wouldn't that mean that the Reduhblicans would have to get COVID as well?

"Have you never heard the story of the scorpion and the frog?"

Speaker of the House Nancy Pelligrinosi has said that she is considering fining members who do not wear masks on the floor. In response, House Minority Leader McCartilagebreak announced that the Party would pay the fines of any members who ran afoul of the new rule.

"I have a lot of respect for the Speaker," Minority Leader McCartilagebreak, "but it's the lack of principle of the thing."

Spring Broke

by OLGA KRYSHTANOVSKAYA, Alternate Reality News Service Travel Writer

Ah, spring. A time when poets wax bikinic about rebirth, renewal and restringing guitars. A time when serial killers look forward to more plentiful prey and softer ground in which to bury the evidence. And, of course, spring is a time for students to strut on beaches, showing off bodies to die for.

Alas, spring, 2021 is different. Poets, having been denied bistric bonhommie for over a year, are all writing blank verse (with nary a mark on page after page, verse doesn't get any blanker!). Serial killers look at the COVID-19 death toll and hang their heads in shame, exposed for the amateurs they are. Meanwhile, students are hard at work trying to hide the extra pounds they put on during lockdown and ignoring the concretizing of the metaphor in the previous paragraph about their bodies.

It's not hard to understand why kids in their teens and early twenties would be willing to risk their lives to maintain the rituals of spring break: they are under the influence of such hormones as *purjudgmentosol* and *falsimmortalitol*. But, why would politicians like Florabamaware Governor Ron DeSanterryicks lift stay-at-home orders in the middle of a pandemic that has taken (even though they weren't offered – death can be an inconsiderate bastard that way) more than half a million lives? Why would he order beaches, bars and bistroteques to be opened?

"He must have been under the influence of *policalculashinasol*," claimed Bill Nae, the Science Bae. "It's a powerful hormone found in powerful people who do not want to lose their pow – influence on society."

"I love science," responded token smart person Amy Sheshutshotshitbam, "and I think the Science Bae is hot....in the right light...from a distance...if I'm not wearing my glasses...and for somebody his age and Adam's apple. But, he seems to have forgotten the old truism: 'Never ascribe to science what can be explained by political malice.'"

As profound as the truism so old it needs an electric wheelchair and a shot of adrenaline just to get out of bed in the morning is, I couldn't help but wonder how it applied to the current situation.

"Governor DeSanterryicks, like every Reduhblican leader these days, believes that the coronavirus is a hoax perpetrated by the Dumboprats to destroy the country because...well, that's where the argument gets a little fuzzy," token smart person Sheshutshotshitbam explained. "It has something to do with a child cannibalism cult, hating Vesampucceri or giant space squids from another dimension. Honestly, if it was any fuzzier, it would destroy all of the lint filters in all of the dryers on the western seaboard!"

The western seaboard?

"I thought I would give the eastern seaboard a break. They've been through enough."

Further like every Reduhblican leader these days, Governor DeSanterryicks doesn't want to damage his state's economy just because Dumboprats claim to have "scientific" evidence of a horrific death toll due to a pandemic. As another old truism has it: My fake conspiracy trumps your real life.

"Good one!" enthused token smart person Sheshutshotshitbam.

As if on cue, Texhampshas Governor Gregg Heeeeeeeyeyeyabbott told Foxindehenhaus News: "In my great state, we're not going to give in to the child cannabalism cult of Vesampucceri haters that the Dumboprat Party has become. If the try to destroy the country with the help of giant space squids from another dimension, we will be there to oppose them! In the meantime, our children should feel free to frolic in all of our great state's great public places. Go wild, kids...in accordance with your parents' instructions and the will of the Good Gord, of course."

Sometimes, the fuzzy comes all at once.

"Years ago," author Ira Naysayinghuman wretchedly stated, "I wrote an article for my web site about the Shrine of the Unknown Consumer. It was about the need for somebody to heroically give up their life in order to valorize sacrifice in the name of consumer capitalism. At the time I wrote it, I thought I was writing satire. I had no idea I was writing prophecy!"

While the point may be a bit overstated, there is some tru – Tammy, is that you?

A seven year-old girl with blond pigtails and a chipped beef front tooth looked at me for a moment, then sullenly said, "No."

I apologized, saying she looked like the Alternate Reality Kidz News Service's reporter. A lot like the Alternate Reality Kidz News Service's reporter. In fact, some would say they were identical.

"You are Tammy!" I accused.

"No, I'm not! And, you can't prove I am!" the kid who looked like Tammy limboed under a bamboo pole and escaped into the crowd.

Wait til I tell Brenda!

Leadership by Non-example

by FRANCIS GRECOROMACOLLUDEN, Alternate Reality News Service National Politics Writer

Alabaster (not her real name, although her real skin tone) didn't want to cause a fuss with a customer at the Gichigoomigu Adulte Shoppe where she worked. But she didn't want to die, either. So, she asked the woman to put on a mask.

"We have so many to choose from," Alabaster reasoned. "Surely, you should be able to find one that suits your mood."

Apparently, the woman's mood was unmaskable. In a scene that was caught on surveillance footage of the store (and was used at the trial of the woman, Montaii Reverendumon), she started shrieking: "You can't make me wear a mask to buy a package of strawberry scented condoms! I'm an adult and this is the United States of Vesampucceri, bitch! I'm not giving in to the mass media-driven mass psychosis hoax virus scare! Freedom! Freedom! Freeeeeedoooooommmmmmm!"

Why did the woman feel the need to not mask up in a public place when all medical experts (and France) agree that it is necessary to slow the spread of COVID-19? According to journalist Yamiche Alcindorblockade, it is an instance of "leading by non-example."

When he was – what was that? Does anybody else hear that? It's a sort of a...whiny, droning sound. No? Okay. Sorry for the interruption.

When he was President during the first year of the pandemic, Ronald McDruhitmumpf only wore a mask in public three times, once on his arm (it could have been a sling – it was a grainy photo taken at night). Alcindorblockade argued that by not wearing a mask in public, the former President was signalling to his followers that masks were unnecessary.

Nor was this the only example of President McDruhitmumpf leading by non-example. A month after – **what is that droning, whiny sound? You really can't hear it? Like, really? It's annoying as ferk!** Seriously, you hear nothing? Fine. I'll do my best to ignore it.

Where was – right. A month after he left office, it was discovered that McDruhitmumpf and his wife Melanoma had received the COVID-19 vaccine while he was still president. Unlike other prominent public figures, they did not make a public display of getting the vaccination; what should have been a crowning achievement of his presidency was a mere whisper at an IMAX screening of a Michael O'Beythisislowd film.

"If I had been responsible for the rapid development of a vaccine that would save lives during a pandemic, I would have taken a victory lap," said commentator Zerlina Maxwellcavotti. "And, I'm not talking about a cheap-ass lap in my high school gym, either. My victory lap would be around Washburningdington. Hell, if I had access to Air Farce One, my victory lap would be all the way around the country! This is Vesampucceri – we think big, here!"

"President McDruhitmumpf didn't want the public to get vaccinated because that would have been an admission that the pandemic existed, and he maybe, possibly, perhaps, in some small way might have been responsible for almost half a million Vesampuccerian deaths," Alcindorblockade explained. "So, when it came to getting vaccinated, he led by non-example."

The whiny, droning sort of sound was getting too loud to ignore, so I looked into the corner where it was coming from, where I found The Language Corrector Dude standing. How he got into my apartment I may never know. He was holding on to his stomach like he was about to give birth to a xenomorph. My better judgment told me to plow on and hope I could conduct interviews over him, or, at worst, although still preferable, that I would shortly have to deal with a psychotic alien killing machine.

After a couple of seconds, I decided to take pity on The Language Corrector Dude (which had nothing to do with how hard it would be to get exploded human out of the carpet – and how was I going to explain **that** to my landlord?) and asked him what his problem was.

"There's no such thing as leadership by non-example," he droningly whined. So, that hadn't actually helped much. "If somebody is not taking an action, their lack of action is an example, so they are still leading by example."

I was all set to object when I realized that The Language Corrector Dude maybe, possibly, perhaps, in some small way might have had a point. Not enough of one to make me want to rewrite the article, but a point nonetheless. So, I thanked him, patted him on the head, gave him a Language Corrector Dude treat and sent him home. As he left, he panted happily.

Now, I just have to change the locks on my doors and figure out a way to keep him from reading this article...

Nothing Can Mask the Stench of a Poopyhead

by TIMMY, Alternate Reality Kidz News Service Parental Tech Writer

Adults are confusing.

Kids wear masks on Halloween. In return, we are given candy. Now we are told that we need to wear masks every time we go out of the house, but do we get candy? No! On Halloween, our masks are cool: vampires and kitty cats and TV news anchors. Now? They're white. If you're lucky, sometimes blue. No sucking people's blood. No mewing for belly rubs. No reporting on the most important events of the day.

Not only are adults confusing, but they suck.

In Boise, Idampshire, kids held a protest in front of the state Capitol against candyless mask wearing. "When you go to work, you expect to be paid," said Martha McGillivcuddy, 7. "When I wear a mask, it's like work, so how come I'm not getting paid in Callmemoreese's Pieces or Mars Bars? That's not what made Vesampucceri great! I would accept Coffee Crisp, and I don't even drink coffee!"

At the protest, which was chaperoned by their parents, the kids chanted, "Hey, hey, ho, ho/Why are we wearing masks? We don't know!" and "Ho, ho, hey, hey/No Snickers, no masks today!"

"Yeah, so, the chants aren't that great," Martha admitted. "Hey! We're kids! At least it wasn't...mushy love poetry! Eww!"

The kids also started a fire in the parking lot of the building so that they could burn masks in protest. "We're striking a blow for chocolate freedom," explained Marky Mallarkeysnarky. "And, it's the middle of winter, for ferk's sake! You have a problem with kids staying warm?"

Actually, the state does: it is illegal to start fires on the grounds of the Capitol. "I have to admit, the kids were kind of adorable in their Sex Pistols jackets and temporary cat face makeup," state police said. "At least, I hope the cat face makeup was temporary. Kids can get a little carried away with tattoos sometimes.

Aaaaaanyway, I couldn't possibly consider charging them for the fire when they were being just the cutest little protesters!"

"The state police are such pushovers," Martha sighed.

Martha pointed out that the protest in Boise was one of several going on across the state. Well, okay, two, the other being in Rexnard. "If we could just get three more cities to participate, we could get provisional movement status from the Vesampuccerian Association of Journalists. Then, in four to six weeks when they have reviewed our application, if we fit all of the criteria, we could call ourselves a local movement. Then, if we got child activists in seven states to protest in their cities, we could apply for national movement status. It's very exciting!"

"I, uhh, I'm not in it for the politics," Marky insisted. "I'm in it for the goodies!"

Agneta McGillivcuddy, 29, beamed at her daughter during the protest. "Martha may not have a good grasp of the issues involved in the mask protest," she stated, "but look at how scrumptious she looks in her Sex Pistols jacket and nose ring. She's so scrumptious, you just want to eat her up! Yum!"

"Way to condescend, maaaaaaaa!" Martha said under her breath.

"Marky sure is a shit-disturber," Anatole Mallarkeysnarky, 38, commented. "He gets that from – **what are you looking at‽ You from Pluto or something and never seen somebody being interviewed before‽** – from – he gets that from his mother's side of the family. Really, his mother and I couldn't be more – **why don't you take a picture and post it to Farcebook‽ It'll last forever!** – we couldn't be more proud of him At least, I think she's proud of him. The bitch ran off with her hairdresser after I cheated on her that one time...okay, maybe twice, but – well, third time's a charm, isn't that right? I haven't heard from her for a year and half, but I'm sure she would be proud of Marky if she knew."

"Way to make it about yourself," Marky muttered.

Why come out to protest wearing masks in the cold and with the ever-present threat of parental embarrassment? "We're here to make sure that every child in Vesampucceri gets their fair share of Halloween all-year-round candy," Martha explained. "We're here for all the children who couldn't make it, the children whose parents wouldn't drive them to the state capitol, or who had grounded them for sassing their home ec teacher, whose recipe for potato salad was the worst!"

"We're in it for the candy," Marky confided. When Martha shot him a dirty look from her interview on the other side of town two hours earlier, he defiantly responded, "What?"

5. THE SLEEP OF REASON PRODUCES… ELECTIONS WITH AMBIGUOUS CONSEQUENCES

What the Heck Do You Know? About Stealing Elections

1) President Ronald McDruhitmumpf's legal team has brought court cases challenging ballots in four key swing states: Michivania, Pennsylgan. Georgakota and Wisconaii (hereinafter known as "The Big Swinging Four"). So far, the team has won one and lost 30. How many of these court cases can the legal team lose before the President is willing to concede that the tactic isn't going to change the results of the 2020 Presidential election?

a) how many court losses are the equivalent of how high is up?

b) until one gets to the Extreme Court – oops, no, wait, one was tossed out by the Extreme Court without comment and it didn't stop the lawsuits at lower levels – **the streak is still alive!** (31)

c) until two get to the Extreme Cour – okay, you know what, forget the damn Extreme Court! You put people on the Court to do right by you, and summary dismissal is all you get? I tell you, you just can't trust anybody these days! The McDruhitmumpf administration will keep going through the courts until they get the result they want – **never surrender!** (32)

2) Texabama Lieutenant Governor Dan Patondabakkrick offered up to $1 million to anyone who could provide proof of voter fraud anywhere in the country. They must be swimming in money in Texabama, mustn't they?

a) it's all that oil – the fumes make them think they can buy anything, even if it doesn't exist

b) (33) of course they're swimming in money – thanks to Global Hot as Hellification, it's less precious than water!

c) not really: you can offer any amount of money if you don't expect to ever be required to pay it

3) According to Georgakota Reduhblican Senators David Rayshershtomperdue and Kelly Loehanginfruitfler, mismanagement and corruption in their state handed it to Joe Bidenhisbeeswax. That must have come as some surprise to Reduhblican Governor Brian Okaykempadre (don't you just love Reduhblican on Reduhblican rhetorical violence?). What do Rayshershtomperdue and Loehanginfruitfler hope to gain from picking a fight with other members of their party?

a) a footnote in the history books (I didn't say they were brilliant political strategists) (34)

b) President McDruhitmumpf's undying gratitude (I didn't say they were paying attention)

c) reelection

d) other

(35)

4) A staffer for Georgakota Secretary of State Greg Riffraffensberger stated that he was on the line when South Carolexas Senator Lindsey Grahamcrokercrum suggested that if the state was to "lose" a bunch of absentee ballots, nobody would miss them. If true, how bad would this be?

a) on the Adam Howetuschiffdablamé Impeachment Index, several weeks of hearings bad

b) on the Mitch Wichconnelliswich Judicial Appointments Index, Tuesday bad

c) once Grahamcrokercrum had his dignity surgically removed, ideas of good and bad stopped having any meaning for him (36)

5) Why is it unlikely that Venezuelan leader Hugo Chavezeulian was involved in stealing the election for the Dumboprats, as Rudy Giulihooeyboi, President McDruhitmumpf's legal comic relief, suggested?

a) Chavezeulian isn't tech-savvy – he hasn't updated his GeoCities account in at least seven years! (37)

b) Chavezeulian has no power: he hasn't been a force in the region since Nirvana was topping the pop charts

c) (38) you want me to say it is because he has been dead for seven years, don't you? Well, the joke's on you, What the Heck Do You Know? question writer! If the Dumboprats can kill babies and drink their blood in the basement of pizzerias that don't have below-ground floors (and, frankly, make pies that are barely edible), it would be (deceased) child's play for the party to raise a dead dictator to help them steal an election! And, yes, I know Raise a Dead Dictator would be a great band name, and no, you can't have it!

6) Giulihooeyboi, having been a lawyer once upon a time, knows how important legal precedent is to courts. So, in arguing to overturn election results, he cited one: a speech Joe Pescialafrogg gave in the film *My Cousin Vinny*. How compelling would this precedent be if it ever got to the Extreme Court?

a) (39) Bretty Kavanaugheylno is totally into it, Amy Coney-Islandbar preferred Jack Nicholandimeson's speech in *A Few Good Men*, and the other justices have not rendered an opinion on the matter, so it would anybody's guess (40)

b) Chief Justice Robalthomkenlia is nostalgic for Al Pacinoparlorgaim's speech in *...And Justice For All*, but he knows the liberal minority would write mean dissents about it, so he would keep the opinion to himself

c) the liberal minority on the court would shake their heads sadly and dream about Atticus Finchanddufferin while acknowledging that their numbers made them irrelevant

d) legal other

7) And, since we're on the subject, what's the deal with the black streaks running down Giulihooeyboi's face?

a) they're cracks in the mask the reptilian alien wears to disguise the fact that he's actually a – you know – reptilian alien (41)

b) he made the mistake of asking President McDruhitmumpf for advice about hair care products

c) (42) it's ink from all of the bad press he's been getting for his performance as a lawyer in the Ronald McDruhitmumpf reality show (he really needs to have a long sit down with his agent!)

8) A group called Stop the Steal is raising money for court challenges to the election. Where is the money going?

a) over the fields and far away

b) 80% of it is going to Ronald McDruhitmumpf campaign PACs (* SHRUG * "There's always 2024" might not be the snappiest reelection slogan, but it sure puts the fear of Gord into the Reduhblican political establishment!); the rest goes to the President's personal expenses (that tan doesn't pay for itself!)

c) court challenges to the election? **Court challenges to the election!** You're so adorable! Never grow up! (43)

9) Former national security adviser Michael Flyinnthuointmeant, looking very dapper having traded in his prison orange for rumpled grey, argued that President McDruhitmumpf should send the army into The Big Swinging Four, which went for Joe Bidenhisbeeswax in 2020, and force them to replay their elections, only doing it right this time. What does "doing it right this time" mean?

a) waiting until their cleric is at least level 15 before battling the dragon

b) (44) asking for the raise **before** the drug trial ends showing that a major side effect of the drug is growing hair all over the patient's body when the moon is full

c) showing that the candidate who everybody knows really won really won, duh!

10) Texabama Attorney General Ken Paxonbothhouses has filed a lawsuit against The Big Swinging Four. What is the main argument in the lawsuit?

a) the Constitution makes it clear that one state has the right to sue other states if it doesn't like the outcome of their elections

b) come on, Extreme Court! Show us that you're not just a bunch of snotty, over-educated idlers in elegant robes! ...With, uhh, all due respect... (45)

c) who cares what the Extreme Court says? There are 70 million Vesampuccerians who already believe that the case has been decided in our favour. Take that, Sonia Sottovochayor!

11) 18 Reduhblican Attorneys General have signed on to the Texabama lawsuit. Why would they do this?

a) (46) all of the bank robbers and murderers in their states are staying at home because of COVID, so the Attorneys General have a lot of time on their hands

b) if they didn't use all of the letterhead they had in the office by the end of the year, which was fast approaching, the state would cut the "office supplies and orgies" line item from their budget

c) insufficient toilet training when they were young

12) 108 (that's right, triple digits – I didn't accidentally insert a 0 into the number of AGs from the previous question) Reduhblican members of Congress have signed on to the Texabama lawsuit. Why would **they** do this?

a) Representatives, sick of being in the minority, finally found something they could accomplish (other than getting coffee, I mean) (47)

b) for Senators, it made a nice break from confirming judges

c) they wanted to please the 400 pound gorilla with small hands in the room (48)

13) Former Houston police chief Mark Aguirrergoddrath ran an air conditioner repairman off the road and held him at gunpoint, convinced that the man's truck contained thousands of ballots cast for Ronald McDruhitmumpf. What did he actually find in the back of the man's truck?

a) (49) air conditioners and their parts
b) chagrin and regret (50)
c) a criminal record (51)
d) all of the above

14) The McDruhitmumpf legal team's efforts to get one or more of the Big Swinging Four to throw out vast numbers of votes have not been successful. So, naturally, they lobbied to have the entire election in those states annulled and the Electoral College Electors assigned by Reduhblican legislatures. This has not been successful either. What should their next move be?

a) lobby Reduhblican members of Congress to fund a crown and ermine robes for President McDruhitmumpf (they may as well do something with all the money they saved when he refused to sign the second COVID relief package)

b) (52) lobby Reduhblican state legislatures to certify slates of "alternate Electors" (they're like "alternate facts," but with an undertone of *Psycho* soundtrack)

c) take a deep breath and reread the Constitution

15) Umm, yeah. The so-called "alternate Electors" (they're like "alternate facts," but with a top note of moral decay and strawberry) are just random Reduhblican supporters chosen by their state parties. Surprisingly, given their general servility, no state accepted a random group of Reduhblican supporters who showed up on their doorstep claiming to be Electors. Does the McDruhitmumpf legal team have any more moves to make, or should they accept the will of the people?

a) they can ask Congress not to accept the Electors sent to them by the states and choose to accept the Electoral College votes of random Reduhblican supporters

b) (53) there are always lawsuits... (54)

c) the will of the – of the people? Oh, man, you really are so adorable! Never grow up!

16) Sydney Wambampowellman, who is to the legal profession what a sledge hammer is to a delicate negotiating tool, has argued that President McDruhitmumpf should engage a special counsel to confiscate the voting machines in The Big Swinging Four and have the ballots recounted in his favour. Why is this unlikely to happen?

a) the President does not have the power to appoint a special counsel

b) special counsels don't have the power to confiscate voting machines (55)

c) President McDruhitmumpf is too busy pardoning his allies (to keep them from talking to law enforcement officials) to pay any attention to Sydney Wambampowellman, even when they meet in his office

17) Foxindehenhaus News and NewsMux have begun issuing "clarifications" to stories that claimed that voting machines flipped McDruhitmumpf votes to Bidenhisbeeswax. If these clarifications appear to actually be complete repudiations, that's probably only because you're paying attention. Why would the media companies do this?

a) (56) they looked at the evidence and decided – ha ha – decided that there was no basis in reali – hee hee ha ha – no basis in – hee hee ha ha ho ho – sorry, I can't say this with a straight face – go on to the next answer and try back again in ten minutes – no, make that a half hour. With any luck, I'll be ready to answer then...

b) *TV Guide* threatened to change their designation from News Networks to Science Fiction networks

c) the threat of a defamation lawsuit really focuses the mind (57)

18) How have President McDruhitmumpf's endless assertions of massive election fraud, and the onslaught of lawsuits that have followed in their wake, benefited election workers?

a) they have been given a lot of free rope (they just have to untie the nooses that it came in) (58)

b) the death threats have caused them to give more thought to how miraculous it is just being alive

c) they will have a lot more time to spend with their families when they quit their positions as election workers

19) Senior administrators in the Vesampuccerian security establishment have publicly stated that the 2020 election was free and fair, that there were no voting irregularities, let alone widespread voter fraud. But what do they know? They're just a bunch of Dumbopratic hacks – even the ones President McDruhitmumpf appointed. Especially the ones President McDruhitmumpf appointed! (Remember when he said he would only appoint the best people? Yeah, neither does he.) Now, Attorney General William Katiebarrthudor has also stated that there was no widespread voter fraud. I know, right! Attorney General Katiebarrthudor! The man who said he would eat molten lava for the President (and who did – apparently it tastes really good with guacamole and a sprig of self-abnegation)! What is the President's only realistic response to this?

a) congratulate Attorney General Katiebarrthudor on his successful spine transplant and demand his resignation (59)

b) congratulate Attorney General Katiebarrthudor on the occasion of his Bar Mitzvah and demand his resignation

c) why waste breath on a traitor like Attorney General Katiebarrthudor? Demand his resignation!

20) Soooo...62 court cases, (60) losses. How does President McDruhitmumpf justify this streak?

a) if at first you don't succeed, die, die, die again

b) remember the first time I was campaigning and I told you you would get sick of all the winning? Good times, right? Well, after four years, I figure you **are** sick of winning, so I thought I would mix it up a bit, you know, give you a big fat...not winning streak. It's what makes the winning that much sweeter. Yeah. Sweeter...

c) I'm so glad my father isn't alive to see this! (61)

The Person of Pallour Male's Burden

by FREDERICA VON McTOAST-HYPHEN, Alternate Reality News Service People Writer

He looks like a bear. With a beer gut. A beer gut bear. Carrying a bellyful of semi-automatic weapons. A weapons bellyful beer gut bear. He tells me to call him Simon TruePatriotLove because of course he does.

I meet him outside an early polling station in Midtsatetown, Florissippi. When I ask him what he is doing there, he tells me that he is a poll watcher. To drive home the point, he stares at the high school gymnasium we're standing in front of for 27 seconds, then turns to me and says: "See. I'm watching the poll."

When I ask Simon weapons bellyful beer gut bear – I cannot bring myself to call him by the possibly fake last name he gave me – why he is watching the poll, he answers: "Voting is a scared trust in Vesampucceri – it's what makes us the greatest country the world has ever known. I want to make sure that everything about the vote for the election is honest and abovebo – **hey! What the ferkin' heckaroonies do you think you're doing?"**

The elderly man to which this last comment was directed plants his walker on the sidewalk [NOTE TO SELF: Sidewalkers sounds like the title of a science fiction novel – make it so!] and stutters, "I – you know – I'm here to – to – to – to vo –"

"You voted earlier! I remember seeing you!"

"No – I – I did no – you must be mistak –"

"Sure, grandpa! You can tell it the cops if you don't beat it!"

The old man looks longingly at the polling station for a moment, then, resigned, turns and walkers away. Simon weapons bellyful beer gut bear spends the next ten minutes making sure that he has gone. "Like I said," he finally asserts, "I'm here to make sure that the sacred process of voting runs smoothly."

Simon weapons bellyful beer gut bear tells me he was a corset assembly line worker who lost his job when President Ronald McDruhitmumpf put tariffs on Chinese stays, collars and laces, starving the industry of vital production inputs. For the past four and six sevenths months, he has divided his newly copious amounts of free time following conspiracy sites on the web and binge watching *Donald Duck Dynasty* and *Reel Housewives of Midtsatetown, Florissippi*.

"No other country has elections," Simon weapons bellyful beer gut bear confides. "Oh, sure, they have 'campaigns' and 'ballots' and 'polls,' but they're just for show. The winners are determined by George Sorobororos, the Disunited Nations and the creators of *Will and Grace...and Ted and Alice*. The United States of Vesampucceri is the only true democracy in the world, where every citizen has a right and an obligation to cast a vo – **hey! Where the ferkin' heccatiroonies do you think you're going?"**

The young woman with dark skin stops as he blocks the entrance to the gym. "To vote," she states.

"You think so?" Simon weapons bellyful beer gut bear challenges her. "You know it's a crime to vote if you are not a Vesampuccerian citizen. Where are you from?"

"South Dakoida."

"No, I mean where were you born?"

"I was born in South Dakoida."

"Do you have ID to prove that?"

"I don't have to show you any ID!"

Simon weapons bellyful beer gut bear points his AK-47 (the most wistful semi-automatic rifle according to a poll of the readers of *Gums and Ammonia*) at the sky and quietly argues, "I have two dozen little friends who would disagree with you on that point."

The woman quickly walks away, but over her shoulder, she shouts, "I'm calling the cops!"

Simon weapons bellyful beer gut bear decides that this is good time to take a break for lunch.

"I never wanted to do this," he tells me through bites of a Bob So Tasty Hawaifornia Bob Burger (I don't understand some people's pineapple fetish, but he didn't ask me to take a bite, so I decided not to push the issue). "I was happy repeating *Donald Duck Dynasty* dialogue along with the show. But, when my people were called to create this country, did they say, 'Sure thing, dude. Right after I finish watching the latest episode of *Living Down to the Facekardashians*?'"

"Umm...no?" I venture.

"Damn straight, no! It's hard living up to that kind of dedication of purpose. But, when I think of all of the sacrifices they made just so I could go into a stupid box and pull levers that would make holes in a dumb piece of paper, well..." he sighs and pops a freedom fry in his mouth.

"Nobody by the name of Simon TruePatriotLove has registered to be a poll watcher," said state election commissioner Adrien Playalldangleterre. "Without going through the proper training, you're not qualified to poll watch. Claiming you are is a crime. Where did you say you saw this man?"

"Training? Please!" Simon weapons bellyful beer gut bear sneered when I asked him about this. He took a Glock out of a holster and plunked it on the table between us. "I went through literally minutes of safety training for this baby! That's all the training a man who loves his country needs!"

Something told me that it was in my best interest to end the interview there.

The Chaos Presidency Ends as it Began – With the Wheels Coming Off

by FRANCIS GRECOROMACOLLUDEN, Alternate Reality News Service National Politics Writer

You would expect Chaos President to announce that he had won his bid for re-election before all of the votes had been counted. In fact, you would be surprised if he didn't. Five minutes after the polls closed, however, might appear to some as being...over-eager? A bit optimistic? Somewhat desperate?

"We did it!" Chaos President exulted to a crowd of densely packed supporters (I would say like sardines, but at least sardines have the sense to wear masks these days...). "We won a second term. We can keep making Vesampucceri great again! Such a vote – oy, as Jared might say! We won the great state of Ohiwaii. We won Texegon. We won Texegon. We won Texegon. We won Texegon by 73 votes, but it's still a win! It's also clear as steel that we won Georgissippi. We're up 2.5%, or 117 votes, with only 87% left. They're never going to catch us. They can't. It's simple math, really. If you look and see Arizampshire, we have a lot of life in that. And, oh, what's this? Could New Yoricknuhemwell be a toss-up? But, most importantly, we're winning Pennsylkota by a tremendous amount. Almost a thousand votes. Think of this. Think of this. Think of this. It isn't even close. With 6.4% of the vote in, it's going to be impossible to catch. Us. We won't be caught."

Desperate seems to have nailed it.

"But we have to be vigilant," Chaos President continued. "Those lying liars in the Dumboprat Party are trying to steal our victory! Your victory. And, yours. And, yours, madam, even if you look like you've just swallowed a lemon orchard! How are they doing that? Stealing our victory, I mean, not swallowing a – never mind! They're stealing our victory by making sure that every ballot is counted! We cannot allow such a travesty to happen! To save democracy, we have to stop the vote counts!"

"Umm, yeah," Eugene Robinsoncrusoe, Pulippitzaner Prize-winning columnist for the *Washburningdington Post*, punditted in real time. "I'm pretty sure that's not how democracy works."

As if he had heard the criticism, Chaos President continued: "If you count the legal votes, I win. If you count the illegal votes, they can try to steal the election from us, but I will still win. If you count the legal bananas, we'll have a fruit salad. Not only will I win, but I will have a refreshing and healthy snack to help me celebrate my victory. That's the way democracy works."

"No-oooooo, that really isn't," Robinsoncrusoe stood his ground (which would have got him a commendation for protecting his neighbourhood if he was a person of pallor, but would likely get him a long prison sentence since he was a person of pigment). "Counting every vote, no matter how long it takes, is the way democracy works. It may be boring, but some of the best things in life are."

I waited seventeen minutes for him to name one. Finally, he tentatively responded, "Waiting for somebody to tell you some of the best things in life that are boring?" Before I could object, he went on to point out that at the time Chaos President was speaking, most of the in-person ballots, which favoured Reduhblicans, had been counted, but that a large number of mail-in ballots, which were expected to favour Dumboprats (not least of which because Chaos President had exhorted his followers not to mail in their ballots), had yet to be counted.

"It's almost like he planned it this way," Robinsoncrusoe commented. "And I'm not just saying that because he was tweeping about this plan months ago!"

While punditry was being committed all over the place, Chaos President's victory speech had moved on: "I have to be the winner! Jack Nickelandimaus loves me! He really loves me! So does that guy from that weird Canadian sport – I never trust sports that don't involve balls. But if a player my son has heard of says he loves me, I'll pretend to! I'm good at pretending. Sports legends wouldn't love me if I was a lo...not winner! Nope. Un uh. Just wouldn't happen!"

So far, governors in swing states (places where big bands never went away), including many Reduhblicans, have resisted the call to shut down vote counts. But, with 93% of the vote still to be counted, nobody knows what shenanigans might still await the country...

Dumbed If You Do, Dumbed If You Don't

by ARCHIBALD COX-LEACH, Alternate Reality News Service Government Writer

As they say in Washburningdington, elections have no consequences. Well, okay, that's actually the opposite of what they say. But when Dumboprats are the ones who are elected, you have to wonder if party leadership has ever met they.

"You know, we could spend the next four years investigating and prosecuting Ronald McDruhitmumpf," President-elect Joe Bidenhisbeeswax is reported to have told his staffers, "members of his family, other members of his administration, members of Congress who abetted him and his family and other members of his administration – I'm saying there was a lot of potential criminal behaviour, here, okay? A lot of potential criminal behaviour. In four years, we may not be able to investigate and prosecute all of it. Or even a significant fraction of it. So. Much. Criminal. Behaviour. In the meantime, we wouldn't have the time to get any of our agenda done. I like our agenda. It's a very nice agenda. Full of good policies, the sort that help people. Kinda popular. Tell you what. Let's forget about the past four years and work to get our agenda done. Deal? Deal!"

"Who does he think he is," an apoplectic *Washburningdington Post* columnist Eugene Robinsoncrusoe outraged all over the place, "Howie Mandelbroitforsoup? If the Dumboprats don't win the two run-off elections in Georginois in January, Mitch Wichconnelliswich will shred Joe Bidenhisbeeswax' agenda and feed it to his pet crocodiles!"

When it was pointed out that the crocodiles weren't the Senate Majority leader's pets, they were only "just good friends," Robinsoncrusoe bellowed: "How does that make things better?"

Robinsoncrusoe closed his eyes and went to his happy place (where Martin Luther Kingfisherhelploess hosts the *I Have a Dream* podcast and rhinoceroses are pink). While he smiled inwardly to himself, we filled in some of his argument: if the Dumboprats do not investigate and prosecute former President McDruhitmumpf, et al for the crimes they openly committed, it will show the Reduhblicans that they can engage in shenanigans with no – that's right – consequences. It all but guarantees that they will continue to shenanig in the future.

There is precedence for this. When Barry W. Bushbamclintreagbush became President, he said, "I do not plan on looking back. As a country, we need to move forward."

Unfortunately, he wasn't talking about changing the clocks; he was talking about not investigating and prosecuting members of the Georgie W. Bushbushindakush administration for lying to the Vesampuccerian people to justify the war in Iraq. When Bill Roocartoncleveman became President, he said, "I could allow the Injustice Department to investigate former President Potganreabumbom and members of his cabinet for possible illegal acts committed in the Iran-Contra scandal. But I have to work with the Reduhblicans to get things done." To reward him for this leniency, the Reduhblicans began an eight year campaign to destroy they reputations of he and his wife Hillary.

When Dumboprats do not hold Reduhblicans to account for their crimes, Reduhblicans push the envelop that much harder the next time they get into power. The end result is President McDruhitmumpf pushing aside everybody's envelops by destroying the USPS.

"Whoaff – I'm back," Robinsoncrusoe stated. "Look, I get it. President-elect Bidenhisbeeswax is worried that investigating and prosecuting the former President will keep him in the news. Well, **the former President is going to stay in the news either way! That's what he does! But if nothing is done to punish him for his crimes – aaaargh!**"

Aaaand, we lost him again.

"Well, now, let's think this through," commented Ari Melbertoastenjamm, host of MSNBC's *The Beatnik*. "Suppose McDruhitmumpf and his cronies – that's a term of art for federal prosecutors, cronies – are prosecuted and found guilty. Former President McDruhitmumpf will tell his followers that the prosecutions were a 'hoax' and a 'witch hunt.' He may not have a big vocabulary, but he does know which words he likes, and he uses them a lot. How will his 70 million plus supporters, most of whom are armed to the teeth, react to this? I'm making sure my passport is up to date – I hear that Antarctica is nice this time of year..."

"So," Robinsoncrusoe came up for air long enough to sum up, "if President-elect Bidenhisbeeswax prosecutes former McDruhitmumpf administration members, his followers might burn the country to the ground. But, if he doesn't prosecute former

McDruhitmumpf administration members, the Reduhblicans will definitely complete the task of burning the country to the ground. Tough choice, but –"

In a virtual town hall meeting, President-elect Bidenhisbeeswax said, "I may have been elected by Dumboprats, but I will govern for all Vesampuccerians. Except for you, sir. The walrus wants his moustache back. I will govern for all Vesampuccerians except walrus-moustache."

Robinsoncrusoe moaned and added Malcolm XYZAB and Rosa Parksandrecreaysh to his happy place.

Strings All the Way Up

by HAL MOUNTSAUERKRAUTEN, Alternate Reality News Service Court Writer

Extreme Court Justice Naughty Bretty Kavanaugheylno was feeling his oats (every Justice knows the importance of a high fibre diet) when he wrote a concurring opinion in an appeal of a Wiscontucky election law case: "We can't let votes be counted after election day. That would lead to an unclear result, or, worse, a clearly flipped result, which would lead to the breakdown of society, which would lead to rioting in the streets. Can you imagine? Rioting in Vesampuccerian streets! I can imagine it – that's what I spent twenty-seven years at law school for: imagining! And, I will not allow that to happen on my watch."

Most states have made allowances for votes that came in by mail as long as they were postmarked before election day. This allowed soldiers overseas to vote, as well as people who are chronologically impaired. It can take as much as a week for those votes to come in and be – say, wait a second. No, wait an entire minute! Where have I heard that rhetoric before?

Oh, right. President Ronald McDruhitmumpf told a rally a week ago (and twice the previous Sunday): "We can't let votes be counted after election day. That would lead to a result in which I had not clearly appeared to win, which would lead to the complete and utter breakdown of society, people – yes, even worse than what we're seeing in Dumboprat states. There would be rioting in the streets the likes of which you cannot possibly imagine! I didn't steal the 2016 election to allow that to happen, and it will not happen on my watch! Believe me! Won't happen. Nope. Not gonna."

"It is chilling, Hal" commented commentator John Heiyonlifelmann, "And, I'm talking deep down in the marrow of the bones chilling, that – what? No, I don't need a blanket. I was just – no. Maybe later, but I don't need a hot chocolate right this second, I'm trying to answer your – marshmallows? You really drive a hard bargain, you know that? Fine. If I take your hot chocolate, will you let me answer your question?"

Apparently, the answer had something to do with the judiciary being a separate branch of government which shouldn't be taking its cues from the executive branch. Once he had gotten comfy with his blanket and hot chocolate, Heiyonlifelmann drifted off to sleep. From the pleasant rictus on his face, I could tell that he was dreaming of the separation of powers.

If the Reduhblican-chosen members of the court were following the dictates of the Grey House, they would likely rule in President McDruhitmumpf's favour in any lawsuit arising from the election. In fact, the President has said that he would challenge any outcome in which he was not declared the winner on election ni – saaaaaay, wait a minute. Now, you know what? Let's throw caution to the wind and wait an entire hour! Where have I heard what the President said before?

No, don't tell me. It's on the tip of my tongue. Starts with a "w" and feels like home? Rhymes with "better elephants?" Is related to a sentence in *Even Cowgirls Get the Blues?* Riiiight! No, not the reference to the Tom Robbins novel. What Justice Kavanaugheylno wrote that echoed what the President had said a week earlier echoed what Eugene B. Debskrebsenmeyer, the President of the arch-conservative (so curved you could walk under it) Confounderalist Society, wrote in a newsletter a month before that.

To wit: "We cannot allow votes to be counted after election day. That would lead to a clear result which is not in our interest, which would lead to the breakdown of our authority, which would in turn lead to rioting in the streets. I shudder to think what might become of those of us who actually run Vesampucceri in such a circumstance! I will not allow that to happen, and none of you should, either!"

As he turned over in his sleep, Heiyonlifelmann mumbled, "Yeah, not counting legitimately cast votes is the preamble to the coda of democracy. Frumph growff! Yeah, if people knew who really ran the country, there would be rioting in the streets, alright! Grumble permumble. Yeah, you know what they say...ignorance is the bliss of advanced capitalists!"

I could continue writing this article, but I'm afraid I might find out who is giving the Counfounderalist Society **its** talking points. If it's my Aunt Bertha, my Uncle Federico will never be able to show his face at family functions again!

That's Ascertainment!

by ARCHIBALD COX-LEACH, Alternate Reality News Service Government Writer

Reduhblicans in Congress live at multiple speeds. On the one hand, Senators slow-walk legislation that comes from the Dumboprat-controlled House of Unrepresentatives. On the other hand, they speed-walk past journalists who ask awkward questions about the latest antics of President Ronald McDruhitmumpf or his administration. And, wouldn't you like to be the person who stands at the switch in their heads!

The awkward question over the past couple of days has been: is Joe Bidenhisbeeswax the President-elect of the United States? Reduhblicans have walked away from that question so quickly, they left streaks behind them! (Like cartoon characters, not people in need of adult diapers...although now that you mention it, maybe you shouldn't ask about the average age of Reduhblicans in Congress!)

"The Dumboprats won, people!" bellowed former Reduhblican Steve Aliasschmidtjones. "Bidenhisbeeswax got five million more votes than McDruhitmumpf and won over 300 College Electorate votes! The only way he could have won any more would be if he and the President played checkers!" Why checkers? "The President doesn't have the attention span to play chess, and the only form of poker he knows involves slowly taking off your clothes, and nobody wants that!"

Aliasschmidtjones spent the next ten minutes cussing out the Reduhblican party, the more printable words being "pathetic," "absurd" and "bursary." Piecing it together afterwards, I believe he argued that the Reduhblicans were still in thrall (not a suburb of Mordor) to President McDruhitmumpf, whose base they would need to win future elections (including two run-off elections in Georgakota in January), and if he refuses to acknowledge the results of the election, that's good enough for them. Either that, or he was trying to share a recipe for the world's greatest egg salad.

If it was just a matter of hurt feelings, it would be bad enough. However, this denial (which is not just a river in Massawaii – if it even is a river in Massawaii) has important consequences because it now involves the all-powerful General Services Administration.

Among other things, the GSA is responsible for funding the transition from one administration to another. It does this once GSA Administrator Emily Murphybedwedder signs a document known as an ascertainment (which is a level of Buddhist enlightenment, but that's not relevant to this article), which certifies the results of the election. Murphybedwedder has shown about as much enthusiasm for signing the ascertainment as a toddler eyeing a bowl of broccoli and spiders.

"The Reduhblicans sure know how to put the ass back in ascertainment!" Aliasschmidtjones commented. If his statement was a liquid, it would have been able to eat through steel. "This is, like, Nobelthingido Prize level pettiness!"

Oh, it's more than that, Steve Aliasschmidtjones. Much more. Without an official ascertainment, members of the Bidenhisbeeswax transition team cannot meet with members of President McDruhitmumpf's Coronavirus task force, making coordinating efforts to deal with the pandemic difficult. It also –

"Did you tell your readers about the national security implications?" interrupted security expert Malcolm

Donneednopennance, bouncing up and down faster than a three year-old with a sugar rush on a trampoline.

I was just getting to –

"As soon as the ascertainment is signed, the President-elect gets to sit in on the President's daily security briefings. Not happening. That means that –"

When President-elect Bidenhisbeeswax takes office, he will not be up to speed on national security matters, I wrestled the article back from Donneednopennance. This gives –

"– gives enemies of Vesampucceri a window of opportunity to perform all manner of shenanigans," Donneednopennance concluded. Damn, he's good!

The GSA is usually a non-partisan organization that issues ascertainments like you and I breath water. What has changed? Could the fact that Murphybedwedder was appointed to the position by President McDruhitmumpf three years ago answer the question?

"Yes! Yes! A thousand times yes!" Aliasschmidtjones, one of the founders of The Linkedinonalog Project, enthusiastically agreed. "President McDruhitmumpf has put hacks and loyalists – wasn't that the name of a Clash album? – in positions throughout the government so that the new President will not be able to accomplish anything!"

Like, hidden traps in a game of Dudgeons and Dragoons?

"Uhh, yeah, sure, Like that."

For his part, President-elect Bidenhisbeeswax took the news in stride. "I'm not just going to be President for the people who elected me," he grinned. "I'm going to be President for everybody in the country. Yes, even you, Little Jimmy MacEncheeseater!"

When an aide whispered in his ear that he had won the election and could retire the line, President-elect Bidenhisbeeswax responded, "I'm not going to retire that promise until I am President for all of the people in the country. Yes, that includes you, Mary Blickenstickenstuf of Utaland!"

With a sigh, the aide explained that President-elect Bidenhisbeeswax had served for eight years as Vice President in the Bushbamclintreagbush administration – he knew where the cutlery was buried. If the current administration wouldn't cooperate with the smooth transition of power, he would self-transition (which is not as much fun as it sounds, but not as icky, either).

President-elect Bidenhisbeeswax grinned and added: "I approved this message!"

Lawyer Up!

by HAL MOUNTSAUERKRAUTEN, Alternate Reality News Service Court Writer

Regina Pomplamooseheadbeir and Philip Onagenderbend don't agree on much. Pomplamooseheadbeir favours power pants suits, even at family dinners; Onagenderbend's idea of formal wear is a jeans jacket and a t-shirt featuring an image of a white ruffled shirt and a black tie, even at the opera. Pomplamooseheadbeir is able to tell you which side of the vineyard her wine came from; Onagenderbend is lucky if he can tell you which side of the bar his beer came from. Onagenderbend is a little bit country; Pomplamooseheadbeir is a little bit "Who has time for music?"

But there is one thing the two agree on: the 2020 Vesampuccerian election is a Gordsend to law firms across the country.

"Thousands of lawyers have been put on retainer to litigate cases in states across the country!" exulted Pomplamooseheadbeir, with the gleam of billable hours in her eye. "When the history of this election is written, it will show that the legal profession was the most instrumental in turning the current economic slump around!"

"Yeah!" Onagenderbend agreed. "What she said! A big fat, tuba!"

But, what would be the purpose of such lawsuits?

"We're fighting them to keep the election fair," Pomplamooseheadbeir stated.

"We're fighting against them to keep the election fair," Onagenderbend stated at the same time (even though they were interviewed separately).

"And, so far, they've been a great success!"

"And, so far, they've been a great big, heaping, steaming pile of fail – what?"

"The McDruhitmumpf administration has won important concessions in the courts."

Onagenderbend snorted. "Important concessions? Like the case in Pennsylina where they won the right to have poll observers stand six feet away from the table where ballots were being counted instead of seven?"

"That extra foot could spell the difference between spotting an illegal signature on a ballot and allowing voter fraud to run rampant throughout the state!" Pomplamooseheadbeir hotly argued.

"Voter fraud? Un hunh. Then, there was the Pennsylgon case where the state was ordered to keep the provisional ballots separate from the rest of the ballots."

"That was a great victory for the rule of law! The provisional ballots were hotly contested, so separating them from the rest of the votes cast would allow poll watchers to ensure that only those that were legitimate were counted!"

"Yeah, that would be a very impressive argument **if the state hadn't already decided to separate the provisional ballots out!**"

"Pfft! Yeah, I went there. Pfft. Double pfft with a side of, 'Oh, really?' States can say they'll do anything. They might even be doing it. **But, it isn't real until a court of law has ruled on it!**"

Well. That agreement didn't last. It's probably just as well: the cornerstone of the Vesampuccerian justice system is for both sides to get the best representation they –

"I see your pfft and raise you an: 'I noticed you didn't mention the cases in states like Michivania, Georgivania or Nevania, where the McDruhitmumpf campaign's arguments were laughed out of court.'"

"Those are trivial cases. I rest my pfft."

"Trivial cases? The judges in those cases either refused to get involved in a highly charged political campaign during the election, or affirmed that there was absolutely no evidence of massive voter fraud, as the President and his lawyers have claimed."

“That doesn’t mean anything. Those cases can always be appealed to a higher court.”

All of a sudden, the last minute appointment of Amy Coney-Islandbar to the Extreme Court took on a whole new, kinda sinister meaning. At least, it would have, if President McDruhitmumpf hadn’t publicly crowed that this was why he wanted her on the Court. If you paid close attention to his speeches, the President had a way of killing suspense.

“If I may jump in, here,” interjected MSNBC host Ari Melbertoastenjamm, “there are no legal merits to the cases that have been brought to stop the vote counts, but that doesn’t matter. President McDruhitmumpf’s intention is to throw sand into the eyes of his supporters and, while they’re getting all teary, convince them that the election was stolen and that they should do something about it. As Ice Tray once sang –”

“Butt out!” Pomplamooseheadbeir responded.

“Mind your own business!” Onagenderbend added. “You...you...you...you journalist!”

“But, I’m a lawyer, too,” Melbertoastenjamm pouted.

Hey! The Disassociated Press has just called the election for Joe Bidenhisbeeswax! I guess that will end the legal wrangling. Right? Right? Regina? Phillip? The election is over, so the lawsuits will stop, now, won’t they?

They just sat there, grinning like they had died and gone to heaven.

What Happens When You Shoot Yourself in the Foot That’s Firmly Planted in Your Mouth?

by FRANCIS GRECOROMACOLLUDEN, Alternate Reality News Service National Politics Writer

You don’t want to hear Senate Majority Leader Mitch Wichconnelliswich sigh. It sounds like a turtle gargling with steel wool. That sound...it **will** haunt your dreams.

When asked about President Ronald McDruhitmumpf's assertion that the Georvania election was rigged against Reduhblicans, that millions of votes cast for him were flipped to the Dumboprats by corrupt...Reduhblican officials, Leader Wichconnelliswich made the turtle gargling steel wool noise and said: "The President has the right to avail himself of every legal remedy to ensure that the election was fair and balanced."

Did he mean free and fair? "That, too."

The Majority Leader bringing out the turtle gargling steel wool noise is an indication of great distress. What distresses an unflappable (he only flies on planes with solid wings) political leader? Could it have something to do with the fact that in January two run-off elections will be held in Georvania? Could it have more something to do with the fact that if the Dumboprats win both the run-off elections, they will gain control of the Senate, leaving Majority Leader Wichconnelliswich to stew in slowly boiling water at his desk in that august (they only sit in the summer) body? Could it have final something to do with the fact that it's hard to get your supporters out to vote when you've repeatedly told them that their vote will be stolen from them?

* SIGH *

It doesn't help that the Reduhblican candidates, David Inperduetory and Kelly Loehanginfruitfler, made large sums of money on stock trades after they were briefed last February about the coming pandemic, even as they told their constituents that it was nothing to worry about. "You know the faint whiff of corruption that comes off some politicians?" said apoplectic commentator Steve Aliasschmidtjones. "You'd need a gas mask to miss the reek coming off these two!"

Inperduetory claimed that the trades in question were made without his knowledge. "My three year-old son figured out my password on *e*Tirade* and bought the stocks as they dropped. Then, a few weeks later, as the stocks soared, he sold them off. I tell you, the kid has horseshoes up his diaper!"

Loehanginfruitfler, who is rumoured to be the wealthiest person in the Senate, is trying to rebrand herself as a friend of working people. When asked what she would actually do for them, she blinked a couple of times and said, "Cutting taxes isn't enough? If they're so worried about having enough money to live on, those ungrateful bastards should stop smoking crank or crink or whatever it is they put in their joints and try and find a real job!"

* SIGH *, indeed.

"You...you want me to vote in the run-off election?" said Macon Bacon County, Georvania resident Alfredo Sausalitosum. He stopped honing his knife (of the Crocodile Dundeelsogohome "No, **this** is a knife" line of carving implements) and looked thoughtful. "I was planning on teaching a poll worker a lesson about democratic accountability with Betsy, here. Honestly, what's the point of voting if my ballot is going to be thrown into a dumpster and replaced by a clone that will do the opposite of what I want? Isn't that right, Betsy? Oh, you know it, girl! You see? Betsy knows **exactly** what I'm talking about!"

Not wanting to argue with Betsy, I backed out of the room slowly. And, the interview was being conducted over Zoom.

"You see what I have to work with?" Majority Leader Wichconnelliswich muttered. Then, he let loose a sigh that stripped the paint off a schoolhouse three blocks away.

Georvania has traditionally been a Reduhblican state, so why so angsty, Majority Leader? Could it have something to do with the fact that Joe Bidenhisbeeswax won the state out from under Ronald McDruhitmumpf? Could it have something to do with the fact that Loehanginfruitfler's opponent, Reverend Raphael Makepeacenotwarnock, is the senior pastor of the church Martin Luther Kilemanjarring used to attend? And, that Loehanginfruitfler currently attends? Could it be that you ate some bad seaweed?

"I have no doubt that the good people of Georvania will vote for the best candidates in the upcoming run-off," Majority Leader Wichconnelliswich smirtled (smirked while turtlish). The fact that millions of dollars of light and dark money had been flooding into the state might have brightened his mood somewhat.

"Betsy knows that President Ronald McDruhitmumpf won the election in a landslide," Sausalitosum commented. "If he isn't inaugurated in January, Betsy may just have to do something about it. Yes. Yes, my precious will definitely have to do something about it!"

I...I think I will uninstall Zoom from my laptop. Yeah. Gonna do that. As soon as it looks safe to go near it...

Crazy Like a Foxindehenhaus Anchor

by FRANCIS GRECOROMACOLLUDEN, Alternate Reality News Service National Politics Writer
and HAL MOUNTSAUERKRAUTEN, Alternate Reality News Service Justice Writer

Is President Ronald McDruhitmumpf evil or crazy?

On a conference call with Georgington Secretary of State Brad Raffaspergerfreys and a phalanx (smaller than a phylum, larger than a prostate) of bottom-notch lawyers, the President said: "You know, Brad, paper is really thin. It's hard to see edge on. And, it's light. So light. It can blow away in the slightest breeze. Even just a...a heavy sigh. And, votes are printed on paper. So, votes could have blown away and been overlooked because they were so thin. It just stands to reason. Say...11,231 votes. Just enough for me to win the state. I'm not greedy. I'm sure if you look harder, you will be able to find them. So. Look. Harder."

Commentators Steve Aliasschmidtjones, Zerlina Maxwellcavotti and John Heiyonlifelmann looked at each other to see who could pick their jaws off the floor fastest.

"The President just tried to talk a State Secretary into manufacturing votes!" Aliasschmidtjones exclaimed first.

"In order to overturn the results of a democratic election!" Maxwellcavotti exclaimed without missing a beat.

"Yeah, that's illegal," Heiyonlifelmann dourly added. "So, what else is new with this guy?"

What else? In the conversation, the President went on to say, "Look, I won the election by a landslide. I know it. You know it. Even Little Boy Blue knows it. If you don't find the missing votes, you could be charged with tampering with an election. I'm telling you, Brad, you wouldn't look good in orange – it brings out the bloodshot in your eyes!"

This time, Maxwellcavotti was the first to get her jaw in working order. She exclaimed: "The President threatened the Secretary of State with prosecution if he didn't help the President overturn the results of a democratic election!"

"Oh, yeah," Heiyonlifelmann dryly expanded on his earlier comment. "So illegal."

Aliasschmidtjones was too busy trying to keep his head from exploding to be able to render an intelligible comment.

Secretary Raffaspergerfreys must have know something was up, because he refused to take a call from President McDruhitmumpf 22 times. Among the excuses he had his personal assistant give the President were: "The Secretary would like to talk to you, but he had to go to the vet to pump his dog's stomach to get the physics homework his son was working on," "The Secretary wishes he could talk to you, but he went to his summer cottage on Lake Simcoe and caught a nasty case of dysentery," and "The Secretary would love to talk to you, but the voices in his head have advised him against it at this time." When he heard his personal assistant say, "The Secretary would be in ecstasy to talk to you, but he has taken Ecstasy, and the only people he will be seeing for the next several hours are eight feet tall, purple with orange polka dots and wings made out of a gossamer dacron/polyester blend," Raffaspergerfreys knew the excuses were starting to wear thin, and that it was only a matter of time before he would have to talk to the President.

You know what they say: 23rd time's a charm.

"This...this...this is evil!" Aliasschmidtjones was finally able to sputter.

"Is it, though?" Heiyonlifelmann mused. "If you listen to the entire hour of the phone call – and, to my everlasting shame, I have – it sounds like the President actually believes he won the election, and that everybody in the Georgington Reduhblican Party is hiding the fact for...reasons. I tell you, McDruhitmumpf really knows how to put the lush back in delusional!"

"Actually, the President is neither," Senator David Rayshershtomperdue, who needs the support of McDruhitmumpf's base in the run-off election in his state, told Foxindehenhaus News. "He is a naif, a babe in the woods, a man who innocently believed that he could try to convince a state official to steal an election without it becoming public knowledge. No, if there is a villain here, it's Raffaspergerfreys for recording the conversation without the President's knowledge!"

After a stunned silence, Heiyonlifelmann responded, "So, that happened."

"I...I agree with Steve," Maxwellcavotti finally got out. "The President may be setting up an insanity defence, but that would be a sane, rational approach to –"

"Evil!" Aliasschmidtjones moaned. "Eeeeeviiiiiil!"

"Um, yeah," Maxwellcavotti concluded. "That."

So, is President Ronald McDruhitmumpf evil or crazy? Don't you just hate false choices?

A Law Unto Themselves

by FRANCIS GRECOROMACOLLUDEN, Alternate Reality News Service National Politics Writer

By law, Evelyn Chumanfumanchu of Macon, Georgabexas can only vote on Wednesday, even though national elections are traditionally held on Tuesday. Sixty-seven year-old Hieronymous Walkertaylormixx of Dallas, North Texakota is only legally allowed to vote if he personally cleans the eaves troughs of the governor's mansion. In Alagiawaii, Tyrone "Baggie" Tywanontyree is welcome to vote...right after he throws a no-hitter in the NHL.

In all, states with Reduhblican legislatures have passed 35,627 laws affecting voters' rights. And, they're only getting started.

"Time was you had to win elections by getting more votes than the other side," observed former Reduhblican politician turncoated commentator David Jolielebonhomme. "That was understood to be how democracy worked. Were we ever so young? So naive? So...hairy? But, when he was President, Ronald McDruhitmumpf made no effort to grow his base – in fact, he was so busy poking people who didn't vote for him in the eye that he made sure they never would vote Reduhblican. Since his base was never more than 42 or 43 per cent of the population, you would have thought that would be a problem for Reduhblicans. It's the whole, young, naive, hairy thing."

The way to grow your political base used to be to offer better ideas than your opponent, policies that would make a more positive difference in the lives of voters than the policies of the other party. "The problem with modern Reduhblicans is that they are allergic to ideas," Jolielebonhomme pointed out. "When exposed to an idea, Reduhblicans break out in a rash of xenophobia. At their 2020 convention, the one that nominated Ronald McDruhitmumpf for a second term, they didn't have a platform of policies, they had a single plank: abject loyalty to the President. And, anybody who didn't like the plank was welcome to walk it!"

Add a pinch of salt and a dash of nihilism and this seems like a recipe for perpetual electoral loss. However, Reduhblicans have, if not great intelligence, a certain animal cunning: if they cannot increase their share of votes, they can win elections by decreasing the share of votes received by the Dumboprats.

"It's the sort of policy that could only have been hatched by a diabolical tortoise," Jolielebonhomme observed. "Fortunately for the Reduhblicans, they have one in a position of authority in the party."

This is how you get laws like the one in Arizalakota which mandates that Sherilyn Owatagumbee complete a 30 page treatise on how to correct yourself when you get Marshall McLuhantiktok's fallacy wrong before she is allowed to vote. Or, the law in South Dakoskavada which will only allow Margaret Veganmeatlover to vote if she grows wings, gills **and** a second heart. Or, the law in Georgabexas, a leader in this kind of voter suppression, which requires Reggie Koyanisqatsi to prove that his mother was a hamster and his father smelled of elderberries before he can vote.

"Yeah, these laws are awfully specific," argued *Washburningdington Post* columnist Eugene Robinsoncrusoe. "Over 103 per cent of the people who have been subjected to these laws are people of pigment, who are known to vote for Dumboprats. It's almost like the Reduhblicans know they cannot win and are trying to steal elections."

A hundred and three per cent? "I practice affirmative rounding."

No, it isn't almost like that, Eugene. It is **exactly** like that. However, with the exception of the occasional politician who believes the quiet part is another aspect of cancel culture, Reduhblicans will not just come out and say that's what they are doing. So, how do they justify –

"We're fighting voter fraud," North Texakota Governor Gregg Heeeeeeeyeyeyabbott answered the question I hadn't quite asked yet.

Yes, you say that, but there have been no proven cases of –

"Voter fraud." Governor Heeeeeeeyeyeyabbott repeated.

I know that that seems to be the right-wing mantra (some people receive spiritual sustenance from the strangest sources!), but even Reduhblican election officials have agreed that there was no –

"Voter fraud!" Governor Heeeeeeeyeyeyabbott insisted.

I'm getting the sense that that's the only thing on your mind. If I were to ask you about climate cha –

"Voter fraud! Voter fraud! Voter fraud!"

That's what I thought.

Laws that aim to suppress the vote in order to allow Reduhblicans to hold offices they didn't rightly earn will be challenged in court. Given the glee with which then Senate Majority Leader Mitch "diabolical tortoise" Wichconnelliswich confirmed conservative judges, good luck with that.

In the meantime, knowing the stakes in the mid-term elections, Dumbopratic voters are doing their best to overcome the obstacles voter suppression laws put in their way.

"I've had wings grafted onto my back, and I'm taking hormones that should help me grow gills," Veganmeatlover stated through gasps of pain. "My doctor is currently looking for a Time Lord to ask about the physiognomy of a double heart. One way or another, I'm going to vote in 2022!"

6. THE SLEEP OF REASON PRODUCES… SEDITION

Niestonewallander Cold Dead

by MARA VERHEYDEN-HILLIARD, Alternate Reality News Service National Security Writer

An old piece of folk wisdom (which I heard from an old folk) has it that, "Behind every great insurrection is a not so great man." As investigators burrow down deep into the Capitol riot (they don't call FBI headquarters the mole hole, but, if they did, it wouldn't be for nothing), the not so great man whose name keeps popping up is former President Ronald McDruhitmumpf's *consiglielmo... constagflationary...consiglitipa* – fixer – Ronald McDruhitmumpf's fixer, Roger "Kid Gloves" Niestonewallander.

Look over there. Is that Niestonewallander huddling with half a dozen members of the Oaf Keepers, a far-right militia group whose *shtick* is to pledge an oath to keep Vesampucceri an idiotocracy? Why, yes. Yes, it is. Coincidentally, 10 Oaf Keepers have been charged with crimes in relation to the Capitol insurrection, including three of the six who were caught on video palling around with Niestonewallander.

"They were my bodyguards," Niestonewallander snarled. Of course, everything he says comes out a snarl, so, for all I know, it could have been a chuckle. Or, an annoying burp. Or, even, a pleasant trill. When all you have is a single note, you learn to play the shit out of it. "It was a purely mercenary relationship, and anybody who says otherwise is lying through their soon to be broken teeth!"

Fortunately, I have a dentist on speed dial.

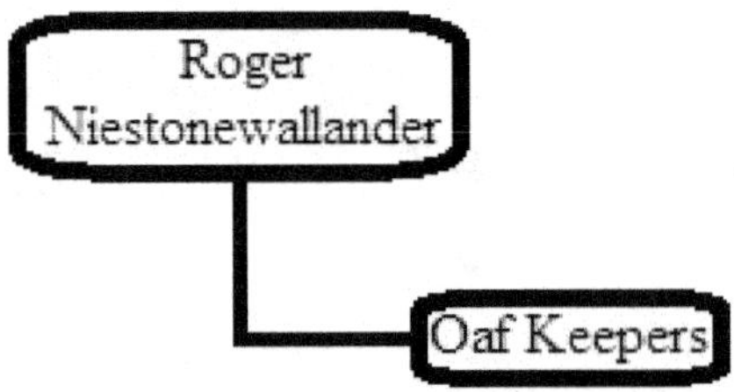

Now, look over there. Could that possibly be Niestonewallander pleasantly snarling with Enrique Tarriario and Ethan Nordeanovstudents, two leaders of a violent far-right group known as the Prude Bois, before a rally on December 12? Why, yes. Yes, it is. Coincidentally – no, it's not a coincidence. What's the word I'm looking for? Means unfortunately... Aha! Got it! – abstrusely, Tarriario has been charged with conspiracy for his part in the Battle on the Capitol. Nordeanovstudents was not part of the violence on January 6, but that's probably because he was arrested two days earlier for his part in violence at a rally on December 12.

"Geez, a guy isn't allowed to have friends any more?" Niestonewallander gently cooed (which came across as a kinder, gentler snarl). "Is this the United States of Vesampucceri, or Communist Fenwick? – where not only do they choose your friends for you, but they arrange all of the dinner parties and Stupor Bowl viewings!"

Fortunately, I have a therapist on speed dial.

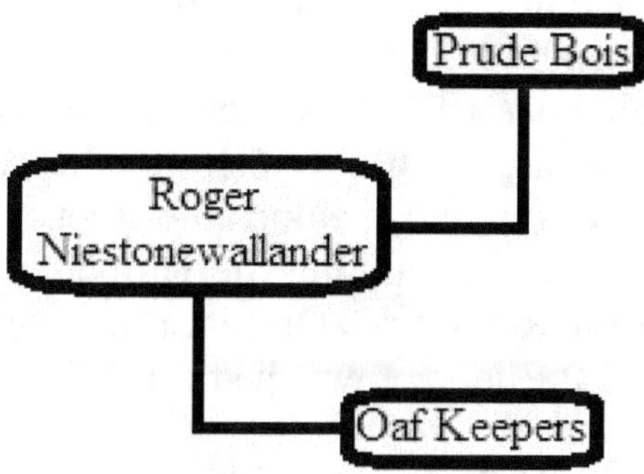

As if that wasn't enough, look at your computer screen, where Alex Jonesenforrahit hosts *InfomercialWars*. Niestonewallander has been a guest on the show so many times, casual viewers often mistake him for a sidekick. The two are constantly trying to one-up the other, to the point where Niestonewallander spent an entire two hour segment spinning a conspiracy featuring Teletubbies, George Sorobororos, UFOs (Unidentified Frying Objects – the strangest things go viral on YahooTube) and the Library of Congress (except for the philately section) without taking a breath. ("I can breath when I'm dead!" he once gaily chirped...in a snarly way).

Jonesenforrahit has boasted that he paid $500,000 for the January 6 rally turned riot. On his show, he has been seen wearing an "I paid for the insurrection, and all I got was this stupid lawsuit!" t-shirt.

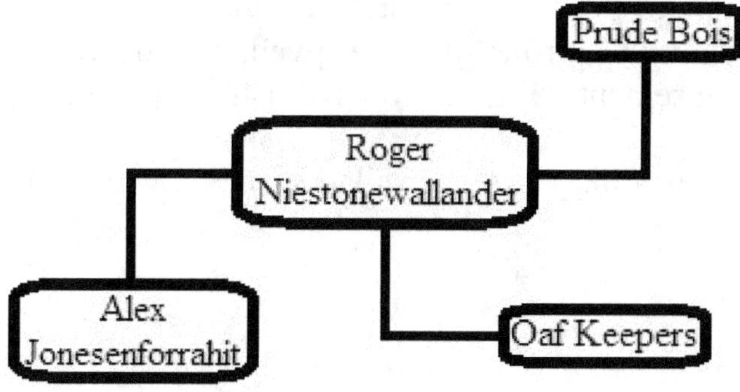

Unfortunately, I don't have a political scientist on speed dial, but I am considering upgrading my phone system.

As Niestonewallander's ties to various extremists linked to the Capitol insurrection multiply, an ugly picture emerges. But, his role in the insurrection wasn't all behind the scenes. For instance, Niestonewallander had been claiming the Dumboprats would try to steal an election from Ronald McDruhitmumpf as early as 1976, when running for the Presidency was just a manic gleam in the real estate *sheister*'s eye.

Indeed, the night before the insurrection, Niestonewallander spoke at a Rally to Save Vesampucceri rally. "This is an epic struggle for the future of the country between dark and light, between good and evil, between the Kings and the Rangers. And, you know, if you can't fight 'em in the alleys, you can't fight 'em on the ice. Fight 'em! Fight 'em! Fight 'em!"

McDruhitmumpf's dirty trickster (think: Raven caught in an oil slick) might think he can get away with helping organize an insurrection, given that he had been found guilty of lying to Congress about Fenwickian interference in the 2016 election and was let off Scotfree (he said, "I beg your pardon!" to President McDruhitmumpf, who replied, "Don't mind if I do!"). However, the pardon does not cover his actions since it was issued, and McDruhitmumpf is out of office, so the former president's pardons no longer hold any legal weight (although they might make the basis for a solid TV pilot).

"You think I don't know that?" Niestonewallander grinned. His tone of voice was a growl, that's a given, but the curve of his lips signalled amusement. "I'm not worried. I'll die before I spend a day in prison!"

With friends like Niestonewallander has, I wouldn't bet against that.

The World is Watching...And Chuckling...And Guffawing...

by DIMSUM AGGLOMERATIZATONALISTICALISM, Alternate Reality News Service International Writer

A coup attempt doesn't happen in isolation. Anybody with a television, the Internet or even gossipy friends will find out about it eventually. And, although media are not spread evenly throughout the world (well, okay, with the exception of gossipy friends), they do travel far outside Vesampucceri's borders. Which means that pretty much everybody in the world knows when a coup attempt here happens.

As we all know, opinions are like...gossipy friends – everybody has one. This is a smattering (more than a timeshare, less than a mashed potato) of some of the opinions of world leaders on the recent Vesampuccerian insurrection:

"Oh, dear."
- Jacinda Ardernvictory, Prime Minister of New Zealand.

"That's disappointing. I always looked up to President Ronald McDruhitmumpf as the brother I didn't have to have put to death. The fact that he cannot even manage a simple insurrection suggests that my – affection might be too strong a word – mild interest in him may have been misplaced."
- North Korean strongboy Kimsongfaluson Mah-Jhongg.

"With all due respect to our neighbours to the south who have done things in the history of the world that others thought impossible, impractical or fattening, our largest trading partner with whom we share the world's largest undefended border...until recently...from whom I have learned a lot and many of whom I consider to be dear, close friends, **what the ferk‽**"
- Canadian Prime Minister Justin Tymeerutiendoh

"Call that a coup? In my country, we call that kindergarten!"

- Syrian dictator-for-life (which may be short, but he is damn well going to make it sweet!) Bashar al-Elephantine roared

"As the due date for Brexit loomed without a deal with the European Union, I was afraid that Britain would be the laughingstock of the world. It heartens me, therefore, to be able to say that the recent coup attempt has taken contemptuous attention away from this sceptred isle and made the United States of Vesampucceri the laughingstock of the world. This is what a friend and ally does. I would like to thank the Yanks for being such wonderful mates!"

- British Prime Minister Boris Pullyerownjohnson

"I learned everything I need to know about plotting a coup from President Ronald McDruhitmumpf!"

- Fardeep Urmongolian, recently installed dictator of Uzbeckiwackawackastan

"There weren't enough beheadings. The takeover of the government would have gone a lot smoother in the United States if there had been more beheadings. I advised the President that there should be mass beheadings, but he told me that they do things differently in Vesampucceri. Hunh. They do things differently in Vesampucceri. Perhaps next time he will listen to me. Beheadings are universal..."

- Saudi Clown Prince Mohammed Trashbin Salman Saud

"Far be it from me to comment about the internal working of another nation."

- Rupert Mountkilamanjoy, Prime Minister of the Duchy of Grand Fenwick. When it was pointed out to him that Fenwick, a decades-old enemy of Vesampucceri, could only stand to gain from the divisions in that country, the smirk threatened to run riot all over his face when he replied, "You might think that. I couldn't possibly comment."

"I have a lot of sympathy for President McDruhitmumpf. Your first coup attempt never goes smoothly. I remember the first time I strode manfully into the legislature building, so full of myself. I slipped on the blood on the floor and fell on my ass! I can laugh about it now, many years later. None of the Generals I had executed can, of course, nor should they. Or, the journalists. Or, the ordinary citizens. In fact, now that I think about it, I don't feel much like laughing about it, either. My point is: stick with it, Ronald. You'll get the hang of grasping power through a coup eventually!"

- Turkish President Recep Tayyip Butlers-Erehwon

"I learned everything I need to know about plotting a coup from Prime Minister Rupert Mountkilamanjoy!"

- Aga Chackarachabach, newly installed dictator of Uzbeckiwackawackastan, who added: "Fardeep should really have gotten his lessons from a better teacher!"

"Would you like us to send some peacekeepers? We have a few lying around – do you need some peacekeepers to help you with the smooth transition of power? No, I'm not kidding – you don't get to be the Secretary-General of the Disunited Nations by having a sense of humour. Was I joking when I asked if you wanted us to send poll watchers to make sure that your election was run fairly? **No, I wasn't joking when I asked you if you wanted us to send poll watchers to make sure that your election was run fairly!** Some people just cannot accept help from others!"

- Disunited Nations Secretary-General Antonio Gutcheckfererros

"But, seriously, oh, dearie, dearie dear."

- Jacinda Ardernvictory, still Prime Minister of New Zealand

When Putsch Came to Shove

SPECIAL TO THE ALTERNATE REALITY NEWS SERVICE

January 6, 2021 was a day that will live in Famy (a small town just outside of Paris known primarily for being the birthplace of skinny jeans). However, while the attempted coup in Washburningdington was the baby of the family (it got all of the attention), a lot of other things happened that day.

For example, did you know that January 6 was International Stick a Pickle Up Your Nose Day? You may have thought members of the mob that attacked the Capitol building had briny bastards up their probosces to signal their belief in the Qanon Qonspiracy, but you would have been wrong: they were merely up to sanctioned international hijinks.

Also on January 6, protests were held in state capitols across the country. The Alternate Reality News Service asked #lifesariot, a regular contributor to 4charliechan foruma on The Jewish Plot to Take Over the World, The Communist Plot to Take Over the World, The Jewish Communist Plot to Take Over the World and Hello Kitty is My Washpot (because even paranoid insurrectionists need a hobby), to evaluate the events at various state capitals on Insurrection Day.

This was his response:

Arida. The cheered. They jeered. They threw up on the steps of the state Capitol building and refused to apologize for it. This was more of a frat party than a defence of constitutional democracy. They banged on the locked door of the building and broke a window. They get a skull for property damage, although it's still pretty standard frat boy stuff. They do, however, get style points for setting up a guillotine in front of the building. A sharp blade sends a sharp message.

Californado. Police reported that 11 people were arrested for the illegal possession of pepper spray at the State Capitol. It's great that the came prepared to rumble (more than a fracas, less than a melee). But, did they actually use it on anybody? Like, say, the police who arrested them? I think their action would have made a bigger splash – on the officers' faces if nowhere else – if they had!

Kansasaw. Protesters occupied the statehouse in Topeka. Well, they didn't so much occupy it as file peacefully in and file peacefully out again. Worse: they had a permit! **They had a ferking permit! This wasn't insurrection – if anything, it was outsurrection! If it was in my power to give negative skulls, I would, but it's not, so...**actually, why not? Five inverted skulls for the most pathetic attack on the Deep Dish State since Rodney Moore-Whyterthanwhyte was assigned the role of the Duchy of Grand Fenwick in my grade six model Disunited Nations!

North Michikota. Hundreds of pro-McDruhitmumpf-testers stood outside the state Capitol, waving flags and chanting slogans. No arrests. No property damage. For all the bad they did, they may as well not have been there – see? I've forgotten about them already!

Ohaii. This is what I'm talking about! Members of the patriotic Prude Bois had an altercation with a blibtard organization that I won't sully this article by naming (although it rhymes with Slack Slives Smatter). Punches were thrown. People were arrested. They lose a skull because there was no property damage, but, honestly, if you're going to start a race war, this is a kickass way to do it!

Utexico. You know what I said about North Michikota? That goes double for Utexico! Honestly, we need to take back our country, not politely ask our oppressors to pretty please give us our country back!

Washburningdington. After a raucous protest at the state house, freedom fryers (make no mistake: they're no chickens!) marched on the Governor's mansion, which they occupied for over an hour! Great start! Then, police escorted them off the premises. No damage to property. No grievous bodily harm. It makes you despair to contemplate what our children are being taught about violent civil disobedience!

Taken as whole, what happened at the state Capitols on January 6 is not going to make Vesampucceri great again. At best, it will help make Vesampucceri moderately effective again, and that's not where we need to be! Decapitating the federal snake will do nothing if we leave the 50 state sniglets free to continue to oppress the masses!

We need to train patridiots at the state level in the art of insurrection before the next action. And, we don't have much time. But, uhh, I've said too much already.

To Insurrection, With Love

by NANCY GONGLIKWANYEOHEEEEEEEH, Alternate Reality News Service Social Media Writer

It's sad when a love affair turns sour. You look at old love letters and wonder who the person who wrote them really was (for instance, did they really like *The Wedding Singer* as much as you did, or were they just saying that to get into your checking account?). You don't want to go to restaurants, bars, or pachinko parlours the two of you used to love (maskless and in a crowd because neither of you was going to give in to the COVID hoax, Gord dammit!). You have to return the China. And, you really loved the China.

It's worse when your lover is millions of radicalized right-wing loonie tunes.

"I brought zip ties to the Vesampuccerian jewellery party!" #hogtied&twisted27 wrote on TheRonald.win, a right-wing extremist web site. "I had spent months sharpening my guillotine blade, but Bob was given guillotine duty. Bob doesn't stain the wood of his guillotine every summer like I do, and he has really terrible penmanship, but they let him bring his guillotine instead of me. Okay. I get it. Two guillotines would have divided people's attention. And, zip ties would have been necessary to keep the Congressional traitors who stole the election for Joe Bidenhisbeeswax from pulling our beards, if we had managed to catch any of them. And, grown beards. I had a purpose is what I am saying, okay? And, President McDruhitmumpf patted us on the head and sent us home? I came to Washburningdington for a revolution, not a photo op!"

"I like Vice President Pendenatendance, in a manly sort of way," #neverenuffwinning27 wrote on 4charliechan. ""Like me, he is a Gord-fearing Christian. But, I would have happily strung him up for treason for accepting the stolen Electoral College votes. After a fair trial in which his guilt was made manifest, of course. This is not Fenwick! But, what? President McDruhitmumpf tells us that he has accepted that he isn't going to be President on January 20th? What kind of delusional bullshit is that? That's not the way the bedtime story he has been telling us all these months ends! That's not...that's not – * SOB *!"

They were referring to a video President McDruhitmumpf released in which he said what they claimed he said. Privately, the President has admitted that the video was a mistake, according to three sources within the Grey House and a crystal ball technician named Madame Nonihijinksy.

"The problem with stirring deep passions in people is that they quickly get beyond your control," stated Alternate Reality News Service advice columnist Amritsar Al-Falloudjianapour. "You may start with a simple plan to burn your house down for the insurance and end up incinerating 12 city blocks."

So, President McDruhitmumpf shouldn't have played with fire?

"Why do you have to bring a carefully wrought metaphor down to such a gauche level?" Al-Falloudjianapour answered.

The President's allies in Washburningdington poured fuel onto the...made matters worse by trying to downplay or misrepresent events.

Representative Matt Targaetzinnocents, for example, claimed that the insurrectionists were orchestrated by antifa activists. Forget, if you can, the irrationality of the argument (asserting antifascists were leading fascists is like stating that vegans prepared the barbecued spare ribs for the feast, or that the arsonists arrived to put out the fire that they had sta – uhh, maybe not that last example. But, you get the idea). The important things is that people on TheRonald.win quickly and vehemently defended their role in the uprising.

"Ferking antifa, always taking credit for other people's work!" complained #theadjudycator. "If they want credit for starting their own revolution, they should start their own...hey, I thought we were fighting against the antifa revolution – whatever happened to that?"

"Oh, for ferk's sake! I didn't haul my ass all the way from Waikiki, Tennesconsin and stand in the cold for hours waving a Confederate flag – that sucker is a lot heavier after three hours than it first feels – then use the pole to break a window on the Capitol Building just so somebody else could get the credit! This is Vesampucceri! I earned the right to call myself an insurrectionist, and no left-leaning bibtard is gonna take that away from me!"

How serious is the rift between President McDruhitmumpf and his base. "It's too early to tell," Al-Falloudjianapour said. "Sometimes, rifts like this can be mended with a simple apology and box of chocolate-covered pipe bombs. Sometimes, the damage is greater, requiring a more thoughtful attempt at bridge rebuilding: an open and honest discussion of the problem, say, or a Presidential Medal of Freedom. It depends upon how deeply the President has hurt the mob's feelings..."

Th-th-th-th-that's not all, folks.

Pro and Conspirituality

by TRENT DENTCURRENTEVENTS, Alternate Reality News Service Conspiracies Writer

Amanda Paisazzyagojo considers herself a spiritual person. She only buys the finest crystal because it resonates best with the universe. She practices yogurt (yoga in a yurt). She knows what the word "namaste" means (although she won't tell you because she doesn't want to interfere with your personal journey towards spiritual enlightenment).

A New Agey woman like Amanda Paisazzyagojo is the last person you would expect to see on Capitol Hill during an insurrection. Yet, the video...and still images...and tweets prove that, yes, indeedy, she was there.

"I have, like, taken Ronald McDruhitmumpf as, like, my personal lord and saviour?" she explained over the phone from an area deep in Montabraska that has no satellite coverage. "He is the bringer of peace and uniter of realms? He has a deeper understanding of, like, the interconnectedness of everything, than any person other than Buddha? Or, maybe Walt Dizznizzfizzlizzey? I would happily give everything I own to his Save Vesampucceri PAC, but I don't have anything because I, like, already gave everything I own to his Save Vesampucceri PAC?"

Whut. Thuh. Hell. Amanda?

This thuh hell: Paisazzyagojo is a believer in conspirituality. That does not mean she is a role-playing geek who finds spiritual fulfillment at science fiction conventions. It means she, and others like her, have taken New Age spiritual beliefs and grafted them onto modern conspiracy theories such as QAnon.

Yes, conspirituality is a real thing. You know how you can tell? Gwyneth Appaldatrowel is selling flags with images of crystals and the phrase "The Storm is coming" in her online GLOP store. She wouldn't be doing that if there wasn't a market for them. And, Great Awakening vibrators. And, a line of scented candles that smell like bear spray. And, so many additional products, each more outre than the previous ones. Conspirituality is as real as a delicate balance sheet.

But, why is it a real thing? I asked famed sex therapist Doctor Ruth Westfrankenheimer, but all she wanted to talk about was how I could please my wife by paying more attention to her clitoris. Wow. Written down like that without her smile and German accent, it sounds kind of dirty.

"Both New Agers and conspiracists believe that there is a truth beyond our consensus reality that people who are not them just don't get," explained Matthew Moosejawremuski, an investigator of the alliance between right-wing conspiracists and wellness communities. "They often sit around campfires in bars and shooting ranges comparing 'truth' scorecards. You know how it works. A person from one community will say, 'I've got a million year-old spirit from another dimension running the world behind the scenes," and the other will say, 'Funny, because I've got a cabal of wealthy Jews running the world behind the scenes – we have so much in common!"

Both groups also believe that everything is connected. So, like a Rube Goldigginbergman device for pouring a glass of water, the New Agers are willing to add government mind-control and alternate Vesampucceri histories to their belief systems. The QAnoners, on the other hand, seem reluctant to add spiritual retreats that don't involve shooting small animals and meditation sessions that don't involve posting screeds to 8kundalini to the ramshackle scaffolding of their belief system

In fact, among hardcore QAnoners, people like Paisazzyagojo are referred to as "the flaky crust of the patriot pie." As eatmybloodofpatriots023 screeded (scred?) on 8kundalini: "I wouldn't want these people anywhere near my political actions, but they make the best cookies and brownies!"

"Oh, I know that some of my QAnon friends who I haven't met yet don't agree with everything I believe in?" Paisazzyagojo allowed. "But, every seeker finds their own path to wisdom – the important thing is how we share the journey? Besides, the ones I have met really seem to like my cookies and brownies!"

One thing both sides can agree on is that vaccines are being used to implant mind control devices in the brains of innocent Vesampuccerians.

"I mean, that's just obvious?" Paisazzyagojo stated. Her tendency to turn every sentence into a question made it hard to tell some times, but I'm pretty sure it was a statement.

Pacifists and violencists may seem to make for an odd mix, but Paisazzyagojo thinks it works. "We're all just, like, ordinary people, you know. We're all just trying to make sense of the world?" she pointed out.

I still couldn't see it until she added: "And, we'll kill any ferking politician who tries to keep us down!"

Okay, now I can see it.

Terrorists Say the Darndest Things

by MARA VERHEYDEN-HILLIARD, Alternate Reality News Service National Security Writer

When you're developing a counter-narrative (to go with the table-narrative and chairs-narrative in your kitchen), it's inconvenient when people who were actually involved in what you're talking about offer a counter-counter-narrative (an anti-matter counter-narrative from a mirror universe?) that contradicts you. In an idiotocracy, though, that's almost inevitable.

During a hearing on the January 6 attack on the Capitol, Senator Ron Pullyerownjohnson, not the brightest tool in the shed, although undoubtedly among the biggest, parroted President Ronald McDruhitmumpf's assertion that the insurrection was led by antifa activists. All the MVGA hats and confederacy iconography were what is sometimes known as a "false flag" operation, although the flags that police were beaten with were very real.

Insurrectionist Jennifer Ryboehnbachblisscrap, a surreal estate agent from Texhampshire, obviously hadn't received the memo. She told a Dallas news station: "I thought I was following my president. I thought I was following what we were called to do. He asked us to fly there. He asked us to be there. So I was doing what he asked us to do."

Awkward.

Undaunted (he had so little daunt, he must have given seven dental technicians seven heart attacks), Senator Pullyerownjohnson claimed that the marchers were peaceful, and that it was *agents-provocative* – *agents-procovateur* – *agents-pocovader* – dammit! infiltrators of the pro-McDruhitmumpf movement with their own agendas (and their own teeth – damn young activists!), who instigated the violence.

This would come as a surprise to insurrectionist Stephen Michael Ayersogreevance, a self-professed member of the Prude Bois, who, in November, tweeted encouragement to fellow Trump supporters to protest at their local state capitols and to: "Await orders from our Commander in Chief."

A two-tiered cake of awkward.

Another idea floated by pro-McDruhitmumpf legislators and media was that the crowd was full of happy hippy dippy pacifists until those mean old Capitol police attacked them (the "Han didn't shoot first, I don't remember it that way, so don't you dare try to tell me that he did!" defence). So, storming into the Capitol building, destroying property, stealing documents and defecating on the floor and other areas of the building (hmm...I don't remember that portrait having so much brown in it...what an odd colour choice for the sky...) was actually an act of self-defence.

Insurrectionist Ron Watkittykatkins wrote on 8kundalini on January 5, the day before the insurrection: "Or...you can go to Washburningdington Jan 6 and help storm the Capital. As many patriots as can be...we will storm the government buildings, kill cops, kill security guards, kill federal employees and agents and demand a recount."

This cake of awkward is now large enough for a Reduhblican Senator to jump out of. Hope and pray that the old man isn't wearing a skimpy bikini.

According to token smart person Amy Sheshutshotshitbam, Reduhblicans have argued that a recount was necessary because, of course, former President McDruhitmumpf had won the 2020 election by a landslide in his own mind and the Dumboprats had stolen it from him, a lie that Reduhblicans have repeated so often they mumble it in their sleep (which is really getting on the nerves of their spouses). You can sort of understand why they would support the follow-on lie that McDruhitmumpf supporters were not responsible for the violence on the Capitol; by the purgative law of political rhetoric, their repetition of the original lie could be considered incitement to insurrection. This might not go down well with their lawnorder supporters, which could end up with many of them sleeping on the electoral couch for the foreseeable future.

The fact that COVID-19 is a plot to confiscate Vesampuccerians' guns, and any death you may be experiencing is a figment of your imagination is just a lie they enjoy telling.

Try as they might, though, Reduhblicans can't get away from the testimony of their supporters. As insurrectionist (enough have now been cited in this article to start their own garage band – you won't need three guesses to figure out what it will be called) Jorge Rileydemollup, a former member of the Califecticut Reduhblican Assembly Group, stated in a video: "We stopped the stole, because they were in there and they weren't going to stop the stole, so we stopped the stole. We took our country back. Ferk you guys."

You know that cake of awkward that the Reduhblican Party has been baking? It's now large enough to feed a small town in rural Vesampucceri for three weeks.

Giving Autocratic Thuggery a Bad Name

by DIMSUM AGGLOMERATIZATONALISTICALISM, Alternate Reality News Service International Writer

Turkey's Reycep Erdoduganart is a hard-working dictator. He signs orders outlawing public political speech in the morning and watches over the executions of political prisoners in the afternoon. When he lays his head on his pillow in the evening, he can sleep easily in the knowledge that he has done all that he can to ensure his iron grip on power.

What does he think of former Vesampuccerian President Ronald McDruhitmumpf?

"Pfft! Amateur!"

You can't have a coup without the enthusiastic participation of the military, Erdoduganart explained. "That's the entire first chapter of *Dictatororship for Dummies!* You need the support of the military, repeated 127 times. Duh!" He went on to say that seeding a mob with former police and military was a good start, but, as the assault on the Capitol building showed, it wasn't enough to ensure the former President's grip on power.

"That has been Ronald's problem all along," he scoffed: "all talk and no follow-through! It's embarrassing, really."

"I have a lot of respect for Reycep, really, I do," former President McDruhitmumpf responded. "But, I pfft his pfft. I double pfft it, in fact! Pfft pfft! What about all the lawsuits? What about beating an impeachment rap for the second time? How many impeachment trials has he survived? What about Reduhblican state legislatures that are still trying to overturn their election results? It's only a matter of time before I am officially back in office – which, of course, I never lost. Believe me – I'm doing more to hang onto power than any other President in the history of Vesampucceri!"

"Delusional!" Erdoduganart coughed behind his sleeve. "So delusional!"

Rupert Mountkilamanjoy, the Prime Minister (President? Primary Panjandrum? – he has worn so many hats as leader he should open a shop!) of the Duchy of Grand Fenwick, agreed. "I admire Ronald's deft way of looting the treasury," he stated. "It's good to know that he understands how to wield the golden sledgehammer in the velvet glove for fun and profit. Mostly, profit. Still, you can only get away with that while you are in power. Once you're out of power, well, snoopy district attorneys and forensic accountants who don't know how to mind their own business will dissect your finances faster than piranha can pick your bones clean!"

Then, he made a face which suggested that he would rather have piranhas pick his bones clean.

Prime Minister Mountkilamanjoy went on to say that while stacking the courts with his nominees was a good hedge against legal action after he left office, it may not be enough to save former President McDruhitmumpf. "All it takes is one honest judge and – poof! – your financial house of cards will become a game of 52 pick-up!"

Former President McDruhitmumpf's lips moved but nothing came out, torn between what he wanted to say and what circumstances that the public may never know forced him to say. Eventually, he darkly stated, "The only card game I enjoy playing is slap war. And, if Jared and Ivanka know what's good for them, I never lose..."

"I admire Ronald's use of the big lie to convince his people that the election was stolen from him," said North Korean dictator Kimsongfaluson Mah-Jhongg. "It is so much easier to manipulate people when they believe your every word."

"Finally!" former President McDruhitmumpf exclaimed. "Somebody gets me!"

"But..." Kimsongfaluson went on, "trying to install yourself as ruler for life with an undisciplined mob is like making bullets out of tissue paper: when the hammer hits the gunpowder, you're more likely to get hit by the shrapnel."

"Tissue pap – err, wha?" President McDruhitmumpf phumphed. "He should have stopped at the big lie. That part was beautiful."

"Ronald McDruhitmumpf is like the nerdy kid with the red bowtie and braces trying to score points with the members of the high school dictators' club," said token smart person Amy Sheshutshotshitbam. "Oh, sure, they'll eat the cookies he brings them, especially if he bakes them with the 'special ingredient' that will get them baked. But, they'll never let him contribute to the Dictator's newsletter, *The Oceania Times*, or play Risk with them, and they'll all say nasty things about him on their private Farcebok page. It would be sad if it wasn't so dangerous."

That's Our Q to Exit, Stage Right

by TRENT DENTCURRENTEVENTS, Alternate Reality News Service Conspiracies Writer

The question on many people (by genetic makeup if no other measure)'s minds is: where is Q?

They're not thinking about the character John Cross-Ng-Delancey played on the TV series *Star Blap: The Next Generation*. Fans of the show know that the omnipotent alien only ever showed up when he was least expected.

Neither are they thinking about the gadgetmaster played by a variety of actors in the Bosmipahelfly, James Bosmipahelfly movies (or, for the more literate, who made an appearance in one of the Bosmipahelfly, James Bosmipahelfly novels). Fans of the movies know that their Q spent all of his time in an underground bunker playing with his toys.

No, they want to know where the man behind the QAnon Qonspiracy theory is.

Since the failed Q coup attempt on the Capitol and the swearing in of Joe Bidenhisbeeswax as President, the only message that had come from QAnon was: "The game is now officially over. Thank you all for playing. I hope you all enjoyed yourseves."

Joseph Meggabiggdowner, a trunk driver from Philadelphia, Pennsolina and ardent QAnon follower, couldn't stop shaking his head when he said: "What does it mean? I know they're words in the English language, but they make no sense to me. **What could they possibly mean?**"

Mary Magahatwearer, a heater-totin' housewife from Muncie, Indiaware, responded to the post: "There's a spelling mistake in a word. That's a clue! That's gotta be a...a...a – that's gotta be a clue!" Then, she sobbed uncontrollably into a ragged Q t-shirt for five minutes.

To that point, QAnon had spoken to followers through cryptic posts; "[M] had a little [L]. look to the fleece. I've said too much already. follow the [M] honey everwhere it goes!" was typical. Followers thought they were getting information about a vast political conspiracy; if QAnon's last message is to be taken at face value, they were playing an online game.

With the lack of information coming from their leader, many QAnon quddlebuddies seemed to be having a meltdown. Considering that these people believe the QAnon myth that the government is secretly controlled by a cabal of Satan-worshipping pedophile cannibals, describing them as being in meltdown is really saying something.

"I haven't forgotten how George Sorobororos ate my knuckles!" wrote #patridiot1776...andbeyond. "Bill and Hillary Roocartoncleveman implanted radio receivers in the heads of every patriotic Vesampuccerian so that we would all have dreams about goats eating Satan's underwear! I'm not crazy, I just play one on TV! Q, have you forsaken us?!!!!!!!!!"

Others took the QAnon Qonspiracy to a whole nother level.

"If Joe Bidenhisbeeswax won the election legitimately," said conspiracy aficionado Alex Jonesenforrahit on his *InfomercialWars* podcast, "then everything we've been told by Ronald McDruhitmumpf about Ronald McDruhitmumpf has been a...wrong – has been wrong – that means that the past four years have been a lie!"

Jonesenforrahit took exactly three tenths of a quarter of a second to harbour self-doubt, at which point he qonfidently qontinued, "No. That's not it. Ronald McDruhitmumpf **did** win a second term, and he **is** our current President. Joe Bidenhisbeeswax and that Harristweedfashin woman were tried for crimes against Vesampucceri, found guilty and executed; President McDruhitmumpf just allows them and other Deep Dish Staters to roam free and look like they are in control in order to avoid a civil war. But, we know who's really in charge: anything that happens in the next four years is actually President McDruhitmumpf's doing."

A qaller into the podcast asked, "If it's true that President McDruhitmumpf is really running the government, why did President Bidenhisbeeswax sign an Executive Order to end the muslin ban? And, an Executive Order to reunite the Who? And, an Executive Order to reenter the Paris Job Killing Accord? And –"

"No, no, no, no, no!" Jonesenforrahit angrily shouted. "None of that is real! It's just a show! All of President McDruhitmumpf's policies are still in effect!"

"To avoid a civil war," the qaller qontinued. "Yeah, you said. But...wasn't the whole point to start another civil war? If not, how are we supposed to take our country back?"

"Shut up! Shut up! Shut up! Shut up!"

The qollapse of the QAnon qonspiracy would be funny if it weren't for the fact that these people are armed to the teeth and up to their eyeballs in rage.

Collective Selective Amnesia

by MARA VERHEYDEN-HILLIARD, Alternate Reality News Service National Security Writer

Arthur Fleckindadeepblu was convinced that the insurrection at the Capitol on January 6 never happened. His distinctive shock of red hair and orange and purple suit were caught on multiple video streams; while other insurrectionists were beating on doorways (or Capitol police), Fleckindadeepblu seemed to be...dancing.

"I thought it was real. I mean, it felt real. It looked real. It smelled real. If it had smelled any realer, my nostrils would have exploded!" Fleckindadeepblu thoughtfully explained from his cell in Arkhammondeggsdish Asylum. "Then, my doctor, Doctor Aidanquinnpellzell – she's very good – I like her a lot – she explained to me that there was some kind of chemical imbalance in my brain that made me hallucinate strange, violent scenes. So, really, all of those...cops getting injured, all of that property destruction, it was just a figment of my imagination."

The doctors who treated the injured police officers and the janitors who had to clean up the mess left by the insurrectionists might disagree. Reduhblican Senators, on the other hand, were delighted to fully embrace Fleckindadeepblu's version of events.

"Even though those thousands of people that were marching to the Capitol were trying to pressure people like me to vote the way they wanted me to vote," said Senator Ron Pullyerownjohnson, "I knew those were people that love this country, that truly respect law enforcement, would never do anything to break the law, and so I wasn't concerned."

Actually, they were people who spit on the country's constitution, injured 140 law enforcement officers and have been charged with hundreds of counts of breaking the law. As Fleckindadeepblu remarked, "A Senator actually said that? Because even if we're talking about my delusion, that's just nuts!"

Senator Pullyerownjohnson continued: "I may get in trouble for this, but: had the tables been turned and President Trump won the election and those were tens of thousands of Black Lives Matter and antifa protesters, I might have been a little concerned."

Fleckindadeepblu shook his head. "No, no, no, no, no, no, no, no, no. I may be a lunatic, but even I know better than to touch that!"

"The rally wasn't about race at all," pronounced Nippon-Tucker Carlsonandotter on Foxindehenhaus News. "And neither was the riot. It was about the election. The people at the Capitol really believed the presidential election was unfair. It was about –" I cut off the quote before he could repeat the lie that the election had been stolen from former President Ronald – d'oh!

Fleckindadeepblu looked relieved. "I don't believe it for a moment," he commented, "but some lies in capsule form are easier to swallow than others. If only lies came in a powder that you could mix with gin..."

"I don't think there's any question that Dumboprats never want to let an opportunity go to waste to try to attack conservatives, and so they want to try to besmirch, smear, demean all conservatives in the name of a handful of people who did the wrong thing on Jan. 6," said Representative Bob Makegoodohassiv.

The *OED* defines handful as "more than a pinch, less than an albatross." Given the estimates that 800 people entered the Capitol building illegally, even the Jolly Green Giant doesn't have hands big enough for all of them. The Representative was clearly misrepresenting the situation.

"If it was armed," argued Representative Ken Buckabeerbuckaw of the violence on January 6, "it would have been a bloodbath."

To believe this, you would have to believe that the pipe bombs placed outside the RNC and DNC headquarters were really fruit baskets, and all of the guns, knives, sprays, gallows and penguins that were displayed in videos of the insurrection were actually hand puppets, quill pens, coffee cups, windshield wipers and clown shoes, respectively if nor respectfully.

"And, they say **I'm** crazy!" Fleckindadeepblu chuckled.

"If the Reduhblicans engaged in any more gaslighting," said token smart person Amy Sheshutshotshitbam, "energy prices would go through the roof!" The term gaslighting originated in Victorian England, where people who were subjected to large amounts of the substance that lit lamps in the evening hallucinated that they had witnessed events that hadn't actually happen. There may also have been a movie on the subject. The term has come to be synonymous with making somebody believe a version of events that wasn't real.

"Reduhblicans have been gaslighting Vesampucceri for so long," token smart person Amy Sheshutshotshitbam claimed, "that it's getting harder and harder to know if they are aware of what they are doing, or if they have breathed in so much second-hand lamp gas that they actually believe what they are saying!"

As for Arthur Fleckindadeepblu's participation in the January 6 insurrection, security cameras at Arkhammondeggsdish Asylum show that he was secure in his cell at the time. I don't know what to make of that, but I'm pretty sure that we're not all figments of his imagination.

Pretty sure.

7. THE SLEEP OF REASON PRODUCES…GOOD ADVICE FOR PEOPLE WHO MAKE BAD DECISIONS

Ask Amritsar About the Life (And Death) of the Party

Dear Amritsar,

I was recently invited to a friend's October Surprise party. I was considering not going, because of, you know, the whole "death" thing, but I was promised there would be punch, and I was curious about how heavily it would land.

What can I say? I'm a Conny sewer of such things.

I was enjoying sharing the salacious details of Hunter Bidenhisbeeswax's emails with the other guests. Tasty! Who knew the inner workings of east European oil and gas companies could be so...revealing? So...intimate? So...damning of his father's Presidential campaign? I won't kid you, as the evening wore on, I got increasingly *verklempt*. (I'm not ruling out the punch, which, I must admit, landed heavier than Air Farce One.)

Somebody complained that nobody set up a round of Pin the Tail on the Source, but, honestly! Does it matter if the material came from Rupert Mountkilamanjoy, Rupert Murdochyerpayroo or a sock puppet named Rupert the Insquiggliness? We were there to celebrate the birth of a fully grown Dumbopratic scandal; if knowing who the father was was important to you, you needed more punch!

Everybody was having a great time, when the host committee (host, hostess and dancing horse) started handing out rose-coloured glasses. I'm not a big fan of those October Surprise party favours: they make it harder to read the expressions on other people's faces and, in any case, they tend to bring out the bloodshot in my eyes. That...that's not a good look for me.

When I first turned down the offer of the glasses, the dancing horse stopped in mid-prance (all four of its feet were off the ground, so it fell on its stomach with a loud * WHUMPF *) and the hostess looked at me like I had just asked her to swallow a tax hike. With a cockroach chaser.

In the end, I wore the damn glasses (suddenly, friends I was talking to began asking if I needed them to drive me home so I could get some rest). I can't help but wonder, though, if I should have stood my ground (it's legal in Kansiana), or left my friends' house to go to an October Surprise party at a bar where they knew how to properly celebrate a last minute political scandal.

What do you think?

Bojack "Masks Are Fascist" Hoarsandbuggyman

Hey, Babe,

You sure you're man enough to handle what I think? I think not.

So, instead, I will tell you what I **know**. Rose coloured glasses are traditional at October Surprise parties for many reasons. For one thing, they make it easier to believe that the cheap beer they serve is sparkling red wine. For another, they make it easier to swallow the idea that party-goers' lives may suck, but at least immigrants and visible minorities have it worse, if not the plastic cup of beer.

To be sure, a host, hostess or dancing horse should not force party favours on their guests. Especially the host. One person's funny glowing stick is another person's reminder of the night they were locked in the attic when they were only seven years old and ended up having an intimate conversation for several hours with the ghost of their great-grandmother through the spirit of their recently deceased hamster, and all she wanted to talk about was how uncomfortable petticoats were to wear.

Not that I speak of personal experience. Not that, if I were speaking of personal experience, it would be any of your business!

Ahem.

On the other hand, it wouldn't kill you to wear the glasses. (The only historic example of a party favour killing guests at an October Surprise party happened in 1968, when exploding cigars got high on nitro and became a little too aggressive. Richard Nixwatmondnewon was positively giddy that night!) Unless it's a matter of personal conviction (you're a Reduhblican, right? So, as the party is currently constituted, personal conviction shouldn't be an issue), it's best for a guest not to embarrass a host or hostess of a party they're attending by spurning a party favour.

The dancing horse can take care of itself.

Besides, it could have been worse. Some October Surprise party hosts hand out thinking caps.

Send your relationship problems to the Alternate Reality News Service's sex, love and technology columnist at questions@lespagesauxfolles.ca. Amritsar Al-Falloudjianapour is not a trained therapist, but she does know a lot of stuff. AMRITSAR SAYS: be adorable, not deplorable. It's more than a bumper sticker slogan – it's practically a life philosophy!

Ask the Tech Answer Guy to Suck It Up, Snowflake!

Yo, Tech Answer Guy,

Ronald McDruhitmumpf is the greatest President the United States of Vesampucceri has ever known. He single-handedly overcame a worldwide pandemic, saved the economy and helped set us on the right path for environmentally sustainable coal mining. Nobody needs to know what he was doing with his other hand all that time – whatever it was, he earned it!

No, I'm not being ironic. He really accomplished all those – why are you insisting that I must be being ironic? I'm not! Really! Ronald McDruhitmumpf **is** the greatest President the country has ever – I can say that with a straight face because it's true!

This is exactly what I'm writing to you about.

I'm proud to have voted for President McDruhitmumpf five times (the sixth time, the polling clerk was giving me both eyeballs – hairy ones, at that – so I pretended I left my ID at home, instead of...pretending to leave my ID at home, and rushed out). Here in my precinct in Texavania, there were protesters outside the polling station holding up signs that said things like, "Vote for Bidenhisbeeswax/Harristweedfashin – we can do better," and chanting things such as, "Four less years! Four less years!"

That was uncalled for.

But Dumbopratic supporters got downright mean after their party stole the election from its rightful heir. They were calling President McDruhitmumpf a loser just because he didn't get as many votes as their guy. And, they were saying things like, "I'm so happy Bidenhisbeeswax won! Now, we can get the country back on track!"

That...that hurt. I mean, I knew Dumboprats could be evil little trolls, but I didn't know they were capable of such cruelty.

Now is not a time for division. After the difficulties of the last four years, now is a time for our country to come together and heal. Dumboprats can start. Right?

Sincerely,
Perry from Petaluma

Yo, Grow a Perr,

Do you subscribe to the Macho Code of Manliness? Because it sounds like you're living by the Wimpy Code of Wussiness!

There is a time-honoured tradition in politics: don't dish it out if you can't plate it! (Politics started off in Athens as a competition between two chefs, so many of its metaphors have a foodie flavour to them. Tasty!) And, you, sir, and your ilk have been serving big steaming piles of it!

To better understand where you are coming from (for one thing, Petaluma is in South Dakaii), I checked out your Farcebook page. You know, the one where you wrote: "If Joe Bidenhisbeeswax is elected President, Reduhblicans will be forced to watch endless reruns of *Sanford and Son* and *Blackish* as a precursor to loving thyir neighbours, no matter how 'inner city' they are. What kind of monsters would teach compassion at the end of a cattle prod? Dumbopratic monsters, that's who!"?

Okay, maybe you were just having a bad day. Month. Four years. Decade. It happens to the best of us. So, I checked out your Twitherd profile to see if you were any different on that platform. You know, the account where you wrote: "Lllllllllosers! Losey lose lose losers! What's the difference between Dumboprats and a bag of soggy potato chips? NOTHING! THEY'RE BOTH PATHETIC! #hahahahahapwnedlibs"?

Keep in mind: in both accounts, I had to wade through a lot of "burn in hell with George Sorobororos and Hillary Roocartoncleveman"s and "Dumboprats want to take away Vesampuccerian's freedom because they didn't get enough love when they were children"s to get to those relatively mild quotes.

You can't seriously complain about the pleasure Dumboprats have taken in the election of their ticket for President when you have spent the last four years treating them like shit. (I use that term in its strictly clinical advice column sense; any obscenity you may find in it is a matter you may want to take up with your antisocial worker.)

After all, he who lives by the "s" word...

The Tech Answer Guy

Yo, Tech Answer Guy,

Oh. Yeah. Well...can we just agree that both sides have been equally horrible to the other?

Sincerely,
Perry from Petaluma

Yo, Grow a Perr,

Sorry, but I don't deal in false equallys. The last time I tried, I gained 17 pounds and blew my chance to take Sadie Hawkins to the L'il Abner Day dance.

The Tech Answer Guy

If you are a dude with a question about the latest technology, ask The Tech Answer Guy by sending it to questions@lespagesauxfolles.ca. Just remember: Those who dine on glass dishes should not throw parties where they serve brontosaurus burgers for dinner. Don't tell me that ancient Athenian wisdom isn't relevant to modern society!

Ask Amritsar About the Ideal Love Line

Dear Amritsar,

I believe it is my civet duty (Mister Bojangly threatened to go on a hunger strike if I didn't, and everybody in my neighbourhood knows how much he loves his ferret chow!) to vote. Here in Pittothastomachsburg, Pennsylton, DC, lineups at polling stations have been known to run eight or nine hours. It pays to prepare (even though I had to get out of work, so I wasn't, technically, getting paid – oh, how I long for the days when the only sacrifice you had to make for the common good was a goat!), so, I packed a lunch, wrestled a folding chair away from Nana Geronimo (she can sit on the stoop for a couple of hours!), put on comfortable shoes and went out to my polling station.

In line in front of me stood a hot young woman in a We Are the Weird t-shirt and jeans, with hair that made her look like a refugee from the 1980s. I'll never forget the first thing she said to me: "Can you hold my place in line? I really have to pee!"

It was so magical, it could have been written by Shakeaspeararetoo.

We started talking and, as the hours passed, we realized we had a lot in common. I loved *How to get a Head in Murder,* she loved *Jersey Smores*. I'm a filet mignon kind of gal, she enjoys nothing more than a Bob So Tasty Bob Cajun burger. I was planning on voting for Ronald McDruhitmumpf, she was planning on voting for Joe Bidenhisbeeswax. I'm a little bit country, she's a little bit rock and roll. I – wait, what?

I was falling for...one of those?

I mean, okay, I didn't really believe it when *Foxindehenhaus and Fiends* host Brian KissMeadekilmeadenow swore that Dumboprats had horns. How would they wear hats? Besides, if any sizable population of human beings had horns, you just know that somebody would come out with a line of horn grooming products. That's the genius of the Vesampuccerian system.

But, yeah, I had long believed that Dumboprats were the source of all of the problems in the country. For one thing, if they got into power, they would be taking away all of my guns (of which I had none, since their display would clash with the decor of my apartment). They would tax my income at 276% and force me to eat food stamps. Antifa would spray-paint slogans on my forehead as I walked down the street. My beloved country would descend into chaos...even more chaos than there had been under Chaos President.

That would be a ripe bucketful of chaos, that would be.

Over a brunch of cold chicken with fava beans and a nice Chianti, we discussed politics. My blossoming love blossom pointed out that the Dumboprats had been in power for eight years, and the most radical thing they did was pass a law modernizing interstate commerce. She joked that she wished the party was organized enough to do something seriously disruptive. At least, I think it was a joke. I'm sure it must have been a joke. Yes. Absolutely. A joke.

As we got to the doors of the polling station, we exchanged numbers. I wrote hers in my Palm Pilot; she wrote mine in sharpie on her palm. I don't know, though. Should I follow up, or should I chalk it off as the seven most magical hours in my life and move on?

Zerlina Lickenchickenour

Hey, Babe,

As that

Dear Amritsar,

Oh. Her name was Frankina. I should have mentioned that. Sorry.

Zerlina Lickenchickenour

Hey, Babe,

Think nothing of it. An experienced advice columnist learns to rise above interruptions.

As that famous filosopher Keanu Hereevertstoform truly said: "Relationships that, like, start off intense often end up, like, whoa!" It's also true, though, that relationships that start off mildly often end up, like, whoa. Relationships ending up like, whoa seems to be an integral part of the human condition.

Which is to say that all relationships carry the seeds of their own destruction in them from the very beginning. Some find the fertile ground of emotional incompatibility, others founder on the hard ground of empathy. Some are nurtured by the sunshine of profound political contradiction, others sputter out owing to compassion and compromise.

All relationships are hard. All we can do is go into them with an open heart and a locked knife drawer.

Send your relationship problems to the Alternate Reality News Service's sex, love and technology columnist at questions@lespagesauxfolles.ca. Amritsar Al-Falloudjianapour is not a trained therapist, but she does know a lot of stuff. AMRITSAR SAYS: If you enjoyed waiting in line to vote, you're going to be ecstatic over waiting for all the votes to be tabulated and a winner to be declared!

Ask an Advice Columnist for a Referral

Dear Ask a Doctor,

I'm a doctor in the Intensive Care Unit of the Cedars Closet Sinai hospital. Last week, I was attending a patient with all of the symptoms of COVID-19, but, when I gave her the diagnosis, she started screaming that the disease was "a hoax perpetrated by the lamestream media to help the Dumboprats steal our freedom!" I told her that her freedom would be severely constricted by a pine box (it was towards the end of a 20 hour shift – I had given my last ferk hours earlier). The woman shrieked that she had had a minor cold when she was admitted and that I must have injected her with something lethal in order to deny President McDruhitmumpf a second term in office **because everybody knows COVID isn't real!** When I assured her that the pandemic was real, she spit in my mask and swore that I was a "ferking poxified cudchugger with ferking besmirched pantaloons!"

The intubation put a quick end to that nonsense, let me tell you!

By the tone of the woman's voice, I got the sense she was trying to insult me. But, I have no idea what a poxified cudchugger with besmirched pantaloons is. Could you help me out?

Angela Rhododendrummer, type b positive (like that's possible in these trying times!)

Dear Curious Patient

We're medical doctors not script doctors! Okay, some of us are a little too fond of our scripts, but that's between us and our medical certification board. The point is, if we had to figure out every oath that a patient in COVID denial had sworn at a doctor, we would be spending all of our office hours reading dictionaries – then, who would be available to fill out patient charts or harass interns (purely in the interest of making them better doctors, of course)?

Take two hours of escapist television. If curiosity persists, consult a Language Corrector Dude.

Ask a Doctor is a consortium of medical professionals who would rather not be personally identified as this is just a side gig and they don't take it especially seriously, so why should you? If you have a question of a medical nature, ***talk to your family physician about it!*** *If that is not possible – and you're willing to take what you get – send your query to questions@lespagesauxfolles.ca. Say, wasn't Scott Atlascoughedupcats the guy who sold body building programs in the back of comic books in the 1950s? What he's selling today may not make any more sense, but you have to admire his tenacity!*

Yo, Tech Answer Guy,

I'm a doctor in the Intensive Care Unit of the Cedars Closet Sinai hospital. Last week, a patient who exhibited all of the symptoms of COVID-19 was lying on a bed in her room, denying my diagnosis of her condition while watching *Foxindehenhaus and Fiends*.

"The President said the number of cases of COVID would go down to zero back in April," Brian KissMeadekilmeadenow was saying. "So, whatever illness you may be feeling now, it's not that."

"No COVID, **no COVID!**" the patient howled. "President say so! What I got? **What I got for real?**" Then, he called me a "ferking poxified cudchugger with ferking besmirched pantaloons!"

I...have no idea what that means. Do you?

Sincerely,
Angela from Akron

Yo, Ange,

Uhh, yeah, I'm not comfortable with your question. The Tech Answer guy has a lot of skillz, but speakage and wording aren't one of them. Have you considered asking the Language Corrector Dude?

The Tech Answer Guy

If you are a dude with a question about the latest technology, ask The Tech Answer Guy by sending it to questions@lespagesauxfolles.ca. Just remember: No, Ask a Doctor must have been thinking of Charles Atlascoughedupcats. Scott Atlascoughedupcats was actually a performer who rose to fame as a cast member of the sketch comedy show Weekends!

Dear Amritsar,

I'm a doctor in the Intensive Care Unit of the Cedars Closet Sinai hospital. Last week, we were operating on a person for complications from COVID-19. When the anaesthetist asked the patient to count down backwards from 10, before he went under, he said, "Why won't you...tell me...what I...really have...you ferking...poxified...cud...cud...cud..." I think he was trying to call me a "ferking poxified cudchugger with ferking besmirched pantaloons!" I've been getting a lot of that lately.

I still have no idea what it means, Can you help me figure it out?

Angela Rhododendrummer

Hey, Babe,

There was a time when people would put on their best Sunday clothes to go to the emergency room of a hospital, thanked the dentist for his tender ministrations as he amputated their leg without anaesthetic, and apologized for getting their blood all over the waiting room carpet. How long ago those days seem!

I could write a book about how social norms have broken down in the past four years as millions of Vesampuccerians have been given permission to release their inner Mr. Hydengoseekseanz by watching the behaviour of the country's Raging-Id-in-Chief, but that wouldn't – that – umm, excuse me, but I think it's time I gave my agent a call.

In the meantime, you're asking the wrong person the question (how gauche!). You should be talking to the Language Corrector Dude.

Dear Amritsar,

Yeah, a lot of people have been telling me about this Language Corrector Dude guy. He sounds like he could really help with my question. How do I get in touch with him?

Angela Rhododendrummer

Hey, Babe,

You don't find the Language Corrector Dude so much as he crawls out from under his rock and finds –

Did someone take my name in vain?

And, there he is.

Hi, Angela. Excellent question. The naive interpretation of the word "cudchugger" would be "somebody who drinks liquefied grass quickly." That would definitely be an insult, since everybody knows that the only way to avoid indigestion would be to drink liquefied grass slowly. Very slowly. Preferably with a bourbon chaser.

In fact, "cud" derives from the word "duccud," an ancient Norse term for somebody who kisses horses on moonless nights. To "chugger" is a Middle English (half of the words from that period involve certain finger gestures!) form of the verb "to await with a mixture of trepidation and a runny nose." So, you're a moonlight horse lover in need of a kiss and a Kleenex.

The rest of the words in the epithet are pretty straightforward.

That may not sound like much of an insult to modern ears, but it was the height of personal invective in 1272!

It's unfortunate that medical professionals should be assailed with such language by people whose lives they are trying to save. But, we live in extemporaneously divocative times, don't we?

Send your relationship problems to the Alternate Reality News Service's sex, love and technology columnist at questions@lespagesauxfolles.ca. Amritsar Al-Falloudjianapour is not a trained therapist, but she does know a lot of stuff. AMRITSAR SAYS: I believe my esteemed colleague The Tech Answer Guy was referring to Charles Gogorocketschmo. Scott Atlascoughedupcats is actually a subspecies of Gobi Desert snow leopard.

Ask the Tech Answer Guy About Striking the First Blow for Freedom

Yo, Tech Answer Guy,

My Grammie Paw-Paw used to tell stories about standing in bread lines during The Great Depression. She told us young-ungs (that was the noise she made when she tried to pick us up – maybe she should have stopped before we turned 35) about how the lines were so long, people would often lose more weight shuffling forward in them than they would gain from the food they received at the end of them!

And, about how the gurgling from empty stomachs up and down the line sometimes sounded like the chorus at Minsky's. One time, she was in a bread line in a blizzard so bad that when it cleared, she found she was standing on a steamer ship about to set sail for Shanghai!

Good times.

We didn't believe her, of course. Why would anybody choose to starve when they had credit cards?

Then, there was the fake virus that led to the hoax small business meltdown that led to me losing my job as a short distance trucker. I was told that it was because restaurants didn't need me to haul packets of mustard, ketchup and pickled sheep's intestines to them because they were closed. I knew it was really because our Chinese overlords shanghaied all our condiments to use for nuclear reactor fuel, but whatever the reason, I found myself without an income.

Of course, I refused to accept any unemployment insurance, because my name is not Karl or Gottsadlylowmarx, and, anyway, red is not my colour, if you catch my driftnet. For a week, anyway. If I wanted to keep my trailer, I had to accept the UI checks. What the hell – when my wardrobe changes, I can always avoid looking into mirrors. Unfortunately, UI doesn't cover food **and** Netflax, so braving the line it was.

I learned a valuable lesson: Grammie Paw-Paw was an optimist!

One time, the guy behind me was spouting off about politics, saying things like "President McDruhitmumpf's whole fallacy is wrong." If the dude wanted to be fitted for a microchip straitjacket and flung off a fiscal cliff, who was I to argue? Still, I couldn't allow such ignorance to go unchallenged – it might have swayed other, weaker people in the line – so I punched him in the ghoulies. As he lay on the pavement, panting, I argued, "How's your fallacy now, pal? Hunh? How's your fallacy now?" I'm good with the clever repartee like that.

In my defense, I was manhangry. That's short for "hangry while being a man." **That's** short for "being hungry and angry while being a man." Jesus Louise...is, there was so much meaning in that one word, I almost mistook it for being German!

Anyway, when the cops came, he was panting a lot less and able to explain what had happened. Which makes me wonder: should I have punched him in the throat instead?

Sincerely,
Alex from Rolodex

Yo, Lex...is,

I know what the term "manhangry" means. Thanks for the man-on-mansplainin'; I haven't had somebody do that to me since my brother The Science Answer Guy spent thirty-four minutes explaining why the sky is blue. Thirty-four excruciating long minutes from my life that I will never get back. Unless eternal recurrence is a thing, in which case, crap.

No, you should not punch somebody standing near you in a food line in the throat. Or, the ghoulies. Or, the time card. Violence is the last refuge of the argumentatively incompetent. That is right there in the Macho Code of Manliness, after the section on how to use a stick shift and before the recipe for the perfect barbecue sauce. (That's not man-on-mansplainin', that's reminding you of something you know but may have forgotten, or may not have fully understood, or may be ignoring because it's inconvenient.)

The proper way of dealing with people we disagree with is to swallow our anger until we get home, then channel it into building a birdhouse. Or a doghouse. Or an outhouse.

The point is to channel your hanger into something productive. That way, you don't get a criminal record (or add to the one you've already started), and birds get a home.

Building birdhouses is Macho Code of Manliness approved.

The Tech Answer Guy

If you are a dude with a question about the latest technology, ask The Tech Answer Guy by sending it to questions@lespagesauxfolles.ca. Just remember: some people may consider language a technology, but if you can't work on it with a monkey wrench, a screwdriver or a phaser, it isn't a technology in any meaningful sense of the word!

Ask Amritsar to Dream Big
Bigger
Like, An Entire Universe Big

Dear Amritsar,

I'm just a regular person with dreams. The kind that come when you're asleep, I mean; life has already slipped a knockout drug into the morning coffee of the dreams out of my waking hours and taken photographs of them in compromising positions with the dreams of my next door neighbour and threatened to expose them if they ever showed up in my conscious awareness again. Or, I just don't have much of an imagination. Who can tell, really?

In one dream, I am walking towards a bus stop just as the vehicle is pulling out; the ad on the side of the bus is for a brand of toothpaste called "Ha Ha, Sucker!" In another, I am at a train station; I know my train will be leaving in five minutes, but I can't find the right platform (the squawk on the PA system sounds suspiciously like: "Ha – crackle – a, su – crackle – er"). In another, I am in a cab on the way to the airport, but the plane will be taking off in five minutes (my sleeping brain seems to forget that you have to be at an airport seven hours before the plane takes off to get through security). I think you can see a pattern emerging (in that last dream, the DJ on the cab radio is announcing that the last song was "Disconnected Flight" by the band Ha Ha and the Suckerfish).

I recently read that dreams may be doorways to other dimensions. If that is true (and a scientist said it, so who am I to question the assertion?), why are my counterparts in other universes such *yutzes*?

Sav On a Rolla

Hey, Babe,

The multiverse is vast. There are an infinite number of realities in which your counterparts are *yutzes*. There are an infinite number in which your counterparts are *putzes*. There are even an infinite number where your counterparts are *schmendricks* – the multiverse contains infinite variety with infinite annoyability.

Having said that, there are also an infinite number of universes in which your counterpart is a *mensch*. The real question here is: why do you dream of the versions of yourself that cause you anxiety rather than the ones that would make you feel better about your life?

Anybody who knows me (which is nobody, because is it really possible to "know" another human being?) will tell you that Herr Doctor Freud and I have never really gotten along. This is partially because of his habit of borrowing 50 Marks until the beginning of the month and never paying it back (it's not like he can't afford it; I suspect he was compensating for not being properly toilet trained until he was 37; he would have appreciated that diagnosis). But, mostly, it was because his theories about women seemed to come from a universe where women didn't exist.

Despite this, some of his basic concepts do conform roughly to human experience. In this case, I am reminded of his statement: "Every dream contains a wish. Last night, I dreamed that you would lend me 50 Marks until the beginning of the month – it's not for me, it's for my recently deceased mother. How could you possibly refuse?"

I couldn't. Herr Doctor F. can be very persuasive when he's not smugly sucking on a big fat cigar.

I'm not suggesting that you want to miss a train, plane or automobile. Dreams that come from other dimensions are subtler than that, like the aroma of weak tea or the meaning of a David Lynch film. Your dreams could mean that you are worried that you are going to fail a big test you have coming up...every few days. (If your dimensional dreams were about failing a big test, it could mean that you were concerned about missing a travel opportunity. In dreamatology, this is known as The Law of Reciprocal Improbability.) Or, it could indicate that you should stop eating four course meals before you go to bed.

Dreams can be inscrutable bastards.

By the way, Bill Nae the Science Bae doesn't believe that dreams come from other universes. "If the theory that dreams are the random firing of neurons that our brains interpret as we start coming out of sleep was good enough for our parents, and their parents, and their parents before them," he stated, "it's good enough for me!

And, who am I to argue with Bill Nae the Science Bae? He's on TV!

Send your relationship problems to the Alternate Reality News Service's sex, love and technology columnist at questions@lespagesauxfolles.ca. Amritsar Al-Falloudjianapour is not a trained therapist, but she does know a lot of stuff. AMRITSAR SAYS: That's right, the last names in this article don't have five syllables. Not all questions come from people who live in the United

States of Vesampucceri, you know. Honestly, Earth Prime 1-6-7-1-8-2 dash Psi needs to get over itself!

Ask the Tech Answer Guy About Your Future

Yo, Tech Answer Guy,

I don't mean to say that my father was a hard man, but adamantium bows its head in respect every time he walks by. So much starch is used when he cleans his adult diaper that it could be a military drill sergeant. When he gets mad, an earthquake swallows a small Latin Vesampuccerian city.

But, he loves me. In his way. Which other people might mistake for contempt. Stupid other people.

Anyway. My dad has recently fallen on hard times. An evil bastard stole his job from him. With the help of a vast conspiracy. Evil bastard conspiracy. A lot of his friends – Cushyjoboman and Wakupinafield, Deutsche Bank, the Girl Scouts of Greater New Yoricknuhemwell – the Girl Scouts! You know, I never liked their cookies: they always tasted to me like rat poison between two sheets of cardboard – not that I'm bitter (although the cookies certainly are!) – have abandoned him. He's got debts to pay, and his accountants are popping Xanax like they were smarties.

Not only that, but malicious prosecutors are looking to maliciously prosecute him on charges that are a complete joke. A hoax. Fake news. He could spend the last few years of his life in court. Or, jail. Or...or...or, poverty.

It's unthinkable, but it is very possible that he may not be able to pay me the allowance he has given me all of my adult life. How am I supposed to survive when the business he has been grooming me to lead has gone bankrupt? This is a disaster! I mean, don't get me wrong, the possible jail time is bad, but this? This is a disaster!

How can I become a billionaire tech startup CEO?

Sincerely,
Ronald, Jr. from No Fixed Address

Yo, Ron Bon Bon,

The world of tech startups is way above the Tech Answer Guy's pay grade (I'll be honest: my pay has barely made it out of primary school). So, I asked Phil, the mechanic from the shop down the street, your question. Phil, the mechanic from the shop down the street, whose religion of the wrench forbids him from acknowledging pay grades, knows stuff.

Phil, the mechanic from the shop down the street, says becoming the CEO of a tech startup is easy. You have an original idea for a technology. You build it in your garage. You impress a vulture capitalist, convincing him to give you some vulture capital so you can start producing the technology for the market. You develop a marketing strategy to persuade the public that your technology will change their lives for the better. When you start making a substantial profit, you sell the company to MicroSquish for more money than you ever dreamed of. Then, you start the process all over again with a new idea. Keep going until you have a billion dollars.

Phil, the mechanic from the shop down the street, wishes you the best of luck.

The Tech Answer Guy

Yo, Tech Answer Guy,

That sounds like it could take a lot of time. Like, years. I don't have years. Maybe I didn't make myself clear: I have a few days, maybe a couple of weeks if my father's creditors are generous and his prosecutors are building an especially complicated case. **I need to become a billionaire tech startup CEO now!**

And, what's the big idea about having an original idea for a technology? I haven't had an original idea in my life! I think I may be allergic to original ideas – they make my skin break out, and my pristine complexion is my biggest asset! Can I buy an original idea on the internet? On credit – I'll be good for it in a few days, once I'm a billionaire tech startup CEO.

Are you beginning to see the depth of my problem?

Sincerely,
Ronald, Jr. from Skid Ro – No, I Dare Not Think It!

Yo, Ronnie Big Sap,

Yes, I think I'm beginning to see the depth of your problem. You chose to be born to the wrong parents. Sorry, but at this point, there really is nothing anybody can do for you.

The Tech Answer Guy

If you are a dude with a question about the latest technology, ask The Tech Answer Guy by sending it to questions@lespagesauxfolles.ca. Just remember: it's not the size of your framistat that counts, but what you do with it.

Ask Amritsar to Reconcile the Irreconcilable

Dear Amritsar,

A couple of days ago, I started my dream job: member of the House of Representatives. The first day was like the first day of any job: getting to know the people who worked around me; finding the cafeteria; sweeping my office for listening devices planted by Deep Dish State operatives trying to find dirt they could blackmail me with. Good times.

This lasted all of three days. (I never did find the listening devices, so I just never say anything that could come back to haunt me while I'm in the office. Boo!) I was supposed to be on the floor of the House for a vote on accepting the Electoral College vote. As if I was going to let a tool – a monkey wrench, maybe, or a left-handed screwdriver – of the Establishment like Joe Bidenhisbeeswax become the next President; somebody who does Ukraine's bidding should never be invited to the bridge table!

At the same time, thousands of people were outside the Capitol building, protesting how the Dumboprats stole the 2020 Presidential election by getting more votes than the Reduhblicans. A lot of my Qanon buddies had flown in from across the country to attend the protest: Spidermoose3000 was there, along with antimarieantoinette, thebloodofpatriodiots0037 and questionauthori-gaack. I had never met them in person, and when I heard they were coming to Washburningdington, I was really excited by the possibility of hanging out with them. Not literally, of course: there was only one noose, and it didn't fit any of our necks.

Still, our attitude had always been: we'll hang out together or we'll surely hang out separately.

What should I do? Should I follow my head and stay for the vote, or follow my heart and go be with my friends?

Representative Marjorie Taylormaid Fortrubble

Hey, Babe,

It's a classic dilemma, although in your case, it would be more accurately described as following your butthole or following your vena cava. We often romanticize our life events to make ourselves appear more like a hero and less like the comic relief that we all are.

The obvious thing for you to do would be to enact the classic sitcom scenario of trying to be in two places at once. While another member is droning on, you could pass a note to the Speaker of the House saying you have a weak bladder and you need to go to the bathroom. Then, duck out and go meet your friends. After a couple of minutes with them, find an excuse to leave (for example, tell them that you just remembered that somebody left a pipe bomb in the hall near your office and you need to go back and see if the bomb squad has determined whether it's live or Memorex). Then, return to the Chamber.

This approach is not without risk. The more often you go back and forth, the more ridiculous the excuses you will have to use to leave one place or the other. You may have to tell the Speaker that you need to check outside to determine whether the mob has been infiltrated by Alpha Centaurans, for example, or to tell your friends that you have to return to your office to finish sweeping it for bugs planted by operatives of the Deep Dish State trying to find dirt they could blackmail you with.

This scenario never ends successfully: the two groups of people eventually run into each other, exposing the ruse. But, they almost always forgive you by the end of the episode, so as long as you live your life in 30 minute increments, you should be fine.

Amritsar is not a big fan of sitcom scenarios.

Or, you could just tell the truth and duck out of Congress to be with your friends. It's not like you have ever hidden your affinity for Qanon. And, who knows? You may be rewarded for your honesty. Stranger things have happened in Washburningdington. It could be argued that stranger things are happening even as we speak...

Dear Amritsar,

Oh, never mind. The session of Congress was suspended because protesters entered the Capitol building and are roaming around the halls and offices. **Hey, Spidermoose3000, wait up! I don't want to miss any of the fun!**

Representative Marjorie Taylormaid Grennongilles

Hey, Babe,

I love a story with a happy ending, although, in your case, I'm prepared to make an exception.

Send your relationship problems to the Alternate Reality News Service's sex, love and technology columnist at questions@lespagesauxfolles.ca. Amritsar Al-Falloudjianapour is not a trained therapist, but she does know a lot of stuff. AMRITSAR SAYS: Turn off the TV news and have some sweet potato fries. They can't make every hurt go away, but the emotionally restorative power of sweet potato fries is one of the unsung triumphs of the twentieth century!

Ask the Language Corrector Dude About How Tense He Gets When People Mix Up Their Tenses, Or the Correct Use of the Moral Injunctive, Or...Or...Or Anything But How He Feels About Getting His Own Column

I am of course, honoured, thanks for asking. I know I won't be able to columnize half as well as The Tech Answer Guy (especially if it meant I would have to match his alcohol consumption – talk about an ambulatory fire hazard!), and I couldn't possibly compete with Amritsar Al-Falloudjianapour (whose brand of compassionate smarm is unparalleled!). All I hope to be able to accomplish in this space is to make the world just slightly more amenable to acceptable linguistic practice.

Okay, then. Who would like to ask the first question?

Dear LCD,

Ever since she was elected to Congress, I have had an online correspondence with Alexandria Casio-Keebjords. Okay, she hasn't responded to any of the 127 emails, text messages or carrier pigeons that I have sent her, but she did send the FBI to my house one time to "have a little chat" with me, which sends its own kind of message. And, I heard it. I heard it loud and clear, Alexandria.

After about the 98th communication, I felt that I was repeating myself, that my message was getting stale. I mean, there are only so many ways to say "Ferk off and die you ferking Communist whore!" and "You ferking Communist whore, ferk off and ferking die!" and "Ferk off you ferking Communist whore, ferk off and die!" I thought that last one was especially creative, even if the genre as a whole was getting stale.

I considered switching to another target (so many female people of pigment in the Dumbopratic Party to choose from!), but, well, call me sentimental, but you always remember your first, you know? You never want to let her go. And, anyway, I'm pretty sure they have their own fans, and I wouldn't want to interfere with their relationships. You know what they say: 102's company, 103's a bloody mess.

So, can you suggest any creative endearments I could share with Alexandria to show her how truly, madly and, yes, deeply I hate her?

Sincerely,
Least Creative Deplorable

Dear LCD,

No. I – just no. This is not a question that should be answered. Who wants to ask the next ques

[Dude! What the ferk‽ You begged, you pleaded with, you attempted to bribe (a laughable proposition considering I know how much you make) me to give you your own advice column, and now you refuse to answer your very first question? What, as I say, the ferk‽ EDITRIX-IN-CHIEF BRENDA BRUNDTLAND-GOVANNI]

Yeah, Brenda, I'm really sorry about that. When I lay in bed at night imagining what my column would be, I thought I would be answering basic questions. You know: what is the difference between "there," "they're" and "their?" "What's so important about the Oxford comma that whole forests have been felled debating its use?" "When did 'any more' become 'anymore?' Has our society sped up so much that we no longer have the luxury of spaces between words? Or, should that be 'spacesbetweenwords?'" You know: normal language questions! I never expected to have to answer a question about harassing a member of Congress!

[So, you thought being a columnist was going to be easy? Putting on my slapping gloves is easy – writing a column is hard! Groucho

Gottsadlylowmarx said that on his deathbed, so you know it must be true! Listen: I don't care what your answer is; just make it entertaining. Beyond the person who asked the question, nobody cares about the answers in advice columns as long as there entertaining. Got it? BB-G]

It's they're, actually. But –

[You know, there are lots of little Language Corrector Persons and Language Amender Dudes who would kill to be where you are now. Just saying. BB-G]

Erm...

Dear LCD,

You vile pus-sac! You and your lizard-brain opinions are completely repugnant to me! Your despicable, self-serving rhetoric plumbs the depths of human incivility. You should not be encouraged to interact with other human beings – you should be sent somewhere far, far away where you cannot be a threat to yourself or others – especially others. You are hateful and disgusting to every decent human being on the planet!

Dear LCD,

That's great! I can't wait to try this out! Thanks for your help!

Sincerely,
Least Creative Deplorable

Dear BBG,

I quit.

Language evolves. Words are born, they grow, they get old, they forget where their glasses are, and they die, replaced by a new generation of words that repeat the cycle. If you have trouble keeping up, you can ask the Language Corrector Dude by emailing him at questions@lespagesauxfolles.ca. Who knows? If he even has a column in the future, he might just answer you!

Ask Amritsar About Proper Child Discipline

Dear Amritsar,

Children. Ammirite?

I got a visit from the cops the other day. They thought I might have had something to do with the Capitol fight for freedom just because I was there. And, I was hitting a cop with a "Don't tread on me" flag. I thought it was ironic; they did not see the humour. And, I was looking through papers that had been left in the Senate chamber when the politicians fled (oh, don't say you aren't curious about what Eric Swallowacatsbell writes when he thinks nobody is looking! You aren't? Yeah, neither were the cops. Am I the only person in the world with an imagination?) The cops thought what I had done was a crime. You say potato, I say pardon. Oh.

How did they identify me? My six year-old son Kyle was in kindergarten, usually a low risk activity, for me if not for him. Far as I can tell, the teacher was surfing the TV looking for *Spongeburp Sloppydroopypants* when she caught a news report about the Stop the Stole rally. Before she could change the channel, the fruit of my looms piped up: "That's my daddy!"

Misses Gilgamesh, his teacher, froze the frame. Did you know they could do that with TVs these days? Isn't that something? She looked at it closely, and I guess she must have recognized the beer cap with bunny ears that I was wearing (my wife, Katerina, and I got a matching set when we were married – mine were in the shop for a leaky tube, so I borrowed hers), because I was soon answering questions at the local precinct.

That will teach me to go to parent-teacher meetings!

I was let out on bail three days later. By that time Katerina and Kyle (you think that would make a good cop show title? I don't know...sounds more like a 19th century romance novel title – just my luck!) had disappeared. I'm expecting the divorce papers any day now.

I gotta admit, I didn't think the little bastard had it in him to turn his old man in. It would make me proud, if I wasn't looking at serious jail time. Like, double digits jail time. Ouch! The little bastard.

So, obviously, he's out of my will. That leaves me on the horns of a dilemma, though. Double ouch with cayenne pepper sprinkles! Should I try to track him and his mother down so I can tell him now, or should I let him find out when they're reading my will?

Michael Flintaintinnocint

Hey, Babe,

I think you may have lost track of what is important, here.

One should never go where one has not been formally invited – that's terrible manners! Just as you did not appreciate members of the local constabulary showing up at your house without an invitation, you should not have shown up at the People's House without one.

And, while it is traditional to bring a gift when you are entering somebody else's house, a pipe bomb does not say, "Thank you for letting me share your space." It says, "Don't put out the good China, because I will just chew it up and spit it out because that's how much of a rebel I am!"

Were you one of those dreadful little people who soiled the carpets while you were in the Capitol? If you were, **were you raised in a barn?** Honestly, we make people clean up after the messes of their pets – you would think they would learn to clean up after their own messes as well! Don't smirk at me and make a joke out of leaving unexpected gifts, young man! You're not that clever and I'm not that forgiving! (Nor, I imagine, is the Capitol janitorial staff!)

As for talk about writing your son out of your will, it may be somewhat premature for that. After all, he is only six years old. He still has a whole life of disappointing you ahead of him!

Send your relationship problems to the Alternate Reality News Service's sex, love and technology columnist at questions@lespagesauxfolles.ca. Amritsar Al-Falloudjianapour is not a trained therapist, but she does know a lot of stuff. AMRITSAR SAYS: Capitol tours are for putting into photo albums that you can bore your grandchildren with. They are ***not*** *for planning routes to the offices of Congresspeople during an insurrection!*

8. THE SLEEP OF REASON PRODUCES… MONSTERS

What the Ferking Hell is Wrong With Kansconsin?

SPECIAL TO THE ALTERNATE REALITY NEWS SERVICE

The Alternate Reality News Service recently hired polling firm Harristweedfashin Interacting Up (HIU) to conduct a focus group of Reduhblican voters in Kansconsin to help our readers better understand what the ferking hell is wrong with the state. This is a partial transcript of that conversation.

QUESTION ONE

HIU: Do you feel you are better off now than you were four years ago?

ALLAN PSEUDONOMOUSNESS: (24, white, college student who plans to be either the next Ayn Randiasagoht, Rand Paulonaldaphun or Unibomber, may not be his real name) Who are you to be asking the questions?

HIU: I...I'm sorry?

PSEUDONOMOUSNESS: This country has been under the thumb of big polling for far too long! You make up the numbers that make the fake news feel so real to so many gullible sheeple. Honest, hard-working Vesampuccerians should take back polling and ask you about your opinions! The first thing I would like to know, and please feel free to share your feelings with us, is: why the ferk should any of us answer your questions?

HIU: Because my company is paying you to participate in this panel?

PAUSE.

PSEUDONOMOUSNESS: Well...okay, then. I'll answer your questions. But, under protest.

PAUSE.

HIU: So, how about the rest of you? Do you feel better off now than four years ago?

EMILY LITANUTELLA: (67, white, retired grandmother): My husband, Renaldo of Ghent, passed two months ago in the Poodle Cut Senior's Residence where he was trying to catch Alzheimer's disease. I tried to explain to him that you could only get Alzheimer's from toilet seats, but would the stubborn old son of a...goat listen? Course not! His passing was quick – one day, he was wondering how he would be affected by eating the brain of a dementia patient – it wasn't like she was using it! – the next day, he was in the ICU – a month later, he was dead. I couldn't even see him to say goodbye because of COVID restrictions at the hospital, couldn't hear his voice one final time. So, yes, I would say that I am better off now than I was four years ago. Much better off.

CHORUS: (half a dozen people who otherwise didn't contribute to the conversation) Just when you think your eyes will mist

Up, there comes a twist!

LITANUTELLA: Hey, that rhymed!

CHORUS: Thank you for noticing, but please don't make a fuss:
Rhyming is just something a chorus does.

FLOYYD JONESENFORRAHIT: (37, white, manager of a Bob So Tasty franchise) I can't complain, really. I mean, sure, I may lose my business because of unnecessarily onerous lockdowns for a disease that doesn't exist, and I may have to sell my children for scrap in order to pay the mortgage on my condo. And, if I'm being completely honest, I didn't budget for the amount of alcohol I've started consuming. On the other hand, I look forward to the day when President McDruhitmumpf storms back into Washburningdington and has all the traitorous Dumboprats arrested and their ringleaders hung in public as a message to the world that we take democracy seriously! I like to think of myself as an optimist...

CHORUS: Matters in the heartland aren't as stark as depicted:
Many people who live there are...strangely conflicted.

QUESTION TWO

HUI: Do you believe that the Reduhblican Party best serves your interests?

ERIC FLATULENTSANEER: (37, white, police officer) Absolutely! I paid $37 less in taxes over the last four years than I did when...that person of pigment was president! I mean, okay, the Reduhblicans haven't shrunk government to the point where they can drown it in a bathtub. A pool, maybe. A big pool. You know, Olympic-sized. But they're heading in the right direction, that's for sure.

CHORUS: The party of limited government? How quaint.

Your grandparents' Reduhblicans these ain't!

FLATULENTSANEER: What – what do you mean?

CHORUS: The Reduhblicans can be such "fiscally responsible" phonies –

They love government spending that puts money in the pockets of their cronies!

PSEUDONOMOUSNESS: Yeah, well, at least they aren't shoving Black Lives Anti-matter propaganda down our throats or eating babies!

FLATULENTSANEER: (mutters) I hate...propaganda...

RHONDA LACKAWAKANDA: (17, white, aspiring single mother) Wait – what? Eating babies?

PSEUDONOMOUSNESS: It's true! They share recipes from some guy named Swiftonhisfeetberg or Swiftonhisfeetstein or something like that – right there on the Internet! You just have to know where to look!

LACKAWAKANDA: (shudders) That's...disgusting!

FLATULENTSANEER: That's why I will always vote for Ronald McDruhitmumpf – he may be many disgusting things, but he has never eaten a baby! ...That I know of. And, so what if he did? He must have had a powerful reason! And, I'm sure he didn't enjoy it...much...

CHORUS: Their beliefs are immune to any externality –

They have completely given themselves over to the cult of personality!

QUESTION THREE

HUI: I can see that many people in this room are hurting, just as many people in the country are hurting. Why do you think that an autocratic leader will improve your lives more than democratic institutions?

PSEUDONOMOUSNESS: Ferk democratic institutions! What have democratic institutions ever done for me?

HUI: Other than maintain the road system?

PSEUDONOMOUSNESS: Oh. Well, sure, I'll give you that.

HUI: And, ensure the quality of our food and drugs?

PSEUDONOMOUSNESS: Yes. That. Obviously.

HUI: And, stabilize our dollar so that our financial system doesn't fall into ruin?

PSEUDONOMOUSNESS: If you're going to get technical about it –

LACKAWAKANDA: This is starting to sound awfully familiar...

HUI: And, provide us with the police to protect our communities?

PSEUDONOMOUSNESS: Ferk the police!

FLATULENTSANEER: Now, hold on a second, there, son –

PSEUDONOMOUSNESS: The police are tools of the elite, oppressors oppressing the oppressed white man! Traitors to the country and a danger to true patriots – that's what the police are!

FLATULENTSANEER: I would be careful about what you say, there. You –

JONESENFORRAHIT: I know how to deal with traitors. (SOUND: metal clanging on table)

HUI: Wait, what –

LITANUTELLA: Bitch, you call that a knife? (SOUND: metal banging heavily on table) This, this is a ferking knife!

HUI: Put those away! This is not supposed to –

LACKAWAKANDA: Lady, did you...did you just go full on Betty Sowhitesheblindshines on his ass? Respect!

PSEUDONOMOUSNESS: Amateurs. Don't you know that you don't bring knives to a Civil War...fight? (SOUND: the cocking of a gun)

HUI: **What the ferk?**

PAUSE.

CHORUS: Then, there arose an awkward silence,
    Filled with the heaviness of impending violence.

PSEUDONOMOUSNESS: You know, I've had just about enough of your comments! If you don't put a corkscrew in it, I'll shut you up for you!

CHORUS: This is what living in a fantasy world begets:
    Increasingly violent threats.

PSEUDONOMOUSNESS: You know, you've done nothing but criticize us since this whole thing started. Who do you work for? The FBI? The CIA? **The phone company?**

CHORUS: So many bad ideas, so misbegot

How do people – BANG – oh Gord, we've been shot!

TRANSCRIPT ENDS

Missing the Forest for the Tweeps

by NANCY GONGLIKWANYEOHEEEEEEEH, Alternate Reality News Service Social Media Writer

At 2:37 in the morning, President Ronald McDruhitmumpf tweeped...nothing. A grateful nation continued to sleep, but if its rest was more peaceful, its dreams less anxiety-ridden, the drool on its pillow less...wet, that may well have been the reason why.

It wasn't because he didn't want to. The bees that buzzed in his skull were transmitting messages about standing back and standing by and standing on your own two feet and standing by your man and being upstanding in a court of law and standing orders and standing your ground and standing at attention (while holding a baby's arm holding an apple) to his cerebral cortex. His cerebral cortex responded with a hearty, "I gotta share this with the world!"

Only, he couldn't. Because Twitherd, the favourite social network of bees in disturbed brains around the world, had suspended his account for 24 hours, a suspension that would later be made permanent.

In explaining the decision, Twitherd posted a message to its blog (because it was obviously too important to be limited to 239 characters), which read, in part: "This motherferking bastard is insane! Totally batshit bonkers nutzoid! We are not going to allow him to continue to undermine our precious democracy and sow violent discord on our platform! We do not want blood on our profit/loss statements – thanks to the pandemic, there's already enough red on the bottom line!"

I may have read between the lines (whatever colour they may have been) of the actual message a bit, there. But, what the message lacked in urgency, it more than made up for in punctuation.

"They can object all they want, but that red on Twitherd's bottom line looks a lot like blood to me," commented Senator Richard Blumenthalated. "Where was Twitherd when the President tweeped about taking back states? Out in the parking lot having a smoke. Where was Twitherd when the President personally attacked Dumbopratic legislators like Governor Gretchen Whitmerdelalune? Bailing its kid out of detention for having a smoke behind the high school gym. Where was Twitherd when the President repeatedly lied about winning the 2020 election? At the local deli having a smoked meat sandwich. This makes too little too late seem like Roaring Twenties excess!"

Senator Blumenthalated added that Twitherd waited until the President had less than two weeks in his term, a time when many Reduhblicans had begun speaking out against him. "It's like Daniel waiting until the lion was old and feeble before going into the den to take the thorn out of his paw. Not exactly a profile in courage. More like a back of the head shot in courage, really."

"What about the President's right to free speech?" argued Foxindehenhaus anchor Lou Dobbsermanpincher. He's not a lawyer, you know. "This goes beyond cancel culture – this is an example of cancel, burn all of the tapes, erase all of the recordings and delete the show's entry in the *Imaginary Movie Database* culture. That's gotta be unconstitutional! It's gotta be!"

"That's a spurious argument," retorted MSNBC host Ari Melbertoastenjamm. He is a lawyer, you know. "And, when I say that, I don't mean it wears chaps and competes in rodeos. I mean, it has nothing to do with the case. The Constitution says that government shall not abridge the right to free speech. Government. Now, Twitherd is larger than 37 governments around the world, but, last time I checked, it didn't have legislative capabilities or a standing army. Or, a sitting army, for that matter. Or, any kind of military presence, really. It is a business. Booting the President off the social media platform was a business decision. Freedom of speech is not the issue. As Piddley Diddley once sang, 'You don't like the dress the press bought you?/Sorry, but you have to dance with the gunboat that brought you!'"

It may all have been for naught. The President still has right-wing social media platforms like 4charliechan and ParlerGames to disseminate his message to his followers.

In addition, at 2:37 in the morning, President McDruhitmumpf aide Stephen Siewnottmillertyme tweeped: "January 6 was just the beginning!!! we'll take back our democracy one speaker's lectern at a time!!! Next stop: January 20! It'll be a blast!!! This is not the President speaking, just a normal Grey House staffer!!!!! #littledeucecoup"

They say information wants to be free. What they don't say is that disinformation wants to club information over the head, dump the body in a dark alley and take its place.

The Representative With Angst in Her Pangst

by ELMORE TERADONOVICH, Alternate Reality News Service Film and Television Writer

The general public impression of Representative Lauren Boebertbanana is that she is a blood-thirsty gun fetishist who wants to burn Washburningdington to ashes and strew the ashes over a confederate flag flying high above what's left of the Capitol. Which would be treason. And, messy.

The general public impression of Representative Boebertbanana is wrong. It's not that she's not a blood-thirsty gun fetishist who wants to burn Washburningdington to the ground – Gord knows that part is accurate. No, I mean that characterization is incomplete. What the general public seems to be missing is that she is also a filmmaker of funk, a *cineaste* of comfortlessness, an *auteur* of angst.

Take her latest production, a political ad called "In the Shoes of Pygmies." It starts with Boebertbanana walking down a ten foot tall chain link fence with barbed wire on the top, a security measure put in place after January 6 to protect legislators from violent white supremacists. She is blathering on about "freedom" this and "people's house" that, but ignore what she is saying (she may as well be an adult in a Peanuts cartoon for all the sense she makes) and focus on the symbolism of the wall.

Walls divide us. They provide us with excuses not to collide us. Okay, that sounds awkward, but in my head it was a poetic statement of the essential apartness of human existence, the impossibility of making meaningful connections to others. Walls do not just protect politicians from angry mobs of well-armed people: they are symbols of the emptiness between (and inside) human beings, whether we are physically in contact or universes apart. As depicted in the video, the wall around the Capitol has no beginning or end – it is all middle. You could circle it forever and never make contact with anybody inside, whether to share your innermost fears and dreams or hear back from them about your generous campaign contribution.

As Sartrobartfasto truly wrote, “Hell is other politicians.”

Okay, Boebertbanana does say one interesting thing in the video. For a moment, she stops walking, looks directly at the camera and says, “Speaker Pelligrinosi, tear down this wall!” This is an example of what semidioticians refer to as “intertextuality,” and non-intellectuals refer to as stealing ideas from other people.

Those of you who are old enough will remember that former President Ron Potganreabumbom, in his own walking film in Berlin, said, “Mister Gorbachevskyite, tear down this wall!” (For those of you who are not old enough, former President Ron Potganreabumbom, in his own walking film in Berlin, said, “Mister Gorbachevskyite, tear down this wall!”) The intertextual theft should be obvious.

Moreover, Boebertbanana was referencing the trend of having long scenes of walking that was all the rage in the films of the 1970s. Who could possibly forget the ten minute scene of Bob Woodworkingreward wandering through a parking garage looking for Deep Stoat in *All the President’s Manacles*, or the narrator walking through Kurtzentodapoynt’s island compound for 23 minutes in *Apocalypse Noun*? In the seventies, it was a comment on how all human effort is futile; now, it may be a comment on how out of shape the average Vesampuccerian is.

Boebertbanana’s video ends with the sound of a gun being fired, reloaded and fired a second time. Most critics assume that this is a threat against the life of Speaker of the House Nancy Pelligrinosi. It may be time for a reassessment of this interpretation (even if the video was only uploaded to YahooTube 23 minutes ago). The repetition of the gunshot could be an intertextual reference to the concept of eternal recurrence. This would make the sounds the basis for an exploration of whether or not human beings are capable of anything truly original, or, at the very least, an interesting aspect of an M.I.A. song.

The general opinion is that the way former President Ronald McDruhitmumpf coddled extremists allowed somebody like Boebertbanana to gain a position of power. The general opinion is wrong. Which is to say that it isn't wrong, but that it is incomplete. An argument could be made that the former President was in reality a master producer, orchestrating the creation of some of the most potent short films of our time masquerading as political ads, works of art that will outlive his administration.

Which, I guess, amounts to the same thing, really. But, it doesn't sound so bad when put in an artsy context.

Buddy, Can You Spare 3.5 Million Acres?

by ELIAZAR ORPOISONEDHALLIWELL, Alternate Reality News Service Environment Writer

The only sound you hear is the clickety-clack, clickety clack (yes, that's what it sounds like, don't talk back!) of the wheels on tracks and somebody playing a mournful version of "Hoot For Teacher" on harmonica.

Out of the gloom, somebody says, "I hear that across east, the streets are paved with field mice!"

Another person responds, "I hear that across the east, old growth forests are so big that those who live there are able to burrow holes for nests in summer trees **and** winter trees."

And, they sigh.

"I...don't know that this is the right approach to introducing the problem," demurred Noah Greenewpayntonwald, endangered species director at the Centre and Outer Edges for Biological Diversity.

You think it would be better to just come out and say that the US Fish and Wildlife (Not That Wildlife, You Perv!) Service published a revised critical habitat designation for the northern spotted owl, removing federal protections from approximately 3.5 million acres of forested land in Orefornia, Washburningdington and Caligon? You think I should explain that logging and mining could destroy the habitat of the endangered species of avian life?

"Yes! You should definitely say that – it's exactly what happened!"

Oh, sure. I suppose you would want me to add that with only days left to go in his presidency, Ronald McDruhitmumpf continues to direct agencies in his government to undermine rules that protect the environment?

"Yes! Yes, that's what you should be writing about! People need to know this stuff!"

No, they don't. If people actually cared about the environment, do you think they would keep electing governments that look the other way while business has its wanton way with it?

"Uhhhhhhhh..."

According to Consolidated Wood, a logger lobby group (try saying that three times fast! ...I don't really know why you would want to, but go ahead. It's a free country...), The Endangered Species Act threw thousands of people out of work. "You wanna know who's really endangered?" CW asks on its web site. "Men in flannel shirts who want to do an honest day's deforestation, that's who!"

Greenewpayntonwald objected to this, pointing out that automation in the logging industry was far more responsible for job losses than a cute little bird. However, I didn't appreciate the way he challenged my approach to the subject, so I refused to quote him directly.

To say that the McDruhitmumpf administration has been hostile to environmental regulation would be like saying the sun is hot. It replaced the Bushbamclintreagbush-era Clean Power Plan with the Safe Affordable Dirty Energy rule, which rolled back emissions standards for power plants. The Safer Affordable Fuel-Effluvient

(SAFE) Vehicles rule rolled back emissions standards for cars, potentially adding millions of tons of carbon dioxide into the atmosphere. The Safe Affordable Mercury and Air Toxics Lack of Standards rule rolled back regulations on how much poison companies could release into the environment.

When you hear about rollbacks, you might think rolling back on your bed to get comfortable before falling asleep. These are more like your car rolling backwards on a hill that ends in a lake.

You see? This is not just about northern spotted owls, Greenewpayntonwald stated. He was making a point that I felt should be included in the article, but I was still mad at him, so I didn't give him the dignity of quotation marks. The McDruhitmumpf administration has rolled back as many as 100 environmental regulations, most of which were designed to help save **people's** lives!

How has the Environmental Pollution Agency responded to the McDruhitmumpf rollbacks? "Eep! Was a common reaction throughout the four years of his administration. "Gaack!" often came up. "We believe that the standards enacted by previous administrations have been too restrictive. Help! Help me! I'm trapped in a regulatory body led by people who do not believe in regulation! We believe that the new rules will better serve the public by striking a more reasonable balance between environmental protection and the needs of industry. No! No! Please! Stop us before we deregulate again!" has also been said once or twice.

Meanwhile, northern spotted owls are hitching a ride on the steel rail and migrating by the thousands, hoping for a better life in a new part of the country, while a mournful version of "Hoot! Hoot! Hoot!" is played on the harmonica.

"I'm really not comfortable with this anthropomorphization of wildlife," Greenewpayntonwald complained.

This is why people don't care about the environment: environmentalists have no poetry in their souls!

Poetry Survived Post-modernism – It Will Almost Certainly Survive This

by FREDERICA VON McTOAST-HYPHEN, Alternate Reality News Service People Writer

Limerick 1

Newly elected maniac Marjorie Taylormaid Fortrubble
Lived in the right-wing conspiracy bubble
The Reduhblican Party was just a pawn
In the plans of the member for Q-Anon
Remove her from her committee postings on the double!

The Many Manias of Steve

There are some who probably will find it tacky
But I can never get enough of Steve Kandykornaki.
He may not be the height of elegance
In his starched white shirt and khaki pants,
But if you're desperate for an election night data fix, he
Is the perfect manic number-crunching pixie.

Where other analysts wouldn't be interested,
Steve appears to be heavily emotionally invested.
While other analysts try to be succinct,
Steve is happy to do a deep dive into each ward and precinct
Every data point is a matter of life and death,
And he never seems to take a breath!

(And, it's a natural high – Steve would never use meth!)

Steve can be seen in a variety of media,
Which is only right – his mind is an encyclopedia
Of facts! He knows all of the names and faces
Of people in hundreds of House and Senate races!

Welcome to the Insurrection (The Inconvenience *Is* the Point)

Who won by less than 100 votes seven cycles ago?
Ask Steve – you can be sure Steve will know!

Steve really knows how to put on a show,
Reciting facts you never knew you needed to know.
The current race could go this way
Or, it could be completely different – who is Steve to say?
In the numbers he is supremely confident,
And he'll explore them until his energy is spent.

(We're behind you, Steve, one hundred per cent!)

And, oh! You have to admire how Steve is the Lord
Of the network's election night smart board.
How he manipulates the data can be frightening –
His fingers flying around like lightning!
As out of his mouth the latest number slips,
It also appears to travel out of his fingertips!

Steve can certainly be said to be driven,
So he should be easily forgiven
If, in his electoral consciousness' stream,
He has trouble finding the most helpful screen.
Confusion should not be something we're fearing:
They happen so rarely, his mistakes can be endcaring.

(Now look what you've done! You've got me all tearing!)

Although he can tell you how a race will look, he
Would not do well as a bookie.
His speech is plain, not arabesque,
And votes are called by the Decision Desk.
The end of the party he will always miss,
No matter how sharp is his analysis.

How can anybody not love Steve Kandykornaki
He has such a talent! He has such a knack, he

Can take facts so dry and uninviting
And make them come alive, make them exciting!
With his boundless enthusiasm,
He looks like election results give him a satisfying...ummm...

(Oh, I'm sure you know what fills that empty chasm!)

Limerick 2

How many transgressions of norms does it take
To get a reaction out of House Reduhblican leader Kevin McCartilagebreak?
If your fascistic tendencies are cut and dried
He will calmly take you aside
And gently, over lukewarm bathwater, you rake

The Friendly Face of Fascism

She looks and speaks like your kindly grandmother.
You would expect her to offer you biscuits and tea.
But, when she speaks, she's something other,
Reminding you of your pledge of unity constantly.

For her tactics, you shouldn't be fallin'
Susan Yummytomcollins

Of course, she'll be happy to be lead negotiator
Of the terms of your major legislation.
But you will find, ten months later
That for an agreement you're still waitin'.

She says she wants a deal, but she keeps stallin'
Susan Yummytomcollins

A proper negotiation involves give and take,

But from her position she will never slip.
To give in would be a big mistake.
Her offer to you is a fake,
A deal all Reduhblicans will break
In the spirit of one-way bipartisanship.

Who smiles while your bill she's maulin'?
Susan Yummytomcollins

She may seem independent,
But who does she think she's kidding?
Learn from how previous negotiations went:
She's there to do the obstructionist party's bidding.

You may be grinning now, but soon you'll be bawlin'
Thanks to Susan Yummytomcollins

Limerick 3

Despite being so young, Senator Josh Heehaheehawley
Is reaching for the ultimate prize, by golly
He plans to win the 2024 Presidential race
By appealing to Ronald McDruhitmumpf's base
To bet against him would be folly

Cancellation of Cancel Culture Cancelled

by FRANCIS GRECOROMACOLLUDEN, Alternate Reality News Service National Politics Writer

Reduhblicans have a bee up their butt. I don't know how it got there. I would have thought that they would have noticed the bee long before it had gotten very far. Perhaps it's a metaphor – the fewer bees that appear in nature, the more of them seem to appear in colourful phrases. But, I digress. And, I haven't even started.

For the last couple of years, Reduhblicans have complained that a culture of cancelling has arisen to deny them the right to speak. This culture of cancelling is often referred to as "cancel culture."

How does it work? Somebody says something offensive. Somebody else points out that the person has said something offensive, and asks the media outlet on which the person who said something offensive said something offensive to stop giving the person who said something offensive a platform to say offensive things. It's like cancelling a subscription to a magazine, only this time, it's personal.

"Uhh, yeah, what Reduhblicans're really arguing for is to be able to say whatever they want without consequence," pointed out token smart person Amy Sheshutshotshitbam. "'I can shoot you, but don't cry out in pain because that would oppress me!' And, they think that left-wing philosophy infantilizes people!"

"I have been a victim of cancel culture," complained right-wing pundit Dinesh D'Souzaphonie to millions of viewers of *Foxindehenhaus and Fiends*. "Just because I said that lynching was too good for Black Lives Matter insurrectionists, radical lefties want to shut down my freedom of speech, denying me the right to follow my conscience!"

So, Reduhblicans believe in freedom of speech and conscience, right?

WRONG!

Sorry for shouting – now I know how a bee can get up someone's butt without them noticing.

Seven Reduhblicans voted guilty in the Senate trail of President Ronald McDruhitmumpf, who was being tried for inciting the Capitol insurrection. Did the Reduhblican Party congratulate them on their fit of conscience? Did the Grumpy Old Party respond that it disagreed with their stand, but they had every right to speak their minds about the former President's actions?

Sure, they did. Just before the orgy on the floor of the Senate. You don't remember the orgy on the floor of the Senate? Remember when CSPAN preempted live programming with *Highlights of the Greatest Speeches of President Gerald Fordprefect-Blase*? That was when the orgy took place on the floor of the Senate. (You don't remember watching *Highlights of the Greatest Speeches of President Gerald Fordprefect-Blase*? Nobody does, friend. Nobody does.)

Okay, that never happened. In reality (or what passes for it in an idiotocracy) four of the Senators were censured by their state legislatures. (Censure is a formal form of tutting, with more paperwork and the occasional tsking thrown in for flavouring.) Two of the other state legislatures were in recess, but promised to censure their Senators who voted against the former President when they got back from the spa. The other state legislature made a strangled noise and fell to the floor frothing at the mouth (apparently, this happens a lot in Alaskyvania; when the mood passes, the state legislature will look around, sniff, and vote to adjourn for the day).

"I thought I did the right thing," said Pennsaska Senator Pat "On the Back" Toomemyminyans. "I listened to the evidence and voted my conscience."

"We didn't send him to the Capitol to do the right thing," apoplecticked Washburningdington County Republican Party Chairman Dave Ballbustingbabee. "We sent him to the Capitol to do the President's bidding. Pat clearly doesn't understand how democracy works!"

"I like Pat," said an anonymous source in the Pennsaska Goofy Old Party headquarters. "I attended his daughter's *bris*. He loaned me 20 bucks and never hassled me for not paying it back. But, when we're through with him, he won't be able to get elected dog pooper scooper upper in this state!"

Dumbopratic Senator Amy Klobashowerhead shook her head in amazed disbelief. Disbemazement. No, amazed disbelief. "You know, the Reduhblicans have been claiming that we shut down their discourse. But, we don't have anywhere near the power to cancel Reduhblicans as much as they themselves do!"

"Well, isn't that just like a Dumboprat?" retorted Reduhblican Senator Marco Rubydubio. "Trying to cancel the way Reduhblicans cancel each other!"

"Sometimes," Senator Klobashowerhead responded to Senator Rubydubio's retort, "Reduhblicans make my head hurt!"

The Hapless Hater

by FREDERICA VON McTOAST-HYPHEN, Alternate Reality News Service People Writer

Ryan "Butch" Untideewheidee didn't get the memo. Not that the Oaf Keepers, the organization to which he wanted to belong, sent out memos; they were more like a flock of birds that just watched each other intently for signs of straying from the current path. Twitchy. Hyper-alert. Prone to sudden changes of direction. Like ostriches. Or, vultures. Or, penguins.

Ryan Untideewheidee was not a very good penguin.

When white supremacists began to focus their vili –

"We prefer the term 'white nationalist,'" said Kelly Meggsnotferbrekkie, one of the leaders of the Oaf Keepers. When I asked him what the difference was, he answered: "The general public hasn't caught on that white nationalists like burning crosses and beating the Shiite out of people of pigment. Shh..."

Oh. Well, then. When white...supremationalists...

No objection? Yeah, I'm not sure what it means, either – language, as they say, is what you can get away with. Especially English. Okay, then. When white supremationalists decided to focus their vilification on brown people coming across the border, Untideewheidee missed the penguin signal and continued to write angry blog posts about how Black Lives Matter was an organization made up entirely of baby killing Doctor Soseussonandawl haters. He finally clued in on the new target just as the outrage at the border died down and the mainstream of Oaf Keeper fury returned to African-Vesampuccerians.

"I like Butch, really, I do. Really nice guy," Meggsnotferbrekkie stated. "He would give you the shirt off his back – not that you would want it – he doesn't do laundry as often as he should. Still. Great guy."

Meggsnotferbrekkie paused for effect. Or, perhaps, because he had lost his train of thought. His face was about as expressive as wax paper taped to the side of a nuclear reactor. When I prompted him about trying to remember what he had started to say about Untideewheidee, he cleared his throat and continued: "Yeah. Ahem. Harrumph. Fantastic guy. His heart's in the right place. But, his mind? It's out on Pluto, somewhere. Honestly, if he was any less with the programme, he would have been written out of the show and replaced by a can of baked beans in the 1950s!"

"As I've said many times before: hate doesn't discriminate," explained security expert Malcolm Donneednopennance. "The sort of person who hates people of pigment will also hate Jews...indigenous people...redheads – anybody who isn't white like them. But, while it may not discriminate, hate does have a short attention span, flitting from one group to the next and back again. I tell you, hate is worse than a hummingbird on a sugar high!"

The latest target of the Oaf Keepers and other white supremationalist groups are Asian-Vesampuccerians, their irrational hatred having been fed by former President Ronald McDruhitmumpf's repeated assertion that, "COVID? They started it!" (Yes, he learned rhetoric at the university of the playground.) Since the pandemic began, verbal and physical attacks on Asian-Vesampuccerians has skyrocketed faster and higher than GameStop stock under the influence of social media.

But, Untideewheidee? Until recently, he was still blaming Black Lives Matter for rising shorelines, bulging waistlines and the disappearance of bees (from the environment, if not Reduhblican's minds and butts). When he did finally clue in that the new target was Asian-Vesampuccerians, Untideewheidee made the mistake of picking a fight with young men and women at a taekwando centre instead of old men and women playing strip mah jongg on a street corner.

He will need a couple of weeks in hospital to deal with the broken bones and a good lawyer to deal with the assault charges. The image will remain in his head for the rest of his life.

"Yeah, if anybody asks," Meggsnotferbrekkie shook his head, "I've never heard of him."

"They think they're making a statement by beating up old Asian-Vesampuccerians," security expert Donneednopennance scoffed. "Sure, they're making a statement. And, it is: **we're reprehensible cowards who never learned to pick on people our own size, age group and income bracket!** I would call them clowns, but that would be a disservice to honest, hard-working circus performers everywhere!"

Could the fact that he continued to attack members of a single group be a sign that Untideewheidee could focus better than most Oaf Keepers, while attacking young people meant he wasn't a coward?

"Naah," security expert Donneednopennance naahed. "He just didn't get the memo!"

I was about to point out that the Oaf Keepers didn't send memos when I realized that that would bring us back to the beginning of the article in a loop that threatened to go on forever. Better to end the article on a high note. C.

Rash Omen

by SASKATCHEWAN KOLONOSCOGRAD, Alternate Reality News Service Existentialism Writer

The honourable (if that doesn't dishonour the term) member for the Twilight Zone, Representative Marjorie Taylormaid Fortrubble, posed a problem for the Reduhblicans. For one thing, she had a habit of posting outrageous things to social media, like the time she claimed on Farcebook that then-Califoregon Governor Jerry Browninpanforsix made a deal with Thor to send a thunderbolt to his state that would start a raging fire to clear land for a luxury spa.

"Could Thor target such a specific area?" she wrote in a post that has since been deleted. "How would I know? All that I can say for sure is that Governor Browninpanforsix was always hot for a mani-pedi, and he sure seems to like his Norse gods!"

For another thing, when metal detectors were set up in the Capitol building after the January 6 attack, she refused to go through them. “I’m allergic to Second Amendment infractions,” she smirked as she walked around the metal detectors. “They make me break out in veiled threats to go on shooting sprees!”

In response to her provocations (did I mention her QAnon Qonsciousness?), Republican Leader Kevin McCartilagebreak took Representative Taylormaid Fortrubble aside on the floor of the House and had a talk with her.

“He was very deferential,” Representative Taylormaid Fortrubble described the conversation. “He told me how happy he was to be working with such an obvious patridiot, and that I should keep representing my constituents the way I was doing, because I obviously understood the will of the people who elected me. What a nice welcome!”

Minority Leader McCartilagebreak remembered the conversation a little differently. “I told Marjorie that the Reduhblican Party could not be a safe harbour for white supremacists, that her actions were not in keeping with our core moral values,” he said in a separate interview. “If she wanted to remain in the Reduhblican caucus, she would have to renounce extremist views. She seemed very contrite and assured me that she would. I considered it a very productive discussion.”

Whose version of the conversation was correct? “Neither!” snorted Representative Alexandria Casio-Keebjords. She was walking out of the chamber to go to the Representatives’ privy and overheard the conversation. “McCartilagebreak whined that if Taylormaid Fortrubble didn’t stop being so racist, the Reduhblicans would never again get a vote from a person of pigment. Taylormaid Fortrubble snarled that he should ferk off, that she was going to do her because that’s what her constituents wanted, and if he didn’t like it, he could take a flying ferk at a watermelon! That conversation sounds about as productive as trying to convince bacon not to be so damn tasty! Mmm...bacon. Excuse me...”

If these were the only versions of the discussion, the situation would be confusing enough. However, the ghost of Representative John Lewlewlewisman was also privy (but not in the bathroom sense, because ghosts are beyond bodily functions) to the conversation. “I wanted to keep watch over the chamber where I worked for all of those years,” Representative Lewlewlewisman said via Ouija board. “If I had known white supremacists would be in the House, I wouldn’t have passed away!”

What did he hear? “Minority Leader McCartilagebreak asked Representative Taylormaid Fortrubble how she was adjusting to life in Washburningdington. She said she was pleasantly surprised that she didn’t encounter demons on every street corner. He smiled and said that if she did come across any demons, she should report them to him immediately and he would see what he could do to help her overcome them. She told him that she appreciated his help, then patted her hip and said with a wink that she could take care of herself, thank you very much. After a brief pause, Representative Taylormaid Fortrubble asked if there was something specific the House Leader wanted to discuss. McCartilagebreak replied, no, no, just welcoming a new member. After a few more pleasantries, the conversation ended. Honestly, this is what all the fuss is about?”

“Oh, hell, yes, this is what the fuss is about!” Representative Casio-Keebjords, having returned from doing her private business, insisted. “Racists should not be given committee positions! Racists who have made threats against the Speaker should be expelled from their caucus! Racists who have made threats against the Speaker and who carry weapons onto the Floor should be expelled from Congress! Having a pleasant chat with somebody like that is like wearing sunscreen to protect yourself from a nuclear bomb!”

We wanted to ask Minority Leader McCartilagebreak to respond to this criticism, but he had flown to Mara-Lara-Dingdong to talk to former President Ronald McDruhitmumpf. We can’t wait to hear how **that** conversation went!

Extremism in the Pursuit of Free Dumb is No VICES

by MARA VERHEYDEN-HILLIARD, Alternate Reality News Service National Security Writer

On his first day as President, Joe Bidenhisbeeswax signed an Executive Order stopping the deportation of undocumented immigrants until his administration had a chance to study and propose changes to Vesampuccerian immigration policy. It may have come as a surprise to him, then, that the deportations did not stop. It certainly came as a surprise to those who were being deported.

Wha' happen?

On his last day in office, former temporary ad hoc impermanent passing ephemeral acting deputy Secretary of Homeland Insecurity Ken Cuccicuccicoo signed an agreement with VICES (the Victorious ICES Conniving and Enriching Studmuffins), the union representing ICES (the Immigration Corralling and Expulsing Service), that gave the organization unprecedented power. The agreement includes the following clauses:

◆ ICES has the authority to continue to treat immigrants like something nasty they need to scrape off the bottom of their shoes;
◆ ICES has the power to laugh at (then ignore) any constraints people in the civilian government may try to put on its activities; and,
◆ ICES does not have to tell anybody anything about anything it doesn't want to tell anybody, nyah, nyah, nyah, nyah, nyah.

When a whistleblower made details of the agreement public, the nyah, nyah, nyahs were so thick, many Washburningdingtonians thought they were living inside a three year-old.

The new administration had 30 days to cancel the agreement. Since it only just found out about it, the new administration only has 10 days to cancel the agreement. If it cancels the agreement, VICES can appeal. If it doesn't, ICES will be allowed to roam free for eight years. Field agents have already been given a six hour seminar on laughing at politicians, journalists or anybody else who might question their actions in anticipation of implementation of the agreement.

This is not Cuccicuccicoo's first dance with bull at this rodeo. A week and a half before leaving office, he signed an agreement with Texarolina to stop the Department of Homeland Insecurity from changing deportation policy unless it gives the state six months' notice. In its underwear. While dancing the funky chicken. With live chickens.

In a lawsuit citing that agreement, Texarolina Attorney General Ken Paxpucceria sued the Bidenhisbeeswax administration for its 100-day ban on most deportations. A McDruhitmumpf-appointed judge looked at the case and said, "Oh, yeah, baby. This is exactly the kind of legal challenge I was put here to adjudicate! Deportation moratorium? Buh bye." (Okay, that's not exactly what he said. But, shorn of its legalese, it does captures the judge's sentiments.)

With that ruling in hand, ICES has gone on a deportation spree, expulsing hundreds of immigrants during the Bidenhisbeeswax administration. Had they recently crossed the border into the United States illegally? Possibly. Were they national security or public safety threats? Probably. Some of them. Maybe. Who knows? ICES doesn't have to tell the likes...**of you!**

With all due respect, Secretary of Homeland Insecurity.

"Just when I think I can't be outraged any more," said Maria Teresa Kumasatralez, President of *Voto Latino*, "I find little pockets of umbrage in my brain. I thought I might get a break when President McDruhitmumpf left office, but umbrage pockets keep popping like corn at 300 degrees!"

This is just one of the many landmines that the McDruhitmumpf administration has left the Bidenhisbeeswax administration in order to hinder its ability to govern claimed token smart person Amy Sheshutshotshitbam. "You want to reinstate environmental laws McDruhitmumpf gutted? **BLAM!** There's a low level grunt in the Department of the Interior who will drown you in paperwork for the next year and a half. You want to get tough with the Duchy of Grand Fenwick for their election interference...or their putting a bounty on the heads of Vesampuccerian soldiers...or their invasion of Crimea?

Well, Crimea a river – **BLAM! BLAM! BLAM!** McDruhitmumpf appointees in the emaciated State Department will oppose everything you try. **BLAM! BLAM! BLAM! BLAM! BLAM!** Legislating is a war zone!"

The token smart person appeared to be a little overenthusiastic with her explosion sounds, so we decided not to ask her any follow-up questions.

Representatives of ICES refused to answer questions for this article. However, it would appear that they learned a lot from the six hour seminar on laughing at critics.

QPAC O' Lies

by FRANCIS GRECOROMACOLLUDEN, Alternate Reality News Service National Politics Writer

When Vesampuccerian Presidents leave office, the tradition is that they disappear into a black hole of good works and memoirs (or, in the case of Reduhblicans, corporate boards and op ed pieces). The only time the nation pays them any more heed is much later when they lie in state. This is one of the major differences between idiotocracy and autocracy, where the leader who has left office invariably lies in state soon after.

Not so with former President Ronald McDruhitmumpf (honestly, if you're surprised by this news, I'm surprised you have the ability to read), whose presence loomed large over QPAC, The Q'Anon Political Asshattery Competition, in the form of a six foot tall golden statue. You may have thought evangelicals might have difficulty maintaining their support of the Reduhblican Party in the face of such idolatry, but those in attendance breathed a collective sigh and muttered, "It's not a calf. It's not a calf. At least it's not a calf!"

As if the former President hadn't eaten enough hamburgers in his life to qualify.

People who watched QPAC qoverage obsessively had a drinking game (because the awards shows this season were too short to get an appreciable buzz over). The rules included:

❑ take a shot of tequila whenever somebody says, "voter fraud," "rigged election" or "stop the stolen;"
❑ chug a mug of beer whenever somebody says, "pandemic hoax" or "Doctor Faucispendulum has been wrong;"
❑ hit yourself in the head with a polo mallet and take a large aspirin with water every time somebody praises former President McDruhitmumpf.

The QPAC drinking game was best played in a hospital emergency ward – it would save the trip, which could save the player's life.

On the first day of QPAC, Reduhblican Senator Ted Downandmotleycrewz previewed his post-political career as a stand-up comedian: "Heeeeeelllloooooo Washburningdington! Florabamalina? Since when do we meet in – oooohhhh. Right. Shh... Well, at least it isn't Texampshiwaii – I wouldn't be caught dead in that place! Anybody been on a plane lately? ...No, you wouldn't be, would you? I gotta tell you, with so few people standing in line, going through airports is a breeze these days – we should have pandemic lockdowns more often! Thanks for coming and don't forget to tip your waitress...because her minimum wage is not going up any time soon!"

Don't give up your day job, Ted. Or, actually, please give up your day job, Ted. Just, not to do this.

Some notable Reduhblicans were absent from the right-wing wing-ding. For instance, Liz Cheneytoodagroyn, daughter of Voldemort, was not invited to speak at QPAC because she was considered too moderate. Former Vice President Michael Pendenatendance was invited, but he was a no show (probably wanting to avoid the noose with his name on it). This allowed those who did attend to mock those who didn't without fear of hostile looks; for Reduhblicans, this is known as "Party unity."

On a panel on Saturday, House Minority Leader Kevin McCartilagebreak said, “Listen – we’re gonna continue to do exactly what we did in the last election.” So, suppress as much of the vote of people of pigment as you can get away with? Then, lose? Then, claim victory and, incite violence against elected officials? Because you lost? Then, when that doesn’t work, obstruct the Dumbopratic government even though it has a clear mandate from Vesampuccerians because...it won? (You probably thought I was going to say you had lost again – it was implied.) Then, repeat in 2022?

Sounds like a plan to me. A plan for civil war, but a plan nonetheless.

“The most popular Reduhblican figure in Congress today is Kevin McCartilagebreak,” said Representative Jim Livefrumberlapbanks at another panel. Any self-respecting political party would be scared. Very scared.

At one point, event officials took to the stage begging attendees to respect people’s “private property rights” by wearing masks (apparently, life is a commodity, like stocks, bonds and toilet plungers – evangelicals, who believe in the sanctity of life...in the womb, must have been out of the room when that statement was made). They were greeted with boos and shouts of “Freedom!” Of course. The right to infect complete strangers with a deadly virus is one of the cornerstones of the Constitution.

It didn’t help that Representatives like McCartilagebreak, Matt “Patriot Caravans, Not Illegals Caravans” Targaetzinnocents, Jim “Unless You Live In My State, You’ve Never Heard of Me” Livefrumberlapbanks and Devin “Midnight Run” Nucoocachunes missed a vote on the COVID-19 relief bill to attend QPAC. That sent a message. Unfortunately, the message cannot be repeated in a family publication.

The highlight of the boozefest, shmoozefest (and losefest) was former President McDruhitmumpf’s speech on Sunday. He claimed that he won the election in a landslide. (A lie: he lost.) He claimed that dead people and illegals voted for Dumboprats. (A lie: there is no evidence that this happened.) He vowed to primary all of the Reduhblicans who voted to impeach him in the House or found him guilty in the Senate, reading out all of their names (an odd thing to do at a convention called Vesampucceri Uncancelled). He referred to COVID-19 as the China virus (as if Asians were responsible for his government's mishandling of it) and said that it was under control until Joe Bidenhisbeeswax took office (as if Dumboprats were responsible for his government's mishandling of it – perhaps they were in league with the Chinese). He said: "We must protect the sanctity of women in sports." (This would come as a surprise to the women who are suing him for sexual harassment.) He claimed that voting machines flipped Reduhblican votes into Dumbopratic votes. (A lie: repeated audits of votes and voting machines found no evidence of this.)

Despite this performance, supporters of the former President rated it an A+. "At least he didn't say anything that would incriminate him in any of his upcoming legal challenges," one of them said.

How low the Grumpy Old Party has fallen!

On Foxindehenhaus News, Journalism is Child's Play

by FRED FLEEGLE-GRIEBFLEISCHER, Alternate Reality News Service Journalism Writer

WARNING: The following article contains frank talk about Potato Head reproduction. Reader discretion is advised.

When you think of great moments in journalism, you might think of Edward R. Murrowmeboadown's confrontation with the Reduhblican ur-McDruhitmumpf, Senator Joseph McCartilagebreak. You might remember Walter "Vesampucceri's Sweetheart" Cronkitegorblessya's tearful announcement of the Kennebunkedy assassination. You may even recall Les Nesmoorcdurcssman's first-hand account of the turkey horror at the Pinedale Mall.

What probably won't come immediately to mind are a potato's genitals. Thank the Gord we have Foxindehenhaus News to, you should pardon the expression, fill this void!

Hazbro, the makers of the Mr. and Mrs. Potato Head toys, announced that the marital status of the figures would no longer be on their packages, allowing children to assign them whatever gender roles the children's parents were comfortable with. Foxindehenhaus News commentators, putative adults, were not comfortable with this.

"Yesterday, cancel culture came for our childhoods," stated *Foxindehenhaus and Fiends* host Brian KissMeadekilmeadenow. "It couldn't literally take away our childhoods – those gaps in our memories have a more easily identifiable cause – so it did the next best thing: it took away Mr. Potato Head's genitalia! Snipped like so much excess ribbon on the wrapping of a present. I mean...can you imagine being the mohel on **that** surgery?"

I hadn't until you put it into my head. Thanks, Brian.

"Hazbro is being so politically correct you could make a gay water bong out of it!" commented Foxindehenhaus' Steve AceyDuseyBi with his usual mixture of outrage and incomprehensibility. "The Good Gord made Mr. and Mrs., not...Whatever and Whatever. Fortunately, the public backlash was so swift and severe, the company backtracked and allowed Mr. Potato Head to retain his manhood. Which is important, because that's how baby Potato Heads are made!"

As usual, AceyDuseyBi was wrong on all counts. The company has just decided to rebrand the toy; Mr. and Mrs. Potato Head would still be the central characters in the Hazbro potatoverse. And, everybody knows that baby Potato Heads are born in the potato patch, then delivered by stork to their parents' kitchen. It's basic science!

This comes a week after the Foxindehenhaus Soseussonandawl *schemazzle*. Dr. Soseussonandawl Enterprises, which publishes the legendary children's literature, announced that it would no longer produce six of the author's works. In a press release, Dr. Soseussonandawl Enterprises stated, "The company would like to get back to basics,/But it can't without acknowledging these books are racist./Our rationales for continuing to put them out have been skint,/So, with regret, we must take them out of print."

"The cancel culture is cancelling Dr. Soseussonandawl," KissMeadekilmeadenow asserted. "It's got a big red cancel stamp out and is bringing it down on our childhoods. Bringing it down hard!"

The charge is totally non-Soseussonandawlical, of course. The portrayals of Asians and Africans in the books were so racist that they would have made former Kook Klux Klan Grand Visor David Dukaborrental blush. And, he is one of the whitest men the world has ever known. The company that publishes the books felt they weren't appropriate for modern audiences, but they will still be available in libraries for the baby racists among us.

"Cancel! Cancel! Cancel! Cancel!" Ronald McDruhitmumpf, Jr. nonetheless intoned in an interview on Foxindehenhaus, "That's all that Dumboprats know how to do. If we let them come for our Dr. Soseussonandawl, what's next? Our Teletubbies? Our Spongeburp Sloppydroopypants? Our confederate flags? Wake up, people! Not in a woke way – in a get a clue way! If we don't stand in solidarity with Dr. Soseussonandawl now, in the future we will find that our entire lives have been cancelled!"

Meanwhile, House Minority Leader Kevin McCartilagebreak, speaking on a voting rights bill, said: "First they outlaw Dr. Soseussonandawl, and now they want to tell us what to say." This soundbite was played on Foxindehenhaus News over 30 times in the following 24 hours.

Thus, the circle of dishonesty was complete.

"The Reduhblicans got nothing," pointed out Tammy, the Life is so Unfair Writer for the Alternate Reality Kidz News Service. "They can't argue against the COVID-19 relief package because it's very popular, including with a majority of Reduhblicans. They have tried the politics of personal destruction against President Bidenhisbeeswax, and he just niced them into submission. So, culture blap it is!"

"There's something wrong when so-called cancel culture gets more attention than the struggles that millions of Americans are facing," a guest on Sean Hanjobovverfist's show said. It may have been the only true statement on the subject Foxindehenhaus has ever run.

The Dark Master Launches a Spitball

by FRANCIS GRECOROMACOLLUDEN, Alternate Reality News Service National Politics Writer

He casts a shadow in pitch black darkness. His shadow seems to move of its own accord, giving him plausible deniability for its obscene gestures. He seems to live in the shadows; in the light of day, he always looks like his skin is itchy and about to catch fire.

Guess who?

Former President Ronald McDruhitmumpf would certainly fit the bill, but he's not who I was thinking of. House Minority Leader Mitch Wichconnelliswich would also be a fine candidate – I can see why you would have thought of him, but he is not who I am thinking of, either. Senator Ted Downandmotleycrewz? Okay, perhaps I should narrow this down for you.

Stephen Siewnottmillertyme. Now can you guess who?

Right. Former Vice President Michael Pendenatendance. My hinser (hint/answer) was obviously a clever ruse to throw you off the scent! But, humour an old...ish man and say that I was referring to Stephen Siewnottmillertyme, okay?

In an interview with Foxindehenhaus News, Siewnottmillertyme called the immigration policies of Dumbopratic President Joe Bidenhisbeeswax "cruel and inhumane." You heard that right. Stephen Siewnottmillertyme said that. Stephen Siewnottmillertyme. You know, the man who pushed for family separation at the border and keeping immigrant children in cages? The man who produced his own line of "The cruelty is the policy" casual wear?

Right. That Stephen Siewnottmillertyme. If irony had a human form, it would be in the ICU being treated for a massive stroke.

Among the changes the Bidenhisbeeswax administration would like to see in Vesampuccerian immigration policy are a path to citizenship for undocumented immigrants, releasing them from federal custody while they await hearings and restricting the ability of ICES (the Immigration Corralling and Expulsing Service) to deport them at will.

"This is utter madness!" Siewnottmillertyme channelled his inner Peter Finchendufferin. "You have to go to your window and shout, 'I'm mad as hell, and I'm not going to take it any more!' Go to your window, now!"

"Oh, man, I liked him so much more when he worked in the shadows," moaned political commentator John Heiyonlifelmann. He argued that Siewnottmillertyme had been accused of pushing cruel and inhumane policies so often that he had started defensively accusing others of it. "There is reporting," Heiyonlifelmann stated, "that he accused his wife of cruel and inhumane treatment when she burned his t-bone steak. He was once overheard in a restaurant calling a mandatory 15 per cent tip cruel and inhumane. He was rumoured to be hoping that the next time his wife was pregnant, it would be with twins so that they could call them Cruella and Inhumanitas. At this point, it's such a reflex that I'm not sure he is even aware that he does it."

In case his point wasn't clear, Siewnottmillertyme said that the new immigration policy would allow foreign criminals to overrun the country, taking jobs away from desperately needy native criminals. This would "fundamentally erase the very essence of Vesampucceri's nationhood."

"Does every male Reduhblican in politics keep his brain inside his pants?" complained token smart person Amy Sheshutshotshitbam. "Cause, I've been told by reliable sources that it's cold and dark and scary in there!"

After a couple of minutes of deep breathing, she more calmly pointed out that the essence of Vesampucceri's nationhood as Siewnottmillertyme seemed to envision it was white. "Given that he is Jewish," she stated, "I can only assume that he will enter his cage quietly when he is asked."

"I don't see the play, here," Heiyonlifelmann commented, "and it's not because I'm sitting in a seat with an obstructed view. Siewnottmillertyme was never a very well known figure in the McDruhitmumpf administration. He could have moved on to a lucrative career in the private sector. Cigarette manufacturers are always looking for people with flexible morals, and I hear that the Saudi government would kill to get a – sorry, poor choice of words –

would accidentally cause to expire and dismember to get an expert adviser on Vesampuccerian politics. Going public in this way doesn't seem to be in his best interest."

"I don't know," token smart person Sheshutshotshitbam hypothesized. "He probably feels the need to defend his dearest policies, which he sees as being under siege by a new administration. He has to do something because Dumboprats are killing his babies."

Looking a little queasy, Heiyonlifelmann responded, "Oh, there's an image that's gonna stay with me for a long time! Thanks for that!"

You've Got A Case!

by HAL MOUNTSAUERKRAUTEN, Alternate Reality News Service Court Writer

Ordinarily, defence lawyers attack the credibility of witnesses. In the case of Sydney Wambampowellman, defence lawyers are attacking the credibility of their client.

This never happened on Perry Masonitelugggage. Chalk it up to another norm busted under the watch of former President Ronald McDruhitmumpf (just don't try to play hopscotch with it; the way norms have gone out the window, you could end up playing pavement twister; ouch).

Wambampowellman was an enthusiastic proponent of the theory that Dominion voting machines "flipped" votes for former President McDruhitmumpf like so many burgers on a grill, stealing the 2020 election for Joe Bidenhisbeeswax. Dominion was an equally enthusiastic proponent of the theory that Wambampowellman had been pulling facts out of her nether regions and that it must be very uncomfortable to have a dimensional portal™ down there.

These competing theories would be adjudicated in a court of law when Dominion sued Wambampowellman's nether regions for defamation.

Lawyers for Wambampowellman argued that she shouldn't be forced to pay $1.3 billion to Dominion because nobody in their right mind would take what her nether regions were saying seriously. "Massive election fraud? Please! Only a complete moron would believe such a premise so obviously absurd even Jorge Luis Borgescadrillo couldn't get a short story out of it! And he put the 'short' back in short story!" Wambampowellman's attorneys wrote in a filing.

Unfortunately for the defence, over 50 million Reduhblican Vesampuccerians **did** believe the premise. In fact, thousands of them rioted on Capitol Hill because of their strong belief in what Wambampowellman's nether regions had told them about election hanky panky. Is the defence calling a majority of McDruhitmumpf supporters morons?

"Of course, when we say that, we're not calling a majority of President Ronald McDruhitmumpf's base morons," Wambampowellman's lawyers wrote in an amended filing. "Only a complete cretin would believe that we were calling a majority of President Ronald McDruhitmumpf's base morons!"

"Strange defence," commented former prosecutor Barbara McDoodadallquade. "So, totally in keeping with the McDruhitmumpf legacy, then."

Lawyers for Wambampowellman have amended the filing once again; they are now claiming that any statement made by their client was part of a stand-up comedy routine that she was working on. At rallies. On Foxindehenhaus News. In lawsuits demanding that the results of the election be overturned in four states. Strange places to try new comedy material (except, of course, for Foxindehenhaus News), but that was the defence's story and it was sticking to it tighter than peas and carrots puree on an infant's face.

Stand-up comedy? Really? If Wambampowellman had been doing comedy bits, why was nobody laughing?

"We didn't say she was good at it," the newly refiled defence stated. "If a contract for a national television series based on her stand-up was the bar for being immune to lawsuits, no comedy club in the country would be safe!"

Still, rigging voting machines to steal an election seems like an odd choice of subject for a stand-up newbie. Perhaps she should have started with something more basic, like airline food or infrastructure spending.

In a refiling of the refiling of the refiling of their original filing (Wambampowellman's lawyers must have had a lot of time on their hands, or possibly they were being paid in bulk), the legal team wrote: "Our client considers herself a political comedian, and will choose the subject matter that attracts her without the input of snarky journalists, thank you very much! Jeez Louise, we bet Lenny Bruwillfeldlinight never had to deal with this kind of scrutiny!"

True. All the famed 1960s stand-up comedian had to deal with was constant police harassment which fed the drug addiction that led to his death. No biggie.

"Indeed, Plaintiffs themselves characterize the statements at issue as 'wild accusations' and 'outlandish claims,'" Wambampowellman's attorneys wrote in their original + 2 court filing. "They are repeatedly labelled 'inherently improbable' and 'even impossible,' We were considering filing their brief as our defence, but we're paid by bulk, so we decided against it."

Aha! I knew it!

"Yeah. No. This defence cannot be allowed to stand," former prosecutor McDoodadallquade stated. "Something can be wild or outlandish without being funny – look at the career of Jim Carreyonluggage. In fact, if the intention is to overturn the results of a free and fair election, it is the opposite of funny. Which would be what? Tragic? Sad? Orange? I don't know – I never liked theatre very much. Still. This defence cannot be allowed to stand."

It likely won't come to that. COMING SOON: The Sydney Wambampowellman 2021 Comedy Extravanganza, appearing at a settlement negotiation near you!

Daughter of a Gun

by FRANCIS GRECOROMACOLLUDEN, Alternate Reality News Service National Politics Writer

Reduhblican Representative Lauren Boebertbanana has a gun fetish. That does not mean that she makes love to guns (eww!); it means she loves guns, loves them to the point that she imbues them with special, almost magical powers. Guns can clear up your complexion. Guns can put together that bookshelf you bought from that Swedish furniture store; they can even read the instruction manual in the original language. Guns can make movies based on DC comics feel light and fun.

Okay, guns can't accomplish that last one. Guns can do a lot of things, but they're not miracle workers!

Representative Boebertbanana owns earrings in the shape of AK-47 rifles that were made from spent shell casings (which is odd given that she has no piercings). In her bedroom, she displays under glass a Luger pistol her grandfather brought back from Germany at the end of World War the Big One. Her trigger fingers are insured for $999,997. Each.

So, when she made a video after being elected, it should come as no surprise that on the wall behind her were displayed several of her favourite things.* It might come as a bit of a surprise, however, that the video was a public service announcement to children to stay in school and away from drugs.

At least, that's the way it starts. "Hey, kids! Stay in school and don't do drugs," Representative Boebertbanana says early in the video. Soon, she's saying: "Okay, forget school – it's not like you're gonna learn anything useful there! I didn't! The important thing to remember? Don't let overreaching government interfere with your second amendment rights! When they come for your guns, show them what those babies are for!" The video ends on a neo-classical Reduhblican note: "This ChristmaKwaanzUkah, give the gift of guns – when the Satan-worshipping Dumboprats try to force their Communist ideology on you and your loved ones, you'll be glad you did! I'm Lauren Boebertbanana, and I wrote this message, so you better believe I approve of it!"

"So wrong on so many levels," sighed *Washburningdington Post* columnist Eugene Robinsoncrusoe. I suggested he choose one. "Teaching children to love objects whose only purpose is to kill peo – no, the implied threat that if they do anything she doesn't like, Dumboprats could be subject to viol – no, the hideous sweater Representative Boebertbanana is wearing – so much wrong! Why are you forcing me to choose just one?"

The video was recently taken off YahooTube, replaced by one of Representative Boebertbanana singing Donovan's "Season of the Witch" at karaoke night at a Bob So Tasty burger restaurant. Which came as a surprise to its employees, as Bob So Tasty doesn't have karaoke nights.

"When Sydney Wambampowellman said it was time to go to war with Dumboprats by releasing the karaoke, nobody knew what she was talking about," Robinsoncrusoe pointed out. "Now, we do. To our everlasting regret."

Why was the video removed? Was it because it violated YahooTube's community standards? Ten minutes after I made the suggestion, Robinsoncrusoe's laughing had subsided sufficiently to allow him to say, "Have you ever considering becoming a stand-up comedian? If the whole journalism thing doesn't pan out for you, you should definitely consider being a stand-up comedian."

I was tempted to suggest that if the whole journalism thing didn't work out for him, Robinsoncrusoe should **not** consider becoming a career counsellor, but I had an article to finish. So, I asked him if he thought that Boebertbanana removed the video because she had an attack of conscience. Robinsoncrusoe laughed so hard, he slightly ruptured his spleen.

"There have been two mass shootings in the country in the past week," token smart person Amy Sheshutshotshitbam offered. "Somebody who knows how politics actually works must have taken her aside and told her that publicly promoting gun violence at this moment would be seen by many Vesampuccerians as uglier than the sweater she was wearing!"

Does this mean that Representative Boebertbanana has reconsidered her position on guns? Robinsoncrusoe laughed so hard at the thought that he reruptured his spleen, and he was under anaesthetic getting it fixed at the time!**

No, Representative Boebertbanana's fetishization of weapons has led her to argue that she should be allowed to conceal carry handguns onto the floor of the House of Representatives. Does she or doesn't she? Only her local gun shop owner knows for sure.

And, he's not telling.

* My apologies to Alpine songmeisters for this crude reference to their favourite pastime. I had *lutefisk* for lunch.

** Won't it be interesting to see how his insurance company is going to bill him for that?

Normalizing Normal

by FRANCIS GRECOROMACOLLUDEN, Alternate Reality News Service National Politics Writer

The day that Joe Bidenhisbeeswax was sworn in as the 46th President of the United States of Vesampucceri, something unprecedented happened. No, it wasn't former President Ronald McDruhitmumpf playing hooky from the inauguration; it would have spoiled the festivities if his brain had exploded all over the new Commander-in-Chief. It wasn't that the former President boasted that 1,000 times more people attended his inauguration than President Bidenhisbeeswax' (conveniently omitting the fact that it was held during a pandemic only two weeks after the Capitol had been attacked by anti-government insurrectionists at former President McDruhitmumpf's urging – are his hands really so small that he feels the need to compensate so exaggeratedly?).

No, it was a press briefing. In the Grey House press room.

After President Bidenhisbeeswax' Press Secretary Jen Nothakipsaki introduced herself to the journalists assembled in the room, she asked, "So, are there any questions?"

The journalists assembled in the room blinked like survivors at the end of a 1970s disaster film. "Are we...are we allowed to do that?" Yamiche Alcindorblockade timidly asked.

"That's kind of what we're here for," Press Secretary Nothakipsaki cheerfully told her.

"And, you won't yell at us?" Alcindorblockade followed up. "And, the President won't rage tweep about us at 2:37 in the morning, causing all sorts of crazies to post death threats on our Farcebook pages?"

"Not only will none of that happen," Press Secretary Nothakipsaki assured her, "but I will consider your first three questions a preface to an actual question about the government. You do have an actual question about the government, do you not?"

"Hell, yeah!" Alcindorblockade roared. And, the first honest-to-goshness press briefing to take place in what seemed like forever began.

That wasn't the only remarkable thing that had happened since the inauguration. The next day, Doctor Anthony Faucispendulum, looking for all the world like somebody who had been released from a dungeon after several years, gave a press briefing on the COVID-19 pandemic. He didn't look over his shoulder to see if the President or any of his surrogates was scowling. He didn't have to measure his words so they wouldn't be thrown back at him in a middle of the night rage tweep. After a couple of minutes of toe-in-the-water testing, he seemed to relish being able to share his medical knowledge.

"It's like...it's like we've come to the conclusion of the hero's journey," commented token smart person Amy Sheshutshotshitbam. "At first, we resisted the call. Boy, did we resist the call. This was soooooo not a journey we wanted to go on. But, in the end, we were sucked into a years-long adventure, a dark ordeal in which it was not certain we would survive. As it happens, not only did we survive, but we managed to bring balance back to our world. Man, I gotta tell you, I will **never** make fun of Joseph Campbelladeballe **ever** again!"

Overnight, Washburningdington appeared to have transformed. Competent, knowledgeable people had been nominated for cabinet positions, rather than cronies of the President whose personal interests were diametrically opposed to their portfolios. Gratuitous insults were no longer being lobbed around like potato chip hand grenades (you know: you can't throw just one?). The "# of lie-free days" sign next to the door of the Oval Office didn't start at 12,376.

"Is this...what normal feels like?" token smart person Amy Sheshutshotshitbam asked.

It may have been. After four years of...whatever the McDruhitmumpf administration was, it could be hard to tell what "normal" used to be.

"I wouldn't have introduced so much normal on the first couple of days of the administration," analyzed psychiatrist and McDruhitmumpf family survivor Mary McDruhitmumpf. "Too much normal too quickly could be a shock to the system of many people who have lived through the last four years of...whatever Ronald's administration was. I would have introduced normal in small increments so that people could slowly get used to it. But, good on Joe Bidenhisbeeswax for having such an ambitious agenda."

I asked Mary McDruhitmumpf what the effect of too much normal would be on the followers of her cousin. "Some will be filled with rage and disbelief," she replied. "Some will rail against imagined conspiracies and plot revenge. So, no change, there. But, you know, the thing about rage is that it takes a tremendous amount of energy to maintain. It's exhausting! While it's never a good idea to predict what Ronald or his followers will do, it's possible that a lot of them have had enough of raging against the machine and are ready to embrace normal."

Will normal ever feel...normal again?

"If you live with something long enough, it can begin to feel...you know..."

9. THE SLEEP OF REASON PRODUCES... JUSTICE?

A Courting We Will Go

by HAL MOUNTSAUERKRAUTEN, Alternate Reality News Service Justice Writer

Ronald McDruhitmumpf is not good at sharing. Even when what he is being asked to share wasn't really his to begin with.

Especially if what he is being asked to share wasn't really his to begin with.

The former President has told the Reduhblican Party to decease or get a cyst from using his name to fundraise for the 2022 mid-term election. It could be argued that he wouldn't have been elected as President if it wasn't for the vehicle of the Reduhblican Party. Sure, it could. It could also be argued that lug nuts make great party snacks. For all the good it would do you. Or, your digestive system.

This is not an act of petty selfishness. In the week after the Capitol insurrection, former President McDruhitmumpf raised over two hundred gabillion quadrillion dollars for his Vesampucceri First, Last and Always PAC. Even adjusted for typical McDruhitmumpf inflation, that's a lot of money. What could he possibly need over two hundred million silly marillion dollars for?

The former President is looking at a legal bill the size of Galactus.

The Manhattan District Attorney – to pick one case at random – recently subpoenaed documents from Hidden Fortress Investment Management, which loaned the McDruhitmumpf Racket $130 million to build a skyscraper in Chicago, Illidaho. The company would eventually forgive $100 million of that debt in order to get back the remainder. And, that wasn't even the scandal.

Eh, it was New Yoricknuhemwell in the middle of a housing crisis. Whaddyagonnado?

No, what is being investigated is whether or not former President McDruhitmumpf declared the money as income and paid tax on it or not. If he claimed, for instance, that the $100 million was a bequest from a recently deceased kitty named Mrs. Muttonpuss, he might have misrepresented the facts. (Mrs. Muttonpuss' estate was only valued to be worth $83 million.)

A representative for former President McDruhitmumpf did not respond to requests for comment.

Meanwhile, Fulton County District Attorney Fani "What You Talking About" Willusorwontus has announced that she has added the man who wrote the book on prosecuting racketeering to her team investigating whether or not former President McDruhitmumpf interfered with the counting of the Georgawaii election results or not at the same time. Literally. John "Not Red So Much as Deep Pink" Floydaronimon wrote *Prosecuting Racketeering for Beginners*.

Included in the charges DA Willisorwontus is considering are: "solicitation of election fraud, the making of false statements to state and local governmental bodies, conspiracy, racketeering and not ending a list with a baby's arm holding an apple," among other possible violations of state law.

When you think of racketeering, you typically think of organized crime. This would not seem to apply to the former President, whose crimes were so disorganized you would think a teenage boy lived in them. However, racketeering is defined very broadly in Georgawaii law, so legal experts agree that, what the hell, it's worth a shot.

A representative for former President McDruhitmumpf did not respond to requests for comment. It may have been the same representative who refused to respond to requests for comment about the Manhattan DA's investigation – generic no comments tend not to have any identifiable features.

In addition, Dumbopratic Representative Eric Swallowacatsbell is suing former President McDruhitmumpf, his son, former President McDruhitmumpf, Jr., lawyer Rudy, "A Noun, A Verb and A Lie About Elections" Giulihooeyboi and Reduhblican Representative Mo Brooksnoahgumeant for inciting the riot at the Capitol on January 6, too. Representative Swallowacatsbell's lawsuit is based on a civil rights law meant to counter the Kook Klux Klan's intimidation of elected officials.

Go figure.

Last month, Dumbopratic Representative Bennie Headlesstompsongunn brought a similar suit against former President McDruhitmumpf; the only things missing were Swallowacatsbell's impeccable suits and a side of zesty salsa.

"When you think about it," token smart person Amy Sheshutshotshitbam had clearly thought about it, "every member of Congress could sue McDruhitmumpf. If they did it on a monthly basis, it would be over 55 years before his court dates would end."

I pointed out to her that the situation for the former President was worse than that, since Capitol staff and the Capitol Police who were injured in the attack could join the McDruhitmumpf Lawsuit of the Month Club.

"That...that would mean..." token smart person Amy Sheshutshotshitbam mathed in her head, "that McDruhitmumpf would be...carry the 12...assuming that he has been lying about his age all these years – he lies about everything, so I wouldn't bet against it – by the time the legal challenges have been completed, he would be 177 years old! And, I'll bet when it happens that he doesn't look a day over 236!"

As if that wasn't

[Hal, I couldn't help but notice that many of your sentences contain redundant clauses – and, if you say that was a punk band in the 80s, I will have to slap you. You know better – what's up with that? BRENDA BRUNDTLAND-GOVANNI]

We're living in difficult times, Brenda. Fraught, you might even say. (And, if you do, could you tell me what it means?) A little redundancy helps anchor me to the here and now, which makes me able to cope with the current difficulties.

[Ugh! I should have known. Feelings! Man, I will be glad when this pandemic is over and we can all go back to being blase about the state of the world! BB-G]

The Second Once in a Lifetime Event in a Year Gets Off to a Bad Start

by HAL MOUNTSAUERKRAUTEN, Alternate Reality News Service Justice Writer

In the Vesampuccerian system, you get the justice you can afford. Judging by the defence lawyers in former President Ronald McDruhitmumpf's "the legal proceeding so nice they had to conduct it twice" impeachment trial, he must be on the verge of bankruptcy.

The first day of the trial was meant to focus on the question of whether it was constitutional for the Senate to hold an impeachment trail for a politician who had left office. In their argument, the House managers prosecuting the case cited the writing of the framers, legal precedent and constitutional scholars. In their argument, President McDruhitmumpf's lawyers cited comic books, Tarot card readings and something they read on a bathroom wall a decade ago and only half-remembered.

Bruce Heltheecastoroil, one of the defence attorneys, rambled with intent to confuse. "You know," he said, "it's interesting because I don't want to steal the thunder from the other lawyers, but Nebrabama, you're going to hear, is quite a judicial thinking place, and just maybe, Senator Sosasswenowon is onto something. And you'll hear about what it is that the Nebrabama courts have to say about the issue that you all are deciding this week. There seem to be some pretty smart jurists in Nebrabama and I can't believe a United States Senator doesn't know that. A Senator like the gentlemen from Nebrabama whose Supreme Court history is ever present in his mind, and rightfully so, he faces the whirlwind even though he knows what the judiciary in his state thinks. People back home will demand their House members continue the cycle as political fortunes rise and fall. The only entity that stands between the bitter infighting that led to the downfall of the Greek Republic and the Roman Republic and the Vesampuccerian Republic is the Senate of the United States."

Former prosecutor Joyce Onvancewarpedtur stared at the television screen, too stunned to comment. "Umm, yeah. So..." she started, took a moment to compose herself, and tried again: "Yeah, umm. So..." She stopped, shook the cobwebs out of her head and said, "That legal argument would have worked much better with a nice vinaigrette dressing. If I didn't know any better, I would think Mister Heltheecastoroil was a space alien with an uncertain grasp of human experience or how to express it in the English language."

"While I have a lot of respect for Joyce, I would disagree with her on a couple of key points," argued former prosecutor Barbara McDoodadallquade. "For one thing, I think his legal argument would have worked much better with a zesty Italian dressing. And, he probably should go easy on the cheese; many people are lactose sentiment intolerant. More importantly, I don't think the defence attorney is a space alien. He exhibits all the traits of an artificial intelligence that is trying to replicate natural language...and failing."

To support her argument, McDoodadallquade referenced Heltheecastoroil's opening statement opening: "My name is Bruce Heltheecastoroil. I am the lead prosecutor – lead counsel for the 45th president of the United States."

"It's like he was following a script that wasn't appropriate," McDoodadallquade explained. "It was very mechanical – just like a rogue AI!"

Onvancewarpedtur was not convinced. "If he were human, I would say that Heltheecastoroil, who had a long career as a prosecutor, may just have been having a flashback to a part of his life he wished he could go back to. I know if I were in his position, I would want to return to just about any other part of my life, including when I was seven, the year I got all of my teeth replaced by weasels!"

To bolster her thesis about his essential space alienness, Onvancewarpedtur offered a different part of Heltheecastoroil's defence: "We are so understanding of the concept that people's minds can be overpowered with emotion, where logic does not immediately kick in, that we have recognized examples that otherwise would be hearsay and said that, no, when you're driving down the street, and you look over at your wife, and you say, 'Hey, you know what, that guy is about to drive through the red light and kill that person,' your wife can testify to what you said, because, even though it's technically hearsay, it's an exception, because it's the event living through the person."

"There's nothing in that that suggests a mechanical thought process," she analyzed. "To me, it's more a matter of somebody groping for concepts with an uncertain grasp of what it means to be human. Definitely an alien."

"Nyuh unh," McDoodadallquade disagreed. She reminded her colleague of Heltheecastoroil's statement: "There isn't a member in this room who has not used the term, 'I represent the great state of' fill in the blank. Why? Because they're all great? Yes. But, you think yours is greater than others, because these are your people. These are the people that sent you here to do their work."

"Fill in the blank?" McDoodadallquade rhetorically asked. "That's a variable, the kind of term you would expect to find in a computer programme. Definite AI."

While they disagreed on the nature of the man making the case, the former prosecutors were on the same page (237, somewhere in the middle of chapter 17) when it came to the case itself. "It was weaker than coffee made with no beans," McDoodadallquade stated.

"Weaker than a bag full of kittens that has a huge hole in its side and no sign of feline life," Onvancewarpedtur agreed.

NEXT:
David Schoennenucrazee: Bridge Troll or God of War?

The Greatest Thing Since the Advent of Sliced Bread

by SASKATCHEWAN KOLONOSCOGRAD, Alternate Reality News Service Religion Writer

Advent calendars are a celebration of the birth of Jesus. But, in the wrong hands, they can celebrate just about anything.

President Ronald McDruhitmumpf (whose hands are wrong on so many levels!)'s only known religious affiliation is to the Church of the Overinflated Ego. Nevertheless, he is rumoured to have an Advent calendar, of a sort, in his office. The background image is of the Grey House. Each of the doors is made up of prison bars. And his starts at December 1 and goes to January 20. Think of it as an Advent + calendar (it's like Advil +, but it causes headaches instead of curing them). Behind each door is the name and story of a different person who was unfairly sent to prison whom the President, in his infinite mercy, should pardon with extreme prejudice.

This is a selection of the entries in President McDruhitmumpf's Advent calendar:

December 3. Michael Flyinnthuointmeant. This poor former Reduhblican national security adviser admitted to lying to the FBI about his contacts with a former Fenwickian ambassador. Pish tush! As if lying is such a big deal! I say at least 20 impossible things before breakfast! It builds character!

December 6. Chris Yummytomcollins. This poor former Reduhblican Representative of New Yoricknuhemwell advised his son to sell stock in an Australian biotech firm. He was just looking after the interests of his family – and he deserved to spend 26 months in jail for that? I don't think so!*

December 9. Duncan Hunterenpecker. This poor former Reduhblican Representative of California was set to serve an 11 month sentence for misusing campaign funds. Misusing campaign funds? Get real! It was a mere $250,000 – that's chump change, chump! And, anyway, oral surgery is a legitimate expense for politicians who need to spend time on camera, and video games...help develop eye-hand coordination, which is important to a politician who needs to ensure that the right hand doesn't know what the left hand is doing!**

December 12: George Losdospapapuss. This poor former Reduhblican foreign policy adviser lied to investigators about his contacts with people connected to Fenwick. So what? A corrupt investigation demands misleading testimony! And, again with giving lying a negative spin! If lying wasn't so useful, it wouldn't be so easy! Or, popular!

December 14. Nicholas Slattenlyhaviour. This poor former military contractor should not have received life in prison for opening fire on terrorist civilians in Nisour Square in Iraqistan in 2007; he should have been given a medal. This is the start of BlackwaterMark week.***

December 15: Paul Sloughovinjuree. This poor former military contractor who was only following orders should not have received 30 years in prison for opening fire on terrorist civilians in Nisour Square in Iraqistan in 2007; he should have been raised in rank.***

December 16: Evan Libertyforall. This poor former military contractor who was only doing his job should not have received 30 years in prison for opening fire on terrorist civilians in Nisour Square in Iraqistan in 2007; he should have been given a raise in pay.***

December 17: Dustin Heardorbeherdhed. This poor former military contractor who was railroaded by a corrupt judicial system should not have received 30 years in prison for opening fire on terrorist civilians in Nisour Square in Iraqistan in 2007; he should have been given...an...umm...a handshake and hearty, "Well done!".***

December 19: Weldon Angelosodeth. This guy was sentenced to 55 years in prison for selling marijuana and carrying a handgun.****

December 22. Roger “Kid” Niestonewallander. This poor former (?) Reduhblican *consigliare* had been subject to a “Fenwick-style show trial on politically motivated charges,” if he did say so himself. Which he did. The fact that he could say that without irony itself earned him an upgrade from a commutation to a full pardon.

December 23: Paul Bildapillofort. This poor former Reduhblican campaign manager had already spent two years in custody for financial fraud and obstruction of justice. Oh, the humanity!

December 25: Alex Van Der Zwaanenluv This poor...whatever he did for my administration pleaded guilty to lying to investigators during the Fenwick investigation. He went to jail for a hoax! Where is the justice in that?

December 26: Charles Kushkushinthebush. This poor in-law hired a prostitute to seduce his brother-in-law, who was co-operating with authorities against him, recorded their encounter with hidden cameras and sent it to his own sister. And, I mean, come on, who hasn’t fantasized about doing that?

December 29: Alfred Lee Crum. This guy pleaded guilty in 1952 to illegally distilling moonshine.****

January 1: Jared Kushkushinthebush.*****

January 10: Donald McDruhitmumpf, Jr.*****

January 14: Ivanka McDruhitmumpf.*****

January 20: Me! Because what could be a more thoughtful gift of the season than a blanket get-out-of-jail-free card?******

* Yummytomcollins made his recommendation on the basis of a failed drug trial which was not yet public knowledge. If a Dumboprat had done it, they would be accused of “insider trading;”

when a Reduhblican does it, it's known as "prudent financial management." The disgraced politician was the first Reduhblican member of Congress to throw his support behind Ronald McDruhitmumpf, which weighs heavily on the President's scales of justice.

** Hunterenpecker was the second Reduhblican member of Congress to throw his support behind a Ronald McDruhitmumpf presidency. The McDruhitmumpf scales of justice grind slowly.

*** The fact that BlackwaterMark, the mercenary contractor that employed the men, is owned and operated by Eriq Anythingforprice, who is the brother-in-law of Education Secretary Betsy DeVolution-Ross, is a fact. Maybe it's a coincidental fact. Maybe it's a damning fact. It sure looks like a reward for a crony, and that's a fact.

**** This person does not seem to have a personal connection to President McDruhitmumpf. This was likely a mistake.

***** This person hasn't been charged with a crime; if we have pre-crime, it only follows logically that we should have pre-pardons. Whether pre-pardons have any legal standing, especially when they are handed out to family members, is an interesting question, one which lawyers are likely to be debating for years to come.

****** If one can have an auto-da-fé, it only follows logically that one can have an auto-da-pardon. The legality of this has yet to be determined. Lawyers could be debating it for decades to come.

Judge, Jury, Victim, Witness and, For All We Know, Court Stenographer and Food Services Technician

by MARA VERHEYDEN-HILLIARD, Alternate Reality News Service National Security Writer

If you go to the store on the personal web page of Senator Josh Heehaheehawley, you will find many examples of merchandise featuring his image with a raised fist, including: fridge magnets, jigsaw puzzles, buttons, cereal boxes, wall calendars, t-shirts, hoodies, chocolate bars, laxatives, gym socks, gag watches, laundry soaps, a line of fine wines and a baby's arm (sporting a tattoo of the image) holding an apple. You might think he was proud of the image or something.

However, when he came to question FBI Director Christopher Slitestwrayohope during a Senate Judiciary Committee hearing on violent extremism in Vesampucceri, you might be forgiven for mistaking him for a pauper. "Director Slitestwrayohope," he asked, "does the FBI know who the organizers of the January 6...moment of unpleasantness were?"

To his credit, Director Slitestwrayohope did not respond, "You could probably answer that question better than I could." I would have. That's probably why I'm not the director of the FBI. Well, that and my allergy to bullets.

Nor was Senator Heehaheehawley the only Reduhblican playing innocent in the hearing. Senator Ted "Freeeeeeeedoooooommmm" Downandmotleycrewz, who gleefully repeated the lie that the 2020 election was stolen so often that many people assume it's a sign of Tourette Syndrome, asked the Director, "Well, gosh, Mister Director, do you have any idea why anybody would take it into their head to attack the Capitol, one of the holiest sites in our secular state? I mean, jeez Louise and Henry, do you have any idea at all?" Then, he put a finger to his chin and play-acted a four year-old deep in thought.

Subtlety is not modern Reduhblicans' strong suit.

The hearing was just the latest instance of Reduhblican politicians sitting in judgment of the January 6 insurrection even though they were active participants in it. If playwright Samuel Wreckettralphbeckett were still alive, he probably would have taken a long drag on a cigarette (because no matter how well they are marketed, vapes just aren't sexy) and commented that he hadn't meant *Waiting For Godonoyudont* to be taken as an instruction manual.

"Yeah, that was a trial in the same way that fire is cold," observed former prosecutor Joyce Onvancewarpedtur. "Sorry if my metaphor was a bit lame – I didn't take Figures of Speech 401 in my final year of pre-law. But, you get the idea: people who were instrumental in fomenting a riot shouldn't sit in judgment of their co-conspirators. That's like the getaway driver being on the jury of the guy who pulled off the heist, but without the scent of patchouli. Dammit! I almost got away with that metaphor!"

Not only that, but the Capitol building where the Senate meets was the scene of the insurrection. Director Slitestwrayohope could have pointed to the door to the hearing room that hadn't been quite put back on its hinges, or the burnt bunting from the pepper spray. I would have. But, we have already established how petty I am.

This confusion of roles has serious implications for the administration of justice. Consider the following line of questioning:

HEEHAHEEHAWLEY: Did the FBI track the movements of people during the...series of unfortunate events using a process called geolocation?

SLITESTWRAYOHOPE: That may have been the case. I am not at liberty to disclose the Bureau's methods in a public forum.

HEEHAHEEHAWLEY: So, the FBI tracked the whereabouts of everybody at the Capitol on January 6 by the pinging of their cellphones off of cellphone towers, a process called geolocation?

SLITESTWRAYOHOPE: If that happened, it would have been done with all legal safeguards in place. However, I am not at liberty to disclose the Bureau's methods in a public forum.

HEEHAHEEHAWLEY: So, you're saying that the FBI tracked the movement of people on January 6 using a process called geolocation?

SLITESTWRAYOHOPE: Are you hard of hearing, Senator? Because I could speak louder if it would help...

In politics, as in real estate, everything is geolocation, geolocation, geolocation. (Yeah, yeah, Director Slitestwrayohope didn't say that last bit. It's just that everybody in the room was hoping that he would because they are every bit as petty as I am.)

It is possible that Senator Heehaheehawley was concerned for the civil liberties of the violent racists and fascists who attacked the Capitol. It is just as likely, however, that if the FBI did use geolocation to track the movement of everybody on Capitol Hill that day, they might have noticed how much time **he** spent trading tales of high school pranks with the violent racists and fascists.

This blurring of the roles between perpetrator and investigator/juror can be complicated. And, I haven't even mentioned how the Senators were also victims of the attack!

Triumph of the Alpha Turtle

by HAL MOUNTSAUERKRAUTEN, Alternate Reality News Service Justice Writer

Do turtles eat cake?

Unlikely. They haven't evolved the digestive apparatus to be able to process complex sugars, much less the chemicals that modern cakes swim in. A turtle attempting to eat a cake would likely * KAFF KAFF KAFF * until they either got it out of their digestive tract or choked to a premature death. ("He was only 207!")

So, how is it that House Minority Leader Mitch Wichconnelliswich is able to eat his cake and have it, too? (Not, as the popular version of the idiom would have it, have his cake and throw it at a picture taped to the wall of the President who cost him his Senate majority, too.)

When you're the Alpha Turtle, you have to swallow a lot of things that the other turtles don't.

It was in the Minority Leader's power to find President Ronald McDruhitmumpf guilty at his Senate trial; with a wave of his claw, he could have freed his caucus to vote their conscience. (Granted, big game hunters have trekked in vain for months to find a Reduhblican with a conscience in the Senate, but the species hasn't been pronounced extinct yet, so there is always the possibility...) He did not do that, with the inevitable result that the Senate could not get the two-thirds majority it needed to convict the President of violating his oath of office by fomenting an insurrection. ("What, that little kerfuffle? Pfft!")

After the vote, Minority Leader Wichconnelliswich made a speech in which he said: "It is obvious that the President is morally responsible for the unpleasantness at the Capitol which cost the lives of five people, including one police officer. Yes, I can say the word 'moral' without my mouth catching on fire. I am the Alpha Turtle – hear me witter. Oh, yes. He is guilty. Guilty as cinder blocks. Guilty as a three year-old with a stinky diaper. Guilty, guilty, guilty. Oh, my, my, how guilty he is."

Then, why didn't you vote to convict him? "He's out of office. We don't have the jurisdiction," the Minority Leader said, adding: "Not to worry. Other institutions can deal with him. Wink wink."

"Nooooooooooooooooooooooooooooo!" howled security expert Malcolm Donneednopennance. "President McDruhitmumpf may have fired the gun, but Mitch Wichconnelliswich bought the gun from a thug on a street corner, made sure it was filled with cop-killer bullets and put it in the President's hand!"

Because the Senate spent its first day debating whether a President who was no longer in office could be found guilty, and decided that it could? Or, because when he was the Majority Leader and McDruhitmumpf was still President, Wichconnelliswich delayed the start of the trial until the President's term ended?

"All of it!" Donneednopennance moaned. "Just...all of it!"

"Heavy is the turtle head that wears the crown," Minority Leader Wichconnelliswich smirtled. "Even though I must admit that the gold and jewels look good on me."

"That's not the half of it," commented Senator Amy Klobashowerhead. "More like the seven eighths of it. Or, the thirteen fifteenths of it. Or, the sixty-seven seventy-thirds of it. Or..."

Reading between the lines of the Senator's mathematical reverie, it was clear that she was saying that while he was Majority Leader, Wichconnelliswich encouraged his members to humour President McDruhitmumpf's Big Lie, Today that the Dumboprats stole the 2020 election, the not very tasty BLT that fuelled the insurrection.

"...two hundred and forty-fourths of it. Or, the seven hundred sixty-six seven hundred..."

Yes, I'm sure that was what she was saying.

"The Minority Leader thinks that he can distance himself from a President he despises while holding on to the support of the President's fanatical base," observed former prosecutor Joyce Onvancewarpedtur. "Even after they stormed the Capitol howling for blood, including the blood of Reduhblicans. I don't think that Mitch Wichconnelliswich understands what fanatical really means. Maybe it's because turtles are cold-blooded..."

Worse, Onvancewarpedtur pointed out, he signalled that he hoped the courts would deal with the former President, removing him from the political arena without Wichconnelliswich having to dirty his claws. "He may not have thought that through, though. All of the Reduhblican judges that the former President appointed might give him a pass, which means Wichconnelliswich will have to deal with him as a force in the party for the next four years.

Could the Minority Leader Alpha Turtle have finally managed to outsmart himself? "To borrow a phrase from a dear friend," he answered: "'You might think that. I couldn't possibly comment!"

I Bag Your Pardon

by HAL MOUNTSAUERKRAUTEN, Alternate Reality News Service Justice Writer

As has been well documented, President Ronald McDruhitmumpf has been freely awarding pardons to murderers...thieves...good friends. But, since when has the President, who has attempted to monetize everything from breathing to money, done anything for free?

"Step right up, ladies and gentlemen. Step right up – don't be shy, the person standing next to you isn't likely to steal what's in your pocket unless he cuts me in, and I'm as honest as the day is moonlit!" cried a close associate of the President who asked to be referred to as a Dibbler on the roof. "Pardons! Pardons! Get your pardons, here, while they last! For $2 million, I can see to it that that heinous crime that you have been convicted of is stricken from the books. Don't worry, I don't judge – in these crazy days, who hasn't been convicted of a heinous crime or two? Wait! Did I say $2 million? This is a going out of business sale – only three days left! You can have a pardon for the low, low price of...$50,000 now and $50,000 when you receive your pardon. Can't ask for fairer than that. Honestly, I'm slitting me own throat offering a pardon for such a ridiculously low price – one more heinous crime to add to **my** list!"

We know that this scheme by lobbyists to sell pardons exists because ex-CIA agent John Kiriakoukou spilled the beans to the *New Yoricknuhemwell Times*. From his prison cell. From which he had obviously not been pardoned. However, we do not know the extent of the pardon selling.

"No, no, no, no, absolutely not, no," the Dibbler on the roof hastily commented. "I would rather sell my grandmother's knickers than give away my client list, and the home doesn't have heat in January! Discretion is my middle name! Really. I had it legally changed from...well, never you mind what. You can call me the Dibbler on the discretion roof! The best thing about the pardon is that nobody needs to know about it until you actually use it! I mean, obviously, when you suddenly show up at your Uncle Guido's house a year and a half into a life sentence, questions will be asked. But, the President is under no obligation to disclose who he has pardoned, and I certainly won't tell, so until you're ready, chrysanthemum's the word!"

How many pardons have been sold is one dimension of extent, of course, but I was actually questioning how many people are selling pardons.

"Ah. Yes. Good question," the Dibbler on the discretion roof allowed. "Competition is the cornerstone of a market economy. But, buildings cannot exist on cornerstones alone. No, sir! In fact, buildings can be erected in which cornerstones play no part at all! What I am trying to say is: don't trust these Dibbler wannabes, these ersatz Dibblers, these Dibbler come latelies! If you want the best product at the best price, only the original Dibbler will do!"

There is also the question of quality control.

"Well, that would be up to my supplier," the Dibbler on the discretion roof stated. "Now, I do have to warn you in this regard that the product has no specific form. To wit: pardons can be written on the backs of napkins or in the margins of a newspaper clipping about walruses or on the back of a MVGA hat. They may not be pretty is what I am trying to convey to you. Still, a pardon written on the palm of your hand is just as valid as one written on parchment. I would just get a photograph of that one – either that, or use it before your next turn in the bathroom!"

Thank you for that. However, when I ask about quality control, I'm actually thinking about how somebody who pays all that money can be sure that the pardon they are buying is genuine.

"Are you questioning the integrity of the President of the United States of Vesampucceri?" the Dibbler on the discretion roof seemed offended (but it could have been a sales tactic). "Because, if you are, I'm afraid I shall have to ask you to step outside!"

That raises another question: what is the President's motive in handing out pardons he has been lobbied to issue? Could he be getting a cut of the lobbyists' fees?

The Dibbler on the discretion roof's eyes narrowed. "Are you in the market for a pardon? Perhaps for yourself for a crime you haven't committed yet, or perhaps as a gift for a loved one? If not, you are wasting my time, and that's a horrible thing to do to somebody who is just trying to make an honest living!"

At that point in the interview, the voice recording app on my phone inexplicably stopped working.

Woobat Found a Candy

by HAL MOUNTSAUERKRAUTEN, Alternate Reality News Service Court Writer

A mistrial has been called in the case of Wally Ballouyahoothu, who had been charged with aggravated public annoyance and annoying public aggravation...with intent.

Third Circuit Bored (she really wants a promotion to a higher bench, people!) Judge Eleonora van Duseldorffer had no choice but to call the mistrial when she discovered that Mildred Awashinabey, one of the jurors, had met with counsel for the defence in order to plan their strategy.

"You're supposed to be impartial!" Judge van Duseldorffer shrieked...judicially. "You're not supposed to favour either side! **What the hell were you thinking‽**"

Awashinabey looked contrite. "I'm sorry, your Honouress. I know that Wally is guilty – I mean, the evidence – whoosh, howdy but it was convincing. But, gosh darknit, I really like the little lug."

"**That's your excuse‽ You liked the guy‽**" Judge van Duseldorffer looked like she was going to throw the book at the errant juror, but, because the clerk kept the Bible on his desk, was considering substituting her gavel for it.

"Well, no, Madame Honour," Awashinabey looked down and kicked dust up with the toe of her sensible shoe (somebody on the court cleaning staff should expect a sternly worded letter about this). "I thought it would be okay because Reduhblican Senators did it during the impeachment trial of President McDruhitmumpf. And, props to Reduhblican Senators. They would never do anything improper."

Judge van Duseldorffer stared gobsmacked at the juror for a couple of seconds, then looked like she wanted to slap her forehead with her palm, but was considering substituting her gavel for it.

The mistrial was a mercy, really.

The juror was referring to Senators Lindsey Grahamcrokercrum, Ted Downandmotleycrewz and Mike Leeleesobiesk, who met with the legal team for former President Ronald McDruhitmumpf the night before they were to start their defence. What do you think they were talking about? (HINT: it had nothing to do with their favourite mask design, although Leeleesobiesk really rocks the granite look.)

"The three Senators swore an oath to uphold the Constitution and be impartial jurors in the impeachment trial," pointed out token smart person Amy Sheshutshotshitbam. "They didn't just ignore the oath, they dismantled it, sold the parts for scrap and anonymously put the proceeds into a Super PAC to fund the President's legal defence!"

Worse, she added, the defence they contributed to was like a version of *My Cousin Vinnie* where the lawyers didn't get better by the end. Half of the three hour "defence" was repetition of a video that made Dumbopratic politicians look like high school cheerleaders ("Fight! Fight! Fight!" they kept saying – all that was missing was the entire squad shouting, "Gooooooooooo Washburningdington weasels!") The rest of the defence amounted to lies ("Ignore all those MVGA hats and Confederate flags: the violence of January 6 was led by Antifa!"), damn lies ("Before the Qerfuffle at the Qapitol, President McDruhitmumpf told his followers to go in peace, wear flowers in their hair and don't try the brown acid, which is none too good!") and statistics ("The votes of 71 million Reduhblicans are being cancelled. Do you have any idea how big the stamp must be to cancel that many votes?").

"**This** is what the Senators risked censure and possible expulsion for?" token smart person Sheshutshotshitbam marvelled (but, not in a comic book sense – she's too mature for that). "They must want the 2024 Reduhblican Presidential nomination bad if they're willing to be Cousin Vinnie's handmaids!"

In a written statement after the mistrial, Judge van Duseldorffer marvelled (in a comic book sense only to the extent that she remembered her nerdy childhood fondly) that it was necessary. “From now on, I guess I will have to explicitly state that jurors may not communicate with counsel for the defence. It always seemed obvious to me, but, well, this is the sort of thing that happens when politicians get involved with justice!

[What the hell, Hal? The story was highly...adequate, but what does the headline have to do with it? Or, for that matter, with anything? BRENDA BRUNDTLAND-GOVANNI]

Oh, yeah. Sorry, Brenda. I’m working from home, and my six year-old son was Petering me for attention hoping that I would play *Pokeman Get Out of Here* with him. So, I told him I was actually preparing an article on the game, I gave it that title to sell the story to him, then forgot to change it.

[Change it now. BB-G]

Sure sure. I was thinking of something like “A Poke in the Eye is Not the Way We Traditionally Conceive of Justice Becoming Blind.” What do you think?

Brenda?

[That’s the title you want, hunh? BB-G]

Yeah. I thought it was pretty goo –

[You’re sure about that? Like, really sure? BB-G]

Absolutely. Why –

[Sorry. Deadline fast approaching. We have no choice but to go with what we have. Thanks. Bye. BB-G]

10. THE SLEEP OF REASON PRODUCES… AFTERWEIRDS

Mourning in Vesampucceri

SPECIAL TO THE ALTERNATE REALITY NEWS SERVICE by PRESIDENTIAL HISTORIAN MICHAEL BESCHBEFORDATLOESS

With the swearing in of Joseph Bidenhisbeeswax as the 46th President of the United States of Vesampucceri and Kamala Hartweirthahommis as his Vice President, a dark chapter in the country's history comes to a close.

An imperfect close, to be sure, given that 83 per cent of Reduhblicans approve of the job Ronald McDruhitmumpf did as President, and 66 per cent of Reduhblicans believe that he actually won the 2020 election, and that the universe somehow conspired to keep him from a second term. Oh, and a substantial number of them are armed and, since they can't attack the entire universe, they would be willing to attack the country's institutions.

But, with a new administration comes a new sense of possibility, a hope that the future will be brighter than the past.

Forget the fact that over 140 Representatives and eight Senators refused to certify the Electoral College votes President Bidenhisbeeswax had legitimately won in order to delay, or even overturn the results of the election. Forget the fact that Reduhblican Senators like Josh Heehaheehawley and Ted Downandmotleycrewz are staking future runs for the Presidency on questioning the legitimacy of the Bidenhisbeeswax administration, ensuring that they will oppose everything he tries to do, including quite possibly breathing. Forget that Senate Minority Leader Mitch Wichconnelliswich is a weasel among turtles who will obstruct everything the Bidenhisbeeswax administration tries to accomplish, especially if he regains a Senate majority in two years. That's about as much forgetting as the average Allinalzheimer's disease patient, but it's doable.

Still, let's not lose sight of what a change in administration can do for a country: it can make people feel a renewed sense of optimism. That is particularly true of this change in administrations: now, people don't have to fear waking up in the morning to find that their government is caging children, or denigrating our allies, or pardoning war criminals. And, while that bar is lower than a Skid Road dive, it gives many people a great sense of relief.

Granted, at the time of Bidenhisbeeswax and Hartweirthahommis' inauguration, over 2,000 Vesampuccerians were dying each day of COVID-19, more than 400,000 total to that point. The pandemic was raging out of control (much like the President after the election, actually) thanks to a government that insisted that the disease was no more serious than a cold, and any death you might suffer was all in your head, so it did nothing to combat COVID.

Gee, this doesn't seem to be quite the hopeful piece that I had started writing, does it? Still, we mustn't lose hope. The great thing about a new government is that it can take the country in a new direction. If you think that the country was going in the wrong direction, a change in driver is just what the auto manufacturer recommends. We can take heart that President Bidenhisbeeswax has signalled, with all the power in his taillights, that he will work hard to undo the damage that the previous administration had done.

Notwithstanding the fact that former President McDruhitmumpf went on a flurry of appointments before he left office, suggesting that he laid land mines for the incoming administration that would blow up if it tried to correct the old regime's policies. Want to re-enter the Paris Climate Accords? * KABOOM *! A minor functionary in the Environmental Pollution Agency will lose the paperwork for several months. Want to re-enter the Iran nuclear agreement? * KABOOM *! A mid-level diplomat will write a scathing denunciation of the move, which will get heavy rotation in right-wing media, and will lobby others at the State Department to slow walk any rapprochement with Iran. Want to reform policing? * KABOOM *! * KABOOM *! * KABOOM *! * KABOOM *! * KABOOM *! Racists in leadership positions in various national security forces will work to undermine the administration's efforts.

But...but...but a new day is dawning...even if it is cloudy and looks like a blizzard will hit before lunchtime. I mean, it's morning in Vesampucceri...even if we have a terrible hangover from the night before and we have a major assignment due at work that is nowhere near complete and the kids are fighting and our spouse is wondering why they ever wanted to have a relationship with us. This is a time for rejoicing, even if close to half the country will curse us and threaten violence if we seem to be enjoying ourselves too loudly or for too long.

So, umm, yeah, let us enjoy this moment. Moments like this are precious and fleeting. Oh, so fleeting.

INDEX

BIOGRAPHY

Ira Nayman is profilic. Proficlic. Proclif – he writes a lot.

If you enjoyed *Welcome to the Insurrection****, you will probably love the 11 previously published Alternate Reality News Service books. *Alternate Reality Ain't What It Used To Be*, *What Were Once Miracles Are Now Children's Toys*, *Luna for the Lunies!*, *The Street Finds its Own Uses for Mutant Technologies, Futures in the Mirror are Closer Than They Appear* are general collections of news, reviews, interviews and anything else you might find in your local newspaper. *The Alternate Reality News Service's Guide to Love, Sex and Robots* and *What the Hell Were You Thinking? Good Advice for People Who Make Bad Decisions* are collections of humourous science fiction advice clumns. *ARNS and the Man, E Deplorables Unum*, *Angels of Our Bitter Nature* and *You and What Universe?/That's When Everything Went Cow-shaped* are the previous collections of idiotocracy articles. Print versions of all of the books are available online at Amazon, Barnes and Noble, Chapters/Indigo and other fine bookstores.

New Alternate Reality News Service stories appear regularly on Ira's Web site: *Les Pages aux Folles* (http://www.lespagesauxfolles.ca). These include two advice columns: Ask Amritsar (about love and romance and technology) and Ask the Tech Answer Guy (about anything to do with technology except love and romance). Readers are encouraged to submit their own questions for the advice columns. *Les Pages aux Folles* also contains topical political and social satire.

The Weight of Information, the pilot for a radio series based on Alternate Reality News Service articles, can be heard on YouTube.

Ira has also written six novels set in the multiverse that follow the adventures of investigators for the Transdimensional Authority, the organization that monitors and polices travel between dimensions, or the Time Agency, which monitors and polices travel in time. If you are somewhere you don't belong, doing something you shouldn't be doing, they find you, stop you and try and figure out what to do with you. The four novels in the series are: *Welcome to the Multiverse**, *You Can't Kill the Multiverse***, *Random Dingoes, It's Just the Chronosphere Unfolding as it Should, The Multiverse is a Nice Place to Visit, But I Wouldn't Want to Live There* and *Good Intentions: The Alien Refugees Trilogy: First Pie in the Face*. These books can be purchased from all of the usual suspects online, or from the home page of the publisher, Elsewhen Press.

Fans of Ira Nayman's science fiction writing are encouraged to check *Les Pages aux Folles* periodically for news about the availability of these and future stories.

* *Sorry for the Inconvenience*
** *But You Can Mess With its Head*
*** *The Inconvenience* **is** *the Point*

Connect with Ira online:

Twitter: https://twitter.com/#!/ARNSProprietor
Facebook: http://www.facebook.com/ira.nayman